**Praise for
MICHAEL PAINE**

STEEL GHOSTS

"Riveting . . . filled with chilling frights and imaginative twists."
—*EXP Magazine*

"Spooky . . . suspenseful . . . a good read."
—*Chronicle*

CITIES OF THE DEAD

"Impressive . . . Fast-moving, scary, and a lot a fun to read. A startlingly good writer. Read him."
—Charles L. Grant

"Terrific . . . really well-done."
—Chet Williamson

OWL LIGHT

"Dark, creepy, and totally satisfying."
—Robert R. McCammon

Titles by Michael Paine

**STAGE FRIGHT
THE NIGHT SCHOOL
STEEL GHOSTS
CITIES OF THE DEAD
THE COLORS OF HELL
OWL LIGHT**

Stage Fright

MICHAEL PAINE

BERKLEY BOOKS, NEW YORK

THE BERKLEY PUBLISHING GROUP
Published by the Penguin Group
Penguin Group (USA) Inc.
375 Hudson Street, New York, New York 10014, USA

Penguin Group (Canada), 90 Eglinton Avenue East, Suite 700, Toronto, Ontario M4P 2Y3, Canada
(a division of Pearson Penguin Canada Inc.)
Penguin Books Ltd., 80 Strand, London WC2R 0RL, England
Penguin Group Ireland, 25 St. Stephen's Green, Dublin 2, Ireland (a division of Penguin Books Ltd.)
Penguin Group (Australia), 250 Camberwell Road, Camberwell, Victoria 3124, Australia
(a division of Pearson Australia Group Pty. Ltd.)
Penguin Books India Pvt. Ltd., 11 Community Centre, Panchsheel Park, New Delhi—110 017, India
Penguin Group (NZ), Cnr. Airborne and Rosedale Roads, Albany, Auckland 1310, New Zealand
(a division of Pearson New Zealand Ltd.)
Penguin Books (South Africa) (Pty.) Ltd., 24 Sturdee Avenue, Rosebank, Johannesburg 2196,
South Africa

Penguin Books Ltd., Registered Offices: 80 Strand, London WC2R 0RL, England

This is a work of fiction. Names, characters, places, and incidents either are the product of the
author's imagination or are used fictitiously, and any resemblance to actual persons, living or
dead, business establishments, events, or locales is entirely coincidental.

STAGE FRIGHT

A Berkley Book / published by arrangement with the author

PRINTING HISTORY
Berkley edition / November 2006

Copyright © 2006 by John M. Curlovich.
Cover photograph by Paul Edmundson/Corbis.
Cover design by Steven Ferlauto.
Interior text design by Kristin del Rosario.

All rights reserved.
No part of this book may be reproduced, scanned, or distributed in any printed or electronic form
without permission. Please do not participate in or encourage piracy of copyrighted materials in
violation of the author's rights. Purchase only authorized editions.
For information, address: The Berkley Publishing Group,
a division of Penguin Group (USA) Inc.,
375 Hudson Street, New York, New York 10014.

ISBN: 0-425-21282-3

BERKLEY®
Berkley Books are published by The Berkley Publishing Group,
a division of Penguin Group (USA) Inc.,
375 Hudson Street, New York, New York 10014.
BERKLEY is a registered trademark of Penguin Group (USA) Inc.
The "B" design is a trademark belonging to Penguin Group (USA) Inc.

PRINTED IN THE UNITED STATES OF AMERICA

10 9 8 7 6 5 4 3 2 1

If you purchased this book without a cover, you should be aware that this book is stolen property.
It was reported as "unsold and destroyed" to the publisher, and neither the author nor the publisher
has received any payment for this "stripped book."

for
John Cook

PART ONE

Prologue

There was this woman, easily available, not quite young anymore and not quite pretty, but young and pretty enough. Her name was Helen, or so she said; nobody much cared, as long as they could pretend she wasn't doing business in their own towns. She rented a bit of space from Portia and took her "clients" out to the island where the old opera house stood, and nobody ever said much to her. A lot of them thought she wasn't quite right in the head.

One kid—young man—no, kid, decided he wanted to educate her. College kid named Mike; he thought she'd be worthy of him if she knew a bit more. He used to bring this portable DVD player and run movies for her, *Never On Sunday*, *Irma la Douce*, *Butterfield 8*, *Rain*, *Klute*, *Nights of Cabiria*, anything he could find with a prostitute in it. He'd take her out to the island and screw her, then he'd make her watch one of these movies. He actually thought the "uplift" he was giving her would make up for the sin.

As long as he was paying, she didn't much care. She'd watch, mostly bored, sometimes not. Whores with hearts of gold, Hollywood style—she knew better. Then when the movie was over he'd want to "discuss" it with her. She'd make things up, pretentious-sounding bullshit about postmodernism and so on, and he'd go away thinking he'd given her a bit of intellectual edification. She used to laugh about it with her friends, of whom she had a few.

It wasn't the best area to be a whore in. There were lots of militant Christians around, heaps of them, as there were in just about any rural area. Helen used to say you couldn't spit without hitting a church. But she was always careful not to do business where they could feel like she was encroaching on their piety, and the island was quite far off, so they pretty much left her alone. Some of them even availed themselves of her services, now and then, when they thought nobody was looking, even a few of the women and now and then a minster or two—she was good enough at this and that to make it worthwhile. But mostly they just left her alone.

Even the ghosts on the island left her alone.

The great thing about the island was that it was nobody's. No man's land, in a very literal sense. It was at a particularly wide place in the Ohio River just at the point where Pennsylvania, Ohio and West Virginia came together. And nobody wanted it, not one of the three states, and none of the municipalities that were within a few miles of it, so it sat there, going to seed and used as a trollop's business address, occupied fulltime only by the spirits of the dead.

Portia thought the island was hers, and since nobody else wanted the place, she pretty much owned it by default. Everyone thought she was crazy, too, and why she wanted it was cause for a lot of speculation around the region. There was nothing on it but the old opera house, and it was pretty much a ruin. But even she had sense enough not to actually try and live there.

So Helen used to take her, er, gentleman callers out there. She never actually took them inside the Imperial—that was where the ghosts were—but there were a few other little outbuildings, too, storage huts and the like. Serviceable enough for what she did; all it took was a blanket or two for the floor. In wintertime, for an extra fee, Portia put a little kerosene heater in one of them, so Helen and her beaus wouldn't freeze their butts off.

And this kid, Mike, the one with the DVD player and the whore movies, used to be very persistent about running them for her. He wanted to show them to her again and again, till she got out of them whatever it was he wanted her to get out of them. But Helen had a short attention span; maybe she really was not right in the head. Once she'd seen a movie and knew how it came out, she couldn't stand watching it again.

So he brought his player and a disc one day. Autumn day, bright sky. The trees on both shores were all pretty much dead, not much more than rotting stumps, so they didn't have that wonderful fall foliage everybody gushed about. There were no trees on the island itself. Upriver and downriver, in the distance, were all the autumn-colored trees, but none were close enough to make much difference to the landscape. It hadn't rained in a while, and the river was running low and slow.

Helen had a rowboat; and she always made her clients do the work unless they were really old or really important, like a preacher or somebody. Mike had a bit of trouble handling the oars, and Helen had to help him tie up securely at the makeshift little dock Portia had built.

He brought *Anna Christie* that day. Helen hated it almost the minute it started. "How old is this thing, anyway?"

"This is Eugene O'Neill, Helen. He was a great playwright."

"Well, he made really bad movies. Look how stagy this is. It looks like it was made around 5,000 B.C."

It was so exasperating for him. "Look, that's Greta Garbo. She was one of the great actresses."

"That ham?" She sneered at the image on the screen.

Mike loved it and said so. It was, he told her time and again, art. She couldn't wait for the damned thing to end.

"This is in black and white," she complained. She sniffed at him and pulled on her blouse. He had already paid for the sex. "It's boring."

"No, you just don't see it, Helen."

She laughed in his face and did a pretty fair imitation of Garbo. "'Gif me a viskey, ginger ale on the side, and don't be stingy, baby.' That's a lot of crap."

"It's art."

"Nobody talks like that."

"She was Swedish, Helen."

"She was nuts."

Under the pile of her clothes was a pint of vodka. She unscrewed the cap and took a long drink. He waited patiently for her to be polite and offer him a drink, but she didn't. She vas beink stingy, baby. "Come on, I've watched enough of this. Let's go."

"Please, just watch it one more time. I know you'll see it, sooner or later."

She pouted and took another long swallow. "Why don't you bring some music so we could dance? Who wants to watch this stuff?"

"I'll pay extra."

Another drink. "Why do you always want to pay me to watch these movies? You some kind of fancy-boy queer?"

He was hurt. "No. I just love them, that's all, and I want you to love them, too."

"What do you care what I love? All I am to you is a piece of ass." She drank.

"You're older than me, Helen. You should be the one teaching me things."

Helen laughed. "I've taught you plenty. Remember how nervous you were the first time you came out here with me?"

Against his will, he blushed and began to stammer. "P-p-please, Helen. N-next time I'll—I'll bring something else, okay?"

"No more of these damned movies. They bore me." She looked him up and down. "You bore me, too."

"No!"

"No!" she mimicked him.

"I'm paying for your time. You should do what I want."

She was not at all young anymore and certainly not very attractive by the usual standards. Her breasts were beginning to sag and her kisses were dry. She wanted to tell him, *I do what I want*. But business was business, and there wasn't as much of it as there used to be, and she had toyed with him long enough. Besides, it was autumn; once the weather turned

Stage Fright 7

cold, and the river ran high or worse yet got clogged with ice, there wouldn't be too many chances for coming out to the island. She remembered the story of the grasshopper and the ants from grammar school, and the moral wasn't lost on her. She held out her hand.

Mike put another twenty in it.

"Fifty."

"Fifty bucks? Just for watching a movie?"

She had learned a long time ago to make them pay real heavy for what they wanted most. If what he wanted was for her to be bored shitless by Greta Garbo, that was fine with her. "Fifty."

"Fine, here, I'll put it on."

He did. She watched. She drank more, and half an hour into it she fell asleep.

He switched it off. Damn. He wanted her to . . . he didn't know what he wanted her to do. But he wasn't going to watch his movie alone.

It was late afternoon. There were long shadows cast by the old dead trees on the Ohio shore. He eyed the rowboat and thought about heading back to the Pennsylvania side and leaving her there. He was from Butler, a town in Beaver County that wasn't too embarrassingly small.

Asleep, she looked a bit more pretty than she did awake. Or maybe it was that drunk she looked better than when she was sober. Whatever. He snapped the DVD into its case and stepped out of the shack.

It would be a cool evening. He could feel it coming. There was a breeze, and the tree branches, dead things that they were, swayed in it like they were trying to reach something. He glanced back inside; Helen was snoring.

What the fuck. He undressed her and screwed her again. It felt good, having her all limp and compliant like that. Why weren't more women that way?

Messy from sex, he took a quick dip in the river. It was a lot colder than he expected so he got out and dried himself with Helen's dress, then got quickly into his clothes. Damned stupid whore, why couldn't she appreciate what he was trying to share with her? Garbo was so wonderful—no, not just wonderful, *luminous*. And it was Eugene O'Neill, for Christ's sake.

For a moment he stood puzzling about it. How could she not want what he wanted? How could she not care about *cinema*? It did not occur to him that Helen might never have used the word *cinema* even once in her life, and that if she'd heard it she'd have thought it was silly to call just plain old movies a thing like that. He shook her, but she was too drunk to do more than open her eyes, stare at him groggily, then shut them again. Her snoring got louder.

So he was stuck there, goddamn it, and he was supposed to be home at six. Almost as bored as she had said she was, he looked around. What the hell, why not check out the Imperial? There was nothing else to do on that damned island.

There it was, ugly as anything, all over the north end of the island. In the marble over the lintel were carved the words IMPERIAL OPERA HOUSE. He stared up at it; it was all of five stories tall, if not more. Who the hell would build a thing like that in a place like this? The cornerstone repeated the theater's name and added the year of its construction. MDCCCXC. God, the place was more than a hundred and ten years old.

Closer, it was uglier. It looked like a whole crew of drunken architects had used every repulsive idea they could think of. The name of the theater, in stone over the entrance, was surrounded by a laurel wreath. On either side of that were medieval dragons. At one corner a grey stone pyramid rose; at the opposite one was what looked like a Chinese pagoda. The main building was black marble or something that looked like it, but the steps leading up to the entrance were some kind of pink stone; even through layers of soot and grime they had the color of rotting meat.

There were six doors; all were made of glass and all but one were cracked. To the sides of them were a pair of Egyptian sphinxes and a pair of Greek ones, ten feet tall or better, staring impassively down the Ohio Valley. Then, descending from behind them, forming handrails for the steps, were a pair of snakes carved out of something green. Mike touched one of them, put a finger into its open mouth. Cold. Stone cold.

"Say 'Ah.'"

It said nothing.

Across the façade were many-armed Hindu gods and goddesses, Greek centaurs, Christian demons. A strong gust of wind blew up. It happened every evening just before sunset; strong wind off the river. Mike zipped up his jacket and looked back over his shoulder at the shack. There was no sign of Helen.

He reached for the handle of the one intact door and pulled. The glass cracked into three large pieces and fell to the ground. Carefully, he stepped through the opening.

The lobby of the theater was huge, much larger than he had expected from the outside. Substantial chunks of the roof were gone, so there was plenty of light. A mural ran the length of the lobby, a desert scene: camels, palm trees, cloaked Arabs and a pyramid on the distant horizon. Opposite it, there was a second one: frontiersmen locked in battle with near-naked Indians. There had been a bar at one end; the enormous mirror behind it was cracked in half a dozen places. The staircases, one at each end of the lobby, were carved from bright blue dolomite. Maybe the architect had been color-blind.

On the floor in one corner lay a faded poster:

IMPERIAL OPERA HOUSE,
Bourbon, Pennsylvania

September 9–16, 1929.
One Week Only.

BERNHARDT
in
ANNA CHRISTIE

by America's Greatest Playwright

Eugene O'Neill.

Funny coincidence. When Helen woke up, he'd have to bring her in and show her this... this bit of theater history.

Sarah Bernhardt. The Divine Sarah, they used to call her. Who knew she'd ever played in a backwater like this?

Backwater, literally—he could hear the river lapping at the rear of the theater. The sound echoed clearly. There was that river smell, fish and moss, no mistaking it.

The doors leading into the auditorium were stuck, their hinges rusted. He forced one, and it gave out an awful creak.

In the auditorium, right at the center, lay the huge chandelier. It had fallen, just like the one in *Phantom of the Opera*. Mike, being an intellectual or something like one, thought of the Lon Chaney film, directed by Rupert Julian, not the Andrew Lloyd Webber musical. The Leroux novel was beyond him.

Most of the seats had been removed, probably sold off for reuse elsewhere, but for some reason a few were still in place. He looked under one. There were a dozen wads of old, dry chewing gum. Wondering if gum ever became fossilized, he folded the seat down—another loud creak—and sat back and took everything in.

The proscenium was lined with monsters. More sphinxes; more dragons, both Chinese and Occidental; a pair of minotaurs, right and left; and chimeras; gorgons; huge bats; enormous serpents. Just at the top of it a cyclops reared; in its right hand it held aloft what seemed to be a human head. And next to it was a representation of the Grim Reaper: a cloaked, hooded skeleton made of bronze, which was quite incongruously still gleaming.

Pillars, great stone columns, surrounded the hall. One of them was carved into a spiral, like the ones at St. Peter's, Rome. Another one was covered with grapevines, climbing up and down, heavy with stone fruit. There were traces of paint; it must have been a riot of color when it was new. Other columns were carved with crocodiles, cherubs, peacocks. At the base of one lay an Arab, lazily on his side, smoking a hookah; the smoke spiraled up the pillar. It was a chaos, a complete mess.

There was more wind. And it made a terrible groaning sound. It took him a moment to realize that under a pile of debris there was a big, heavy old theater organ still in place, and

Stage Fright

the wind was wheezing through it. Maybe the Imperial had been used for silent movies as well as plays? He thought of a dozen old horror movies where the villain played an organ like a madman. Why hadn't they taken the thing out? It must have been worth a lot in its day.

There was still light coming from outside, but it was almost nightfall. Shadows in the corners of the theater were deep and getting deeper. And he realized he couldn't see the back of the stage; it seemed to stretch on forever. It was a bit disconcerting.

Time to go and see if he could wake up Helen. Time to go back to shore. His mother would be staying dinner for him, and he didn't want to keep her waiting any more than he had to.

Someone moved behind him. There was no one there.

He knew, of course, all the stories about the Imperial being haunted. Old wives' tales, preposterous nonsense. Ghosts—be serious.

As if on cue, the organ played. Bach, the D Minor Toccata and Fugue, the very piece Karloff had played in *The Black Cat*, and a score of other movie villains had played in other potboilers.

There was, needless to say, no one at the keyboard.

Time to go, definitely. Ghosts. Piffle. Must be the wind. He got up and there was a strong gust. It came from out of the blackness on the stage. The organ thundered, a rendition of Wagner's "Ride of the Valkyries." It roared, and the roar echoed deafeningly through the Imperial Opera House.

From the stage came a voice, reciting something old, probably Shakespeare or worse. The voice came clearly, despite the sound of the wind and the scream of the organ. For the first time, Mike started to lose a bit of his cocksure confidence.

Then there were people pressing around him. Not visible. But they pressed harder and harder until it began to be painful. He fought to get away from them, whoever or whatever they were. But they were too strong, or there were too many of them. Helpless in their grip, he looked heavenward. But all he saw was the proscenium, with its procession of monsters. They were watching him and grinning.

* * *

Helen awoke. She didn't quite realize where she was for a moment, and the inside of the shack was dark, which didn't help. Then it came to her. She had been doing a bit of business.

It was late, too late to be on the island; it would be night soon. Her clothes were in a pile next to her, still damp. She realized that Mike had fucked her again while she was out. It was sufficiently cool that her wet things were quite uncomfortable, but there was nothing else to wear. Carefully she counted the money in the right pocket, to make sure he hadn't taken any back. That fifty bucks for the movie had really pissed him off, she could tell. She counted, and it was all there.

Outside, it was not quite night yet; but there were clouds and a moon. Frogs were croaking along the riverbank. But the sounds from the Imperial Opera House were louder and impossible to mistake. Organ music, just like she remembered from church. And screams, a man's screams.

Her rowboat was still tied to the little dock. The man screaming was Mike; it had to be. She watched the façade of the theater for a moment in the moon's cold light. Were the stone animals moving? Why was Mike screaming?

But he didn't scream for much longer. A cloud covered the moon, and when it passed, the animals were still again and all the sounds but the frogs had fallen silent.

Helen shrugged. She'd be able to manage the boat herself. Not bothering to look back, she got in and headed for shore as quickly as she could. The Ohio shore. Mike would have to fend for himself, if he was still capable of doing any fending. Right in the head or not, Helen knew better than to stay on that island after dark.

ONE

The Imperial Opera House waited, waited indeed.

There was sufficient time. The theater had stood patiently for more than a century, its inhabitants for two and a half. Its griffins, unicorns, dragons, sphinxes had seen generations come and go, and had tasted the blood of each.

And the ghosts that animated them? They had devoured more, and more substantial things than randy college boys. Tempered by long decades, they knew that they would devour more still.

Waiting was all.

"To be perfectly honest, Mr. Gallardo, I'm looking for ghosts." Joanna Marshall smiled at Vince Gallardo across his desk, which was not quite big enough to be impressive.

"Ghosts." His face was very carefully neutral.

"Yes, ghosts. Every theater has one, at least all these old, ornate, fabulous ones. I'm sure you've heard as many stories about them as I have."

Outside, it was snowing. From the window in his office, at the top of the Fulton Theater in downtown Pittsburgh, Joanna could see snow falling over the Allegheny River, which was being roiled by strong winter winds. She had to force herself to pay attention to Gallardo, who couldn't possibly be as important as he seemed to want her to think. PR people never were. They were flunkies, no more. She had figured that out a long time ago.

He shifted his weight and looked down at the desktop. "I'll be frank, Miss Marshall."

"Ms., if you don't mind." It seemed like a good idea to put him on the defensive.

"Ms., then. We conduct tours for the public every Saturday. You're more than welcome to join one of them. I have a registration form right here." He reached across and handed it to her. "The tour covers all three theaters the foundation administers. But I'm afraid giving you access to them independently, and without any kind of supervision . . ." He spread his hands wide apart in a bureaucrat's "what can I do?" gesture. "I'm afraid that would be quite impossible."

"But it's not the buildings themselves that interest me. I want to look into their history, especially the Fulton's. You must have heard the same legends I have. There's supposed to be a ghost here." She made herself smile as widely as she could manage. "An actress who was killed by a falling spotlight, I believe. At least that's one version. There's a story about a murder, too. There must be archives for this place. And surely they must mention her."

This wasn't going well, Gallardo realized. She was a student. A student for an advanced degree in theater arts, no less. She was supposed to be compliant and bend to the will of the Pittsburgh Arts Foundation and its representatives. He decided to be a bit more forceful. "If there is a ghost, Ms. Marshall, it is the property of the foundation. And I'm afraid that's not the kind of publicity we'd want."

Joanna turned sweet. "But Mr. Gallardo, there's no such thing as bad publicity. You must know that."

"I'm afraid it's out of the question. Our archives are—"

"Listen, I really want this, Mr. Gallardo. I've given a lot of thought to what I want to do my dissertation on, and I want to explore the influence of the irrational on the creative process."

" 'The irrational' meaning ghosts?"

"Exactly."

"But—"

"I was going to do sex, at first. All the ways sexuality has helped shape modern theater. Did you know George Bernard Shaw didn't have sex till he was thirty? If he'd started screwing in his teens, like everybody else, the world might never have had *Don Juan in Hell*."

"Or *My Fair Lady*." Unexpectedly he gushed this out like a true fan.

Joanna had never met a male publicist who wasn't gay. What was it about the job? The female ones tended to be gorgons. She found herself laughing. "Exactly. And if a simple thing like sex can influence creativity like that, just imagine what ghosts can do."

"But really, Ms. Marshall, there's not a thing I can do. We could never trust an outsider with our archives. The board would never permit it."

She frowned, then caught herself and put back the smile. It was time to get tough. "What about those letters of introduction I sent you? Do they really not count for anything?"

"Letters?" It caught him off guard, as she'd hoped it would. If she had any connections . . . Might she be related to one of the board members? It hadn't occurred to him, but it was a possibility.

He picked up the manila folder that contained her letter requesting a meeting. There was only that one sheet of paper in it. Puzzled, he rummaged lightly through the other things on his desk. "I don't seem to . . ." He scowled, opened the center desk drawer, realized they wouldn't be there and closed it again. "I'm afraid we . . . it looks like we never got them."

Playing at bewilderment she said, "I faxed them to you last week. You must have received them. I got a confirmation." She had done no such thing.

"I'm sure they've only been misplaced. Let me check with my secretary."

"Oh, please don't bother. I have the originals here with me." She reached into her purse and handed them to him.

He scanned them quickly. His eyes widened, and he

whistled softly. They were signed by a major Broadway producer, an administrator at Lincoln Center and a world famous actor. "I'm sure I never got these. I'd have remembered, believe me."

Pleased that his conversation had shifted from "we" to "I," Joanna told him not to give it another thought. "You see, I'm not just a student. And I'm not exactly an outsider to the theater world."

"Well . . ." The letters could be phony, of course, but he decided it wasn't worth taking the chance. These were important people. He glanced at his watch. "I have a few minutes free now. Why don't I show you around a bit?"

"Around the archives?"

"No, I'll have to get clearance for that. But it shouldn't be a problem. I thought I might just give you a quick tour of the theater for now."

"Well"—she turned into a coy coed—"if you'll promise me to take care of that other thing."

"You have my word." He checked his watch again. "It's twelve-thirty—lunch time. We should have the place pretty much to ourselves for a few minutes."

She followed him out of his office. He paused to tell the receptionist where he'd be, asked her to have one of the interns bring them some snacks, then led Joanna down a back flight of stairs. They were marble, yellowed and cracked; she guessed they were probably gleaming white when they were new.

Four flights down, they reached a stage door. Gallardo held the door for her, and she strode energetically through the wings and onto the stage. Planting herself firmly at the footlights, spreading her arms grandly like Auntie Mame, she gushed, "I can't tell you how I love these old places. They're all haunted." She looked over her should at him. "I'm sure this one is."

Gallardo watched her, amused. Even in a profession filled with, er, unusual people, Joanna Marshall was quite something. "Do you know how many people I've seen do that exact same thing? People can't resist being theatrically grand." He joined her center stage, still smiling. "There's something about these old theaters that turns everyone into a Barrymore."

She made her voice deep and dramatic, like Dame Judith

Anderson. "A Barrymore? Those vulgar little people." She made a grand, sweeping gesture. "They were all drunks, you know."

The theater was in fact quite empty except for the two of them. In one aisle, a cleaning woman had left a vacuum cleaner, but the woman herself was off on her midday break. Another one had left a mop, in a bucket of dirty, soapy water, leaning against the stage.

On the stage itself, a set of scaffolds had been erected; the set for a new play was being put up. There were work lights on extension cords, drop cloths, ladders, huge boxes of tools. In the wings there was a lot more of the same. Joanna commented on it all. "It looks more like a janitor's closet than the home of art and magic."

"Like all magic," Gallardo told her, "it's nothing but a confidence trick."

"I know," she said in a mock whisper. "My family are among the biggest con artists around."

It clicked for him. Those references—"Marshall? You're not related to Marianna Marshall, are you?"

Joanna nodded, then lowered her voice. "Don't spread it around, will you?"

"The daughter of a bona fide Broadway producer—granddaughter of one of the great vaudeville impresarios—how could I keep a thing like that secret?"

"How about on penalty of death?" She turned grand again, walked in a wide circle, center stage. "No one at school knows." This was another harmless lie. "I really don't want to trade on the family name."

"But—"

"Look, Mr. Gallardo, I'm here doing graduate work. I'm serious about theater, and I want to apply myself. Not the kind of stuff my mother does, but serious theater, important themes. I want to do something significant. Having people ask me about my family would be a—"

"That's right!" He snapped his fingers. "Your grandfather was a producer, too. Call me Vince."

"He was, yes. He produced Cole Porter's last musical. The one that put him in his grave."

Gallardo was a bit shocked. Like a lot of publicists in the city, he was young and handsome; the rest were all middle-aged women who seemed to be direct descendents of Medea. "I've seen so many of your mother's shows. You shouldn't—"

"I shouldn't talk about the theater in anything but reverent tones? Don't make me laugh. My mother produces second-rate Broadway revivals of musicals that should have been left buried, and then turns huge profits with cut-rate touring productions of them."

"She's provided us with a lot of product. Her shows have done very well for us."

Joanna was unimpressed. "This is Pittsburgh."

An intern walked onstage, carrying cups of coffee for them and a tray of Danish. She took the coffee but passed on the pastry. "Please—I have a girlish figure to maintain."

The kid asked if they needed anything else, then left. Gallardo was still watching Joanna, beaming. "A genuine, theatrical Marshall. You're theater royalty."

"Like French royalty before the revolution—ripe for the guillotine." She sipped her coffee and made a sour face. "So anyway, I want you to give me a bit of history. I want to know all about this building. Who played here, when, how often . . . all of it."

He held out a sheaf of papers. "Here—unofficial history of the place. It's the oldest theater in the region that's still standing, you know. Built in 1890. It was a big stop on the vaudeville circuit in its day."

Joanna thumbed through the papers while he went on with his lecture. It was clearly one he'd given many times before, but she didn't mind; and he seemed happy to be reciting it to the daughter of "a real Broadway producer."

"A lot of history happened here, Ms. Marshall. We were on the Orpheum Circuit. And when the Ziegfeld Follies toured through Pittsburgh, this theater was where they played."

"Call me Joanna."

"Joanna." It seemed to please him. "Do call me Vince, then. There were two great theaters here, back in the old days. The other one was a few blocks uptown. It was more of a legitimate house. It's long since been torn down and turned into a parking lot. And paved over three or four times since then. And there were smaller ones, a lot less prestigious. But this house . . ." He beamed. "It used to be called the Pittsburgh Theater."

"Why did they change it?"

"Oh, you know the arts. Different patrons, different funding sources." He shrugged. "It's probably just a matter of time before they start renaming theaters for junkyard owners."

"What do you think they're doing now?"

Vince laughed. "Anyway, all of the greats played here. W.C. Fields, Fanny Brice, The Lunts, the Barrymores, Helen Hayes, even going way back to Lillian Russell. You name a legendary theater performer, we had them here at the Fulton."

She was focusing. "There are photos and programs in the archives?"

"Well, sure." He pointed to the "official history" in her hand.

"There has to be more than this. There have to be old programs, press clippings, collections of reviews . . ."

"All locked away upstairs, I think. I've never actually checked them out. But I'm sure there won't be any trouble about—"

"That's the stuff I want to see. And contracts, production archives, that kind of thing. Whatever still exists. And," she added, heavily, "anything you have about the ghost."

Uncertainly he asked, "Does that stuff really interest you?"

She found his tone a bit condescending—he was talking to a theater student again, not a Marshall—and she put on a tight smile. "This MFA I'm working on means a lot to me. No one in my family has learned anything about the theater before me except by the seat of their pants. Family wisdom, passed down through the generations. There has to be a better way to do it than that. Or at least a smarter one."

"Besides vaudeville and musicals, didn't your grandfather produce Eugene O'Neill?"

"Yeah, and a couple hundred floppo shows nobody remembers. Theater's too important to be done in that haphazard way. I want to produce great art. I mean to learn how."

He wasn't at all sure how to respond to this. "Well, anyway, if you look through that official history, I'm sure it'll tell you a lot of what you want to know. Names, dates, details about the building of the theater and the two major renovations we've done. It's all there."

"And the ghost?"

"Well, no, I'm afraid that's not in there."

Joanna stepped close to him and put an arm around him. She craned her head backward and looked up into the flyspace. In a confidential tone she whispered, "Look up there. Look at all that empty space. Nothing but ropes and wires, but it's essential to the theater—more so than the things that show, really. That's what I want to research, the things that stay hidden from view, the things that never show."

This seemed to leave Gallardo nonplussed. Pulleys and ropes were real; ghosts . . . He was more and more certain she must be . . . the word they used in the theater was *eccentric*. "Well, like I told you, I've never even been through the archives myself. There never seemed to be any reason. But I promise I'll check with someone and let you know."

"Listen, Mr. Gallardo—"

"Vince."

"Vince. I'm not a dilettante. You know that. Aside from my family connections, I'm a credentialed scholar doing research for an MFA in theater at West Penn University. I'll be producing, myself, some day. Maybe even here." It seemed a good idea to remind him of that. "There has to be some way you can get me access quickly, so I can get started."

Her assertiveness caught him a bit off guard. "Well I'll, uh, I'll do what I can."

"Make it happen for me." She was the daughter of a producer, all right.

"I will, Joanna."

"Good. Now tell me what show you're preparing here."

"It's a new stage adaptation of Henry James's *The Turn of the Screw*."

"A ghost story! Perfect!"

"But—"

Unexpectedly, she took him by the hand and led him a few steps upstage. For the second time she looked up into the flyspace and gestured. "You think the theater's empty, don't you, Vince?"

He was lost. "Everyone's on lunch break."

"And the wings. To you, they're nothing but offstage space. A place to park props and scenery till they're needed."

"Well, I—"

"They're not empty. There's life. The life of the theater. Ghosts, the Spirit of Art, call it what you will. Something living and vital comes out of those empty corners."

He looked at her, mildly alarmed. Every theater producer he'd ever met had struck him as a bit crazy, Joanna's mother included. It had never occurred to him it might be hereditary.

Lunch time was over. Cleaning people and the stage crew began to file back into the auditorium, by ones and twos, and take up their work where they'd left off. A few of them had cups of coffee or soda cans. An overweight cleaning lady ate a hoagie. Vacuum cleaners wailed, power tools shrieked.

Vince put on a professional smile. "Now I imagine you want to see the Stanley and the Penn, too."

"Those monstrosities?" She wrinkled her nose. "They were built as movie palaces, right? Not as legitimate theaters?" Her tone suggested that anything as vulgar as a movie was far beneath her. "They're much too large for meaningful theater to happen there. Showy junk like *The Producers*, maybe, but . . ." She let the thought go unfinished.

Vince tried to ignore it all. "If they're larger, doesn't that mean they might hold more ghosts?"

"Don't make fun of me, Vince. They were originally movie palaces." She said the word "movie" with a bit of distaste.

"They were, yes. They were both built late in the silent film era. But you know how things were in those days. Theaters presented live shows between the movies. A lot of great performers played those halls. Dick Powell was the emcee of the stage shows at the Stanley before he made the move to Hollywood."

"Really? I don't think I knew that. Maybe I'll have to check them out, too. When I find the time. But . . ." She let her voice trail off and looked around the theater still again. "Listen, how extensive are the press clippings in the archive for this place?"

"They're pretty thorough, I think. But like I said, I've never really . . ." He looked a bit embarrassed. "A PR person lives in the present and the near future, not the past."

"Behind the scenes stuff? Production memos, that kind of thing?"

"I really couldn't say. I'd have to—"

"I want to know about ghosts."

"Of course." So they were back to that. "I wish I could convince myself you're really serious."

She glared at him, "Believe me, Vince, I am."

"But—"

"You must know the stories. Some of them, at least. My mother used to produce shows in the Belasco Theater on Broadway. It's haunted by the ghost of David Belasco himself."

"That old producer?"

"I come from a long line of old producers, remember?"

"I didn't mean it like that. I—"

"You must know about it. Everyone in theater must. Belasco's ghost used to show up during rehearsals. Especially during long, grueling ones. In the small hours of the morning, when people couldn't get a show or even a scene to work right, and they were exhausted and nerves were frayed, there would be Belasco's ghost, stalking through the theater, watching them all with obvious disdain."

His skepticism registered pretty clearly in his face. "And did he doctor their scripts for them?"

"You think I'm joking. I'm not." She made herself smile again. "I saw him myself. Back when I was in my teens. My mother produced that dreadful revival of that old Sondheim show, and I sat in on rehearsals. And late one night—three, four o'clock in the moring—I saw him. He walked slowly across the rear of the mezzanine. He climbed up to the balcony. He was white and transparent. And he looked down his nose at me as if to say, 'You fools, you think you know how to do a play well, you think you understand art, but you are nothing compared to what we used to do.' "

She seemed to have gone into a little trance. Hoping to bring her out of it, he put a hand lightly on her arm. When she looked into his eyes and he knew she was all right, he let go again and sipped his coffee. "I know everyone says theater used to be glorious, that the twenties were the Golden Age of Broadway. I've heard it all a million times. But I don't see how that can be. We can do so much more today—everything's computerized. We can do lighting cues and scene shifts that would have been impossible even thirty years ago."

"Theater is all about tradition, Vince. If we lose touch with the past, we're nothing."

"Oh." He wanted to like her. But she was . . . well, *eccentric*, even more so than most theater people. "Well, listen, it's going to get pretty noisy in here. Why don't I get in touch with you as soon as I've got clearance for you to examine the archives?"

"That'll be fine." She seemed not to realize she was being given the bum's rush, or else she didn't care. "And remember: ghosts. I want you to give me ghosts."

Uncertainly he told her, "Well, I'll do what I can." Then, quite abruptly, he dropped his professional manner and turned into a human being. "Doesn't it occur to you that if we stay in touch with the past, it might affect us in ways we don't want it to?"

"I'm not sure what you mean."

"I'm not sure what I mean, myself. But mucking around with the past . . . I mean, we have to live in the present."

She shrugged. But she was pleased he was defrosting a bit for her. "It's like I said, theater is tradition."

"That's what they say in *Fiddler on the Roof*. And then the pogroms start." This seemed to catch her off guard. When she didn't know how to respond, he told her, "Listen, it's been a real pleasure meeting you. Let me walk you to the entrance."

He led her up the center aisle, past workers and cleaning people. Unexpectedly, he laughed. "We've had shows that have played to smaller audiences than this."

"You should have seen the houses for my mother's last show."

They made their way through the lobby to the front entrance on Sixth Street. Vince shook her hand. "Listen, I'm sorry if I was a bit distant earlier. When you started talking about ghosts . . ." He put on a nice, warm smile. "We get other people asking about that, from time to time, and they're all crackpots."

"Well, my pot's as cracked as any, I guess."

"No, not at all. You're one of us. You're real theater. It's in your blood, I can tell."

"That sounds mighty inclusive for a PR guy."

"I was an acting major. This is—"

She said it with him: "just till I get my break."

They both laughed, and Vince went on. "I went to West Penn, too. And I did all the things theater students do—acted dreadfully in Shakespeare, looked down my nose at Andrew Lloyd Webber, got drunk with my friends and fantasized about starting our own company. . . ."

Joanna shook his hand. "It was good meeting you, too. And confidentially . . ."

"Yes?"

"I'm still in the 'let's found our own company' phase myself."

"We all do it." He raised his arms over his head, snapped his fingers and sang, "Tradition!"

Now that the ice had thawed, Joanna decided she liked him. And he seemed to feel the same way about her. That was good—he might be useful in any number of ways.

They shook hands again, and she walked happily to her bus stop. The snow was getting heavier, and black clouds were building eerily to the west of the city. She was hungry, but she decided to wait till she got back to school before getting a bit of lunch. With what looked like a big storm developing, she wanted to get back to campus as soon as she could.

The campus theater at Western Pennsylvania University was in a Gothic Revival building next to Gothic Revival Academic Tower which, visitors were routinely told, was the tallest scholastic building in the world. It soared in a way the builders of Notre Dame could never have dreamed. The theater itself was much less imposing.

An hour after her interview with Gallardo, Joanna was back

on campus. The snow was heavier now, and though it was not yet dusk, the sky was dark enough for streetlights to be on; the forecasters were all predicting a major storm that night. A gust of wind nearly knocked her off balance. She wrapped her scarf a bit more tightly around her face, and headed for the theater. Things at the foundation had gone better than she expected.

Gothic. Improbable style for a university theater. Hell, improbable style for a university. There were lancet windows, flying buttresses, heavy doors that might have come off a Renaissance church in Florence, even gargoyles. But inside, the theater was all quite modern. Joanna always found the contrast jarring. Why couldn't the interior have any atmosphere? If there was ever a theater that ought to have a ghost . . .

But a succession of renovations had processed all the flavor out of the place. She thought fleetingly that that was a good metaphor for what was happening to the arts everywhere in the country; but she was too cold for much reflection.

Inside, the lobby was taken up with a huge canvas backdrop, spread out on the floor. It was positively enormous—for a mainstage production of a classic musical. John Bartlett, assistant production designer, and a freshman named Tim something were on their knees, busily painting trees, shrubs and clouds. Even though Joanna pulled the door firmly shut behind her, there were drafts and the lobby was freezing.

John smirked at her. "You just had to do that, didn't you?"

"Would you have liked me to stay out in the storm?"

"Don't ask."

She stopped and inspected their work. "No, those clouds are too fluffy. This is supposed to be an abstract landscape, not an ad for fabric softener." She put on a sardonic smile. "Hi, John."

They both looked up at her, then glanced at each other. John, who looked like he ought to be a linebacker on the football team instead of a theater major, gaped. "Hello, Joanna. Why don't you make yourself useful and turn up the thermostat a few degrees?" There was no sign he was glad to see her. He nodded in the direction of the mainstage auditorium. "Mark's onstage."

"I figured. Can't you guys work in the basement or someplace less drafty? It's like the North Pole in here."

"We don't mind."

She had only met the younger of the two once before, and she wasn't quite certain who he was. Smiling, she held out a hand. "I'm Joanna Marshall. That's my design you're painting."

"Tim Myers." He wiped the paint off his hands.

"Nice to meet you, Tim."

"I'm a freshman."

"Well, don't tell anybody and they'll never guess."

He wasn't sure if she was making fun of him.

Joanna gave them more feedback on the drop; she didn't seem to like anything they'd done. It should be darker, it should be starker, it should have fewer blues and more greys. Hadn't they consulted her sketches?

John got to his feet, crossed to a pile of sketches and pulled hers out. Unrolling it, he put on the biggest grin. "See? Fluffy clouds, lots of sun, not much grey."

Annoyed with him, she said, "Well, the concept has changed. This is a revisionist, postmodern *Oklahoma!*"

"You can't expect us to know that."

"Make the clouds darker and stormier. Look outside and you'll see what I want."

"Yes, ma'am." He got back down on the floor and resumed his work on the drop.

"Less blue, more grey."

"You're in a disagreeable mood, Joanna. Didn't your meeting downtown go well?"

She realized she was still bundled against the cold, took off her gloves and began to unwrap her scarf. "Am I being too bitchy?"

"Let's just say that until you uncovered your face just now, I wasn't sure it was you."

She looked at him, waiting for him to go on.

"I thought it might be your mother."

She laughed. "God, am I being as bad as that?"

"Pretty much, yeah." John turned to Tim and told him, "Joanna's mother is Marianna Marshall."

The kid's face went blank.

"The Broadway producer," he prompted.

It still barely registered. The kid turned to Joanna. "You know someone from Broadway?"

"I know her, all right, but not very well."

He was even more baffled. Joanna decided to let him work it out for himself. Gesturing in the direction of the auditorium she asked John, "You said Mark's in there?"

"Yep. Working with 'Honey'."

"Oh." A look of concern crossed her face. "Why aren't they downstairs in the studio theater? Isn't that where they're doing the show?"

"Tech crew's working there."

"Oh." She seemed to study the backdrop again. "If he's having trouble, maybe I shouldn't go in."

"Nah, I think he'll be glad to see you." He laughed a bit. "At this point, he'd be glad to see anyone who isn't a dumb actress."

"Don't be a sexist. The character's supposed to be clueless, remember?"

"The character, sure, but not the one playing her. About an hour ago I saw her look at her script, scratch her head and ask Mark, 'I don't get it—who *is* afraid of Virginia Woolf?'"

"You're kidding." Despite herself, she broke out laughing, too.

"Is there anything on the face of this planet emptier than an acting student?"

"Shh." Mildly alarmed, she looked around. "They're not supposed to know tech people think things like that."

John put down his paintbrush, got to his feet and stretched. "If we're going to start talking about what actors know, this going to be a mighty short conversation."

Tim had been listening to this with obvious concern. Startled at what he was hearing, he gaped and said, "You mean Nicole Kidman might be dumb?"

They ignored him. John wiped some paint off the back of his hands onto his sweatshirt. "So, tell me about your meeting. Did you find any ghosts?"

She unzipped her coat and dropped it and her bag into a

corner. "No, but I'm working on it. I met their PR guy. He might be useful. And I think you'd like him."

John turned a wary eye to the freshman and decided to save that conversation for later. No use confusing the kid more than he already was. "He actually told you there really is a ghost?"

"No. As a matter of fact, he was pretty skeptical. But he's going to get me access to the theater's archives. There are bound to be old news stories and so on."

Tim gaped still another time. "A ghost in a theater?" He looked around nervously.

"Relax, Tom."

"Tim."

"Sorry, Tim. I was downtown, at the Fulton."

"Oh." He didn't seem to find this reassuring. Again he looked around, quite wide-eyed. Freshmen.

John decided to explain for him. "Joanna's fascinated by irrational influences on art. Why don't we call out for pizza?"

"Irrational?" Tim said the word as if he'd never heard it before and it had an alien sound to his ear. "What's irrational about the theater?"

"You're new around here, aren't you?" Joanna turned wry.

John got between them. "You'd do better to ask what *isn't* irrational. I mean, look at this backdrop. It's not bad, but it's not exactly a masterpiece of realism. We've sketched in suggestions of a prairie and the sky above it. But when we put it up, the actors in front of it will act as if it's real, and the people in the audience will buy it."

"Pizza sounds good." Her hands were still cold; she rubbed them together. "You have a lot more confidence in both our cast and our audience than I do."

"No, I'm serious. Whatever we decide to do—a party in a Beekman Place apartment, the parlor of a professor's house on a small college campus, an angel crashing through the roof of a house, whatever—becomes real. The collective will of everyone involved, actors, director, technicians and audience—"

"Oh, don't forget the audience!" Joanna didn't try to hide her sarcasm.

He ignored her. "Whatever we decide to do becomes real."

"We ought to put up a bank, then."

Tim looked from one of them to the other. "And what does all that have to do with ghosts?"

Joanna said, "Nothing," and John said "Everything!" at the exact same moment.

Tim blinked and stammered, "Wh-what do you want on the pizza? I like sausage."

Joanna put her hands on her waist. "I think I'd better pass. My ballooning hips need some attention. You boys have fun."

"We could get it plain, Joanna."

"No thanks." Without waiting for an answer, she left them and walked into the auditorium.

John turned to Tim, grinned and said, "Welcome to the theater."

The hall was biggish, some five hundred seats plus a balcony. It was dark except for three work lights that bathed the stage in harsh white light. Joanna's boyfriend, Mark Barry, was sitting at the edge of the stage, legs dangling, script in hand. A young actress sat in front of him, in a seat in the theater's front row. They were shouting at one another. One of the work lights flickered a bit.

From the corner of his eye Mark saw Joanna enter, but he kept his focus squarely on the young woman in front of him. "What exactly don't you understand about dancing, Annie? She thinks she can dance like the wind."

"I can't dance." Annie sniffed, loudly. "I'm a legitimate actress."

"You're not supposed to be able to dance. The character isn't supposed to be able to dance. She dances badly but thinks she's good. Get it?"

"No." She shouted the word. "How can I think I'm good if I know I'm bad?"

By this time Joanna had reached the foot of the aisle. She crossed quickly to Mark and kissed him on the cheek, then smiled broadly at the girl. "I believe it's called acting."

Another sniff. "I don't get it. Nothing anybody says makes any sense."

Mark let out an exasperated sigh. "Have you two met? Joanna Marshall, Annie Moore. Look, Annie, why don't you find an empty rehearsal room and work on the script, okay? We'll work on the physical stuff later. You'll be fine."

"Well . . ." she seemed to suspect he wanted to get rid of her, which he did. "All right, I guess."

"Good." He plastered a big, phony smile across his face. Annie gathered her script and personal things and ambled up the aisle, muttering to herself. When she was out of the auditorium, Mark slumped over Joanna's shoulder in an exaggerated way and kissed her. "Christ save me from actresses."

She wrinkled her nose. "Sure. Like male actors are intellectual giants."

He clambered up onto the stage, stood and stretched. "So how did things go?"

"I didn't get past the publicist. Guy named Vince Gallardo. He seemed to like me, though. And he seemed to like mother's name even more."

"Good." There was a plastic coffee cup sitting on the stage. "I like the thought of a useful mother-in-law."

"Don't get too confident. She's hated every guy I've ever dated."

"You are *not* 'dating' me, you're engaged to me."

"Well, what Mother doesn't know won't hurt you."

He headed into the wings and killed the work lights. The only illumination came from the windows in the auditorium doors. Mark decided the effect was romantic; he took her in his arms and kissed her again, longer and harder than before. "Let's get some lunch."

"Let's. I haven't eaten all day."

"A growing girl like you. I've been working with Miss Brain Trust since before noon. I'm starving." Mark got his coat from a corner of the stage.

She gave a slight shrug. "Maybe we can find a stable and eat that horse hungry people are always talking about."

He ignored her stab at wit. "How about the Z?"

"Do we have to?"

"I need grease."

The Z was the campus hangout. It was short for The Zone, and it was always crowded and noisy, and the food tended to be saturated with grease. Mark loved it; Joanna loathed it but

Stage Fright   31

usually went along for the sake of harmony. Trouble in paradise.

The place was crowded with fratboys, all drinking beer and shouting about this weekend's football game. Mark followed Joanna as she pushed her way through the crowd; they got the last free table, at the back of the room. An overweight kid with a buzz cut spilled beer on her. Instead of saying anything to him, she rounded on Mark. "Just once, couldn't we eat someplace where the children's menu isn't the most appropriate thing they have?"

"It'll wash out."

"That's not the point."

"It is." He decided to ignore her mood. "I'll get us a couple of beers, okay?"

"Why, don't I look wet enough?"

He turned and headed through the crowd. A few minutes later he was back with a pitcher of beer, two glasses and a large basket of fries. She grumped; he ate.

When she seemed to be calming down, he asked more about her meeting at the Arts Foundation. She told him about Vince Gallardo and his promise to get her access to the old records and press clips and such. "And he told me that, yes, there are legends of a ghost haunting the Fulton."

"I wish there was some way I could persuade you to stop this chasing after poltergeists. It creeps me out."

She scowled at the fries, then took one and bit into it. "These are worse than usual. Are you afraid of ghosts, then?"

"No, I'm afraid of being married to someone who believes in them."

Against her will she took a few more fries. They were salty, which meant addictive. "I wish I could find someone, anyone who'd take this seriously. Do you know how long and how hard I had to argue to get the department to accept this as my thesis topic?"

"Yes." He was the model of a long-suffering boyfriend.

"John Bartlett kids me about it all the time."

Mark drained his glass and poured himself another beer. "Why single him out? Everybody does."

"Including my loving fiancé." Irritably, she pushed the

fries away. "But you should have heard John just now, talking about the irrational in the theater. The way our collective will makes things that ought to be false become real. I'd think he'd understand where I'm coming from, if anyone would."

A few of the fratboys got out a Nerf football and started tossing it around. It landed squarely in Mark's fries. Annoyed, he tossed it back to them. Joanna rolled her eyes and sighed an exaggerated sigh. "Just once, couldn't we?"

"That 'collective will' makes things real all right. But only for the duration of the play." He repositioned himself to protect his meal from any further foreign objects. "The minute the lights come up, everyone remembers how completely *un*real it all is. Plywood, paint, paper maché and pancake makeup."

Joanna frowned and took a sip of her beer. "This is foul."

"Yeah, but it makes you want something to take the taste out of you mouth, doesn't it? It's a sneaky way to drum up more business."

For a few moments they fell silent. Mark ate, Joanna watched the ruckus around them and wished they were someplace else. Finally something dawned on Mark. Something that made him even more uncomfortable. " 'Collective will'? You're talking about a séance or something, aren't you? About actually trying to make spirits materialize."

Joanna lowered her eyes and didn't answer, which was all the answer he needed.

"Look, Jo, there are no such things as ghosts. All the collective will in the world can't create what isn't there."

She responded with more silence, the silence of the true believer.

"Jo, will you say something?"

"Everyone I've ever heard talk about the theater," she told him emphatically, "has talked about the magic it creates."

"They don't mean that literally."

"I don't think most of us know how we mean it. But we all say it, all the time. Turn on the Tony Awards next June and listen."

"Joanna, will you please stop talking like this?"

"No. Listen to me. Think what this can do for us. We've been talking for months about starting our own company. You, me, John, everyone in our circle. But it's idle talk, and most of us know it. You need something special to make a theater company fly, something to make it stand out from the ten thousand others. A ghost could do that for us."

"If there was such a thing."

"Mark, if we can find a theater with a real ghost, or better yet more than one, we could play up that angle in all our PR. It could make us."

He looked at her sideways as he took another drink. "The pitcher's empty. Should I get another one?"

"Will you listen to me and stop trying to change the subject? Mark, we can attribute everything that happens to the supernatural. The papers and the TV stations would eat it up."

"I want some more beer."

"Not until you tell me what you think."

"I think," he said slowly and emphatically, "that maybe you've had enough to drink already."

She stiffened and didn't say another thing.

"I'm hungrier than I thought. I'm going to get a burger."

"Go ahead."

While he was gone, one of the fratboys got up on a table and started to strip. Joanna watched till he was down to his bikinis, then got up, put on her coat and headed for the door. As she passed the stripper, she pushed a dollar bill into his underwear. It fell out.

Mark saw her leaving but decided he was too hungry to follow her. They'd make up later.

But the discussion continued when they were both back at their apartment. Joanna still resented his not taking her seriously; he resented her not being reasonable. Outside, the winter storm was raging. Snow, ice, wind. The sound of it accompanied their argument.

"Look, Jo, let's say I agree about the PR angle. Yeah, it could get us a few good stories up front. But you know the press. In a few weeks they'd be tired of our ghost."

"A good PR person could keep the story alive."

"Even so, why would we have to find a 'real' ghost?" He

leaned on the word *real* with sarcastic emphasis. "If this is all a PR ploy, why not just invent one?"

"We don't have to."

The argument went on all evening, through dinner and beyond, quieting down, then erupting again at the least provocation. They each had coursework to do; when it was finished they decided to watch a DVD. Joanna suggested *The Haunting*; Mark wanted Penn & Teller's *Bullshit!*

The tension was still there when they went to bed. Mark wanted to make love; Joanna told him there wasn't the ghost of a chance. He sat up with a copy of *Penthouse* for a while, headed to the bathroom, then got back into bed and went to sleep. She was quite asleep herself by then.

Joanna dreamed.

And in her dreams were monsters. And the monsters, some of them, were human.

Scaled serpents breathed fire and burned the eyes out of a man's head. Harpies pinned a woman to the ground, slit her throat and cackled as she bled to death. A child impaled himself on a long knife. And a chorus of men, hidden in shadow, sang a dirge for all the dead.

She cried out softly in her sleep, but Mark was out too soundly to hear her. She tossed violently, but he slept the sleep of the satisfied.

There was something around her throat, choking her. She struggled against it and gasped for breath, but she couldn't get a good grip. Whatever it was writhed and undulated and wouldn't stop moving. A snake. An enormous one.

Then she opened her eyes. Mark was there. He'd been shaking her, trying to wake her up. The room was pretty dark, but he had switched on a small lamp on the nightstand.

Instinctively putting her hands up to her neck, she blinked at him and asked, stupidly, what time it was.

"It's the middle of the night, Joanna, that's what time it is."

She was still shaking off sleep and her nightmare. "Did you have to wake me up so roughly?"

"Yeah, I did." Mark got out of bed and pulled his shorts on.

"Every time you have one of these things, it gets harder and harder to wake you out of it. All this damn talk about ghosts. That's what causes these nightmares."

"Get me a glass of water, will you?"

"Yes, ma'am."

She sat up. "I saw it again."

From the bathroom he called, "Saw what?"

"I've told you. I keep dreaming about this place, this mad old theater with monsters of all kinds crawling about its façade. Each time, a different one attacks me."

"Maybe they're pissed that you keep turning down the electric blanket."

"I'm serious, Mark. Tonight, it was a snake, a huge one, wrapping itself around my throat and squeezing. Then it opened its huge mouth, wider than seemed possible, and poised to sink its fangs into me."

He came back with her water. "Here. I put a shot of scotch in it." He sat down on the side of the bed. "Your snake lore's rusty. Constrictors don't kill with their fangs. Vipers don't constrict."

"Thanks, Mr. Science."

"Don't mention it. Can we get back to sleep, now?"

She took a long swallow. "Mark, it's the ghosts that bring these things on. I know it."

"Don't start, will you?" He crawled into bed beside her, switched off the light and pulled up the covers. "I never have any dreams at all."

"No wonder you decided to work in theater."

"Shut up and go to sleep."

"Mark, I'm telling you, these dreams are real. There's this place, this awful, ugly old place. I keep seeing it."

He was not going to get any sleep. He sat up and switched on the lamp again. "We've been through this, how many times? You've seen every old theater in the city. You've been as far afield as Johnstown and Wheeling. The place you dream about is just that, a dream."

"No. It can't be. It's too real."

"Don't be silly."

"You remember the night I dreamed that the sphinx there

was clawing me? And I woke up and there were all those deep scratches on my stomach?"

"That hasn't happened since you cut your nails to a reasonable length."

She got up and crossed to the mirror. There were marks on her throat. "And am I imagining these?"

"No, but I think you did it to yourself, while you were dreaming."

"Mark, I—"

"There are no ghosts. Only ghost stories. Now if you don't mind, I need to get some sleep. I have an Albee play to direct and a clueless cast to wrestle with. Why student actors always want to do plays that are beyond them . . ."

She didn't move from the mirror. Mark got out of bed, moved behind her and put his arms on her shoulders. "Take something. I think there's still some valerian in the cabinet. You'll sleep better."

"No."

"You want me to light a joint?"

She nodded. He got one out of the nightstand drawer, lit it, took a drag and passed it to her.

"Here. Maybe instead of this damned ghost thing, you should do your research into old theaters in the region. You'll either find this place or satisfy yourself that it's imaginary."

"The theater and the ghosts go together." She passed it back.

Mark took a long, deep drag. Then he stretched out on the bed. "I wish I knew what to tell you. You hit on this ghost idea for your thesis, and then you start having dreams. I don't see how the connection could be any clearer."

Joanna held onto the joint and smoked it all.

The theater in her dreams was real, and she knew it.

Mark switched off the lamp, turned up the electric blanket again and rolled over, hoping he could finally get some sleep.

TWO

The bronze sphinx atop the Imperial Opera House sat unmoving, carefully balanced, looking eastward into the rising sun. She was a Greek-style sphinx, lion's body, eagle's wings, head and breasts of a woman. And she had a long, distinguished pedigree; her ancestor had sat on a rock outside ancient Thebes and devoured everyone who could not answer her riddle. The sphinx at the Imperial had one advantage over the mythical one, though. She was real.

Being bronze, she was not hungry, exactly. The spirit that animated her was gone, for the moment. But it had been awhile since she'd had rich, red blood to drink. Like her companions throughout the theater, she was not inhabited by any ghosts just at that moment. She sat and waited and looked patiently to the sunrise. Or was she watching eternity, knowing that nothing ever really ends?

The Pittsburgh winter was erratic and wildly variable, as Pittsburgh winters tend to be. What can you expect in a city that sits precisely where the East, the Midwest and the upcountry South run into each other? A week after the blizzard, temperatures were in the seventies. Students at West Penn walked around in shorts and sandals. A few professors even held their classes outdoors, on lawns or the roofs of buildings. Despite the warm weather, though, the snow from the storm hadn't melted entirely. Little patches of it still lay in corners, especially shadowed ones. More than one campus type, not paying attention to where he was going, found himself stepping into a puddle of slush. In sandals, not pleasant.

Mo Settles was too short to be an athlete, at least not in any sport his friends would have respected. People took that as the reason he wasn't playing basketball for the school. But the simple fact was, he was bored by sports. And he loved history, really loved it, in a way few people ever did. Especially his own history.

On the warmest of the warm days, dressed in shorts, sandals and a tank top, he made his way to the theater. Some friends were playing touch football on the lawn of Academic Tower, and he stopped to say hi. A few girls were sunbathing not far away, and he took a moment to watch them. They were on a thick blanket, thick enough not to become soaked for a while. One of them smiled back at him. The consensus was, he was cute.

"Mo!" One of his friends was especially glad to see him and dropped out of the game.

"Hi, Jeff."

"What's up? You want to play for a while?"

"No thanks. I'm working on an independent study project."

Jeff smiled. "That girl over there wants to do some independent study with you."

"How can you tell?" He looked at the girl in question, and as near as he could tell, she was indifferent.

"Get a clue, Mo."

He shrugged. "I never know." He looked again. Could she really be interested in him? "Besides, I'm with Tonya."

"Whatever." Jeff suddenly jumped back into the game, just in time to tag an opposing player. A controversy broke out. Unfair. Cheating. Mo, having no interest in the outcome, went on his way.

Stage Fright

The Gothic architecture of the theater—and of Academic Tower—pleased him. There was something old, or oldish, something traditional on a campus that seemed determined to keep up with the most unattractive current trends. Two guys were on ladders, raising a banner over the entrance that announced *Oklahoma!* and *Who's Afraid of Virginia Woolf?* as the first productions of the winter term. A half dozen students came out of the building in a group, and all of them superstitiously avoided walking under the ladders.

The lobby was empty. He put his head in the door of the mainstage theater. The stage was lit brightly with work lights, and a crew was busy hoisting a painted backdrop into place. Prairie landscape, stormy sky overhead. A young woman, about his age, was supervising them; she seemed to be unhappy about everything. At one side of the stage two male dancers practiced what looked like a hoedown; at the opposite side were four girls doing ballet steps.

Mo walked down the aisle to the stage and caught the attention of one of the stagehands, a kid, from the looks of him a freshman. "Excuse me. I'm looking for the Drama Library."

"The—?"

"The library."

The kid looked baffled. "Library?"

"You know—it's an old-fashioned place where they keep books."

"Books?"

The woman who had been supervising overheard this and got between them. She told the stagehand, whose name was Tim, it turned out, to get back to work, then turned to Mo. "Hi, I'm Joanna Marshall." She said this as if it might mean something to him, which it didn't.

"Hi, I'm Mo Settles. I'm looking for—"

She got down on one knee and shook his hand. "I heard. You're in the wrong place. The library's in the department. This is just the theater."

"Oh. I thought—"

"I'll be heading up there myself in a few minutes. You can come with me, if you like."

"Thanks."

"Just give me a few minutes to get this damned drop in place."

She got back to her feet and went back to barking orders at her crew. Mo dropped into a front row seat and watched as the work went on. Joanna was more than a bit, well, bossy; the kind of woman usually called a bitch. But she was getting the job done. Mo wasn't much of a theatergoer, but as near as he could tell, the show would look fine.

A tech guy came in with a ladder and climbed it to adjust a few of the lights. He repositioned some of them and placed colored gels over some others. When he dropped one of the gels, Joanna barked at him. The tech was pissed; Mo was amused.

Another guy came in and sat two seats away from him. Mo smiled and said hi.

"Hi. I'm Mark Barry."

"Mo Settles."

They shook. Mark looked him up and down. "I don't think I've seen you around before. You transfer in this semester?"

"I'm not in the Theater Department." And he was glad of it; on stage, Joanna was yelling even louder. "I'm a grad student in history."

"Well, you may get to see some history here today. The first time a production designer was eaten alive by her stage crew."

Mo looked at her again. "She is a bit, well . . ."

"Yes, she is. She's my fiancée."

"Oh. I didn't know. Sorry."

"It's all right. Her mother's a Broadway producer. As near as I can tell, being unpleasant to co-workers must be genetic."

"Then why do you—?"

"Because I love her." He shrugged slightly. "Besides, she's only like that when she's working. One-on-one, she's terrific." He hesitated, then decided to say it. "Unlike her mother, from what I hear."

Joanna looked at her watch. It wasn't quite time for a break. She decided the backdrop was an inch too low on the stage left side.

Mark focused his attention on Mo. "So what's a history student doing here? Slumming?"

"Nope. I'm—"

"Don't tell me. You couldn't make it to the zoo, and you decided actors are just as good as baboons."

Mo forced himself not to laugh. "I'm doing research. Or at least that was the idea. I thought the Drama Library was in this building."

"It's up in the department."

"So Joanna told me." He glanced at the stage. "This is for *Oklahoma!*?"

Mark nodded. "We thought about doing *Virginia Woolf* in a prairie setting, but it wasn't working, so . . ." He put on a wide grin.

But the joke was lost on Mo. "I've never seen either one of them."

"Wow, you're really in alien territory, aren't you? I thought everyone had to see *Oklahoma!* at least once when they were growing up. As a kind of penance for being American."

"Not me, I'm afraid."

"What kind of theater do you like?"

"Like I said, I'm not really a theater person at all."

Mark found it odd but resisted the temptation to say so. "You should come to some of our shows, sometime. I'm directing *Woolf*."

"Well, now that I know someone here . . ."

"We're doing *Woolf* downstairs, in the studio theater. I had to take a break or I'd have killed one-fourth of my cast."

Onstage, Joanna launched into a wild outburst, directed at no one in particular, or rather at everyone generally. It was Monday, and the goddamned show was due to open on Thursday. How did they expect it to be ready? Dress rehearsal was two days away. Did they expect the cast to play in front of a half-dressed stage?

When she finished and the echoes died down, Mo turned uncertainly to Mark. "Is it always like this?"

"Are you kidding? Compared to some shows I've worked, that was downright polite and parliamentary."

"I don't get it. Why would anyone want to work in an atmosphere like this?"

"Almost every show I've ever worked on has been weighed down with tension and friction. But somehow, out of all the unpleasantness, art emerges. That's what keeps us all going. It's irrational, I know. Downright weird. But . . ." Instead of finishing his sentence, he smiled at Mo still again.

"So, do you act like this with *your* crew?"

"More or less." Mark looked slightly self-conscious. "It keeps them on their toes. I'm nowhere near as ladylike as Joanna, though."

"No, I wouldn't have thought 'ladylike' would be the word for you." He grinned. "Though from what I've heard about theater . . ."

"Don't believe all the gossip. We're all devout saints, here."

Finished with her tirade, Joanna jumped down off the stage and joined them. She shook Mo's hand energetically. "Welcome to the Sooner State." Then she pecked Mark on the cheek.

"Hi." Mo smiled; from all the screaming, he'd been expecting her to be in a foul mood. "Are you heading to the department now?"

"In just a minute. I have to give John a few notes. Then we'll get out of here." She vaulted back up onto the stage and headed for the wings.

Mo looked at Mark. "Busy."

"Good, too. Personally, I can't see doing a revisionist production of Rodgers and Hammerstein. I mean, however dark you may make it, you're still stuck with that score. But the director wanted it and she delivered." He gestured at the stage and the backdrop.

In a flash Joanna was back. She got her coat from one of the house seats, took Mo by the arm and said, "Let's go."

He looked to Mark. "Are you coming, too?"

"Nope. I'm just giving my leads a quick break," He grinned. "They're fucking in a closet and think I don't know. Best to let them blow off steam."

"Oh. Well, I guess I'll see you around, then."

Stage Fright

"Sure thing."

Slightly bewildered, Mo followed Joanna up the aisle to the lobby. So this was what theater was like. He was both fascinated and put off. These shows had to be terrible, just terrible. He'd have to get tickets for himself and Tonya so he could see.

Outside, Joanna paused at the top of the theater steps and took a deep breath. "Just smell the good Pittsburgh air."

"As a general thing, I try to do without."

She strode off down the steps, leaving him to catch up. When he was beside her she looped her arm through his. "So. Do you believe in ghosts?"

The question couldn't have been more unexpected. "Uh . . . I guess I've never given it any thought."

"The more I think about it, the more I think I do."

"Uh, fine. And what leads you to share such intimate thoughts with me?"

Jo giggled. "You have a bit of an attitude. Are you sure you're not a theater person?"

"Reasonably sure, yeah."

"What can you be researching at the department, then?"

"Suppose I say ghosts?"

"Then I'd tell you you're encroaching on my territory. I'm doing my thesis on theater ghosts and their effect on the creative process."

He narrowed his eyes; was she putting him on? He decided it was safest to ignore it. "My research is for my thesis, too. I'm looking into old show business portrayals of African Americans, especially minstrel shows. I thought I might be able to find some useful stuff in the Theater Department's library."

"Ghosts sound like more fun."

He shrugged. "I'm not sure they don't come to the same thing, pretty much. The dead past refusing to stay dead, still affecting us today."

A gust of wind blew up, with a bit of a chill in it. Joanna shuddered. "It looks like this warm spell will be ending soon."

"Everything ends, more or less. But everything leaves something behind when it goes."

Jo stopped walking and looked straight into his eyes. "You see? That's what I mean. Ghosts."

"If the ghosts you're talking about are metaphors, then I'm with you. I'm talking about prejudice and the way it persists. But you mean it literally, don't you?"

"Yes. You might almost say the figures you see on TV and in movies these days are the ghosts of those old minstrels."

The insight startled Mo, coming as it did from a white woman he'd taken for a bit of a ditz. "You're right. In a way. But taking ghosts literally . . . no, I don't think I could bring myself to do that."

"You just haven't tried." She took his arm again; then she sensed it made him a bit uncomfortable and let him go.

There were some dead leaves in the gutter; more wind stirred them, and the sky began to cloud up. Joanna looked up and saw a dark line on the western horizon. "Damn. I was getting used to this weather. Now I'll have to adjust to the goddamned cold again."

"Can I come and see your show?"

This time she stopped dead in her tracks. "You want to see *Oklahoma!*?"

Her exaggerated reaction made him laugh. "You and Mark are interesting. I'd like to see your work."

"Mark's a good director, better than anyone in the department, even the faculty. But he's doing a different show."

"I know. I want to see that, too."

"Well, I can leave a pair of tickets at the box office for you on opening night, if you like."

"Oh, I couldn't ask you to—"

"No, really, it's no trouble. I'll be interested to hear what someone with a history degree makes of a show like ours."

"I'm sure I'll enjoy it."

"Now, Mo." She took his arm again. "We know each other much too well for you to lie to me like that."

"We just—" He realized she was being a dramatic smartass and caught himself. "Well, I'd love to come. Thanks."

"We're previewing on Thursday and Friday, then the opening's Saturday. There'll be a party backstage after the show. You're coming to that, too. As our guest."

"But—"

Stage Fright

"No arguments. Nothing's too good for a friend of Joanna Marshall. Besides . . ."

"Yes?"

"You might see a ghost."

The weather quickly turned ferocious again. There was snow, ice, wind. Everyone was concerned it would keep people from the opening, but to their surprise the performance sold out.

Backstage, the cast and crew were in a frenzy, as they always were on opening nights. Joanna still hadn't got the backdrop adjusted to her satisfaction. Spotlights kept blowing, and the lighting crew worked frantically to replace all the bulbs by curtain time.

Mo's girlfriend was sick with the flu; he brought another friend. Feeling a bit self-conscious about it, he picked up his complimentary tickets at the box office, and they went in and sat down. They had the third and fourth seats off the aisle; Mark was in the aisle seat, and the next one was empty, obviously waiting for Joanna.

Mo and Mark recognized each other and said hello simultaneously. "Mark, this is my friend Andre." Andre looked completely out of his element. He smiled, shook Mark's hand, sat down and fell silent. Mo asked Mark how the show was looking.

"I haven't seen any of it. Jo says the previews went pretty well, but there are a few rough patches."

"I'm surprised to see you here, Mark. You gave me the impression this isn't really your kind of show."

"It's not." Mark looked a bit uncomfortable with the topic. "Musicals . . . Never mind. The department requires us all to see every student production. It's probably a good idea, I guess. I mean, you never know what you might learn, even from a show you hate. But . . ."

Mo enjoyed his discomfort. "When you're rich and famous, you'll be able to see just what you want to."

"Rich and famous?" Mark laughed. "I'm planning to work in theater. There will be church mice living better than me."

"Joanna says you're good."

"I think I am, too. That's not really the issue."

Andre, quite bored, coughed loudly and flipped through his program irritably. Then he looked at his watch. "It's after eight o'clock. Isn't this thing supposed to start?"

"There's a lot to do backstage." Mark explained patiently. "Every light, every body mike, every costume, every prop has to be just right. You wouldn't want them to start before they're ready, would you?"

"It wouldn't matter. I hate this shit."

Mo decided to change the subject quickly. "So, Mark, what kind of plays do you like? I thought everybody in theater liked musicals."

"Not even close. Have you ever seen this show before? It's three hours long, and it's not about anything but a girl trying to decide who to go to the dance with. I like plays that have some substance, some meat on their bones. My *Who's Afraid of Virginia Woolf?* is opening in three weeks. You should come, and you'll see what I mean."

"I'd like to. I guess. I had to read some *Virginia Woolf* for an English class once, and I don't mind telling you *I'm* afraid of her."

Abruptly the house lights dimmed and the curtain went up. An old woman, or rather a coed made up to look like one, very white, sat alone onstage, churning butter. Music began. Andre shifted in his seat and snorted. Mo shushed him.

And so the opening night performance was underway. And it went even better than the previews had. The entire cast was in good form, the scene changes went off quickly and without a hitch, the student orchestra was inspired. And the audience was properly enthusiastic. None of which stopped Andre from claiming he had a headache and leaving at intermission. Joanna stayed backstage and never joined them.

Mo, on the other hand, and quite to his own surprise, enjoyed it quite a lot. When the show ended and the cast had taken their curtain calls, he got up to leave, but Mark insisted he join everyone at the party backstage. Reluctantly, feeling every inch a fish out of water, he went.

Joanna was beaming. "Mo, you came! I hope you liked it."

Stage Fright

"I did." He could hear the astonishment in his own voice and tried to mute it. "It's pretty far from the music I usually listen to, but . . ."

Mark scowled. "It's pretty far from what anyone normal listens to."

"Be quiet, dear. You're being a wet blanket." Joanna stepped between the two of them, hooked her arm through Mo's as she had that first afternoon, and steered him toward the food and the liquor.

The room was crowded with cast members, tech people, students, teachers, relatives. . . . Some of them paired off, guys and girls, guys and guys, girls and girls, whatever. Mo found he enjoyed the energy. One guy from the chorus hadn't bothered to change out of his ranch hand outfit. Mo looked at him, then glanced questioningly at Joanna.

She wrinkled her nose in the guy's direction. "Either he's an enthusiastic freshman, or else he has a cowboy fetish. We get all kinds."

She took him around the room, introducing him to everyone she thought he might find interesting. After a few minutes, realizing he'd never remember them all, he steered her into a corner where they could hear each other over everyone else.

"This is all great, Joanna, but—"

"Call me Jo."

"Jo. But why are you lavishing all this attention on me? I mean, don't get me wrong, I appreciate being made to feel welcome. But I'm a total stranger here, and I don't really fit in with this crowd, and—"

"And you're being mothered by a crazy lady." She grinned at him. "Is that it?"

"Well, no, I wouldn't exactly have put it that way. But—"

Suddenly she turned quite direct. "I have plans for you."

This stopped him. "Plans? What kind of plans?"

"You'll fit perfectly into something I have in mind."

"Now, hold on, Jo. If you think you're going to get me to act or something. . . ." He lowered his eyes self-consciously. "I'm just not cut out for that."

"No, I wouldn't have thought you were. I have something else up my sleeve."

"Would you mind telling me what?"

"All in good time."

For the first time all evening, Mo was feeling uncomfortable. It was not exactly that he was feeling used, but he was not exactly not, either. He looked around the stage, hoping to spot Mark.

John Bartlett came through the crowd toward them, munching a slice of pepperoni pizza. Like Joanna, he seemed in an upbeat mood. "Well, did I build you a fantastic set, or what?"

Jo introduced him to Mo. "John's the genius who executes my designs."

They shook hands, but Mo's mind was elsewhere.

"Has Jo been telling you spook stories yet?"

Finally Mo brought his attention to John. "No, that was the other day." He relaxed a bit and laughed. "Now she's trying to bring me into some kind of conspiracy she's cooking up."

"Conspiracy?" John looked to Jo.

"The plan," she said in a loud stage whisper. "You know."

"Oh." He made his face blank. "The plan."

Mo looked from one of them to the other. "Excuse me for asking, but what plan would that be?"

"You'll have to learn to take everything Jo says with a grain of salt. No, with a whole box of it. We all do." Joanna glared at him, but he went on. "When she's not hatching all kinds of grandiose schemes, she's off chasing the spirit world."

Mo said he'd figured that much out. It was pretty obvious Joanna liked attention—any kind.

An actor came through the crowd and hooked Joanna; his parents loved her designs and wanted to meet her, it seemed. Jo went cheerily along.

"So the Dragon Lady has co-opted you." John watched her go, then turned to Mo. "Sooner or later, she gets everyone she wants."

"You really call her that?"

"Among other, more colorful things, yes. She gets things done, so we all respect her. But, boy, can she be hard to work with."

"What's this plan, then?"

"I doubt if it's much of anything. At least not yet. Some of us like to get drunk and dream about starting our own company once we get out of here."

"Why don't you?"

John shrugged. "We probably will. Everybody does, or wants to. But making it a success, that's the bitch. Are you hungry? There's some great pizza over there."

"No, thanks. But then . . . how do you make a theater company a success? What's it take?"

"Just between us," John said confidentially, "you gotta have a gimmick."

Mo was lost. "What kind of gimmick?"

"That, only God and Joanna Marshall know. She keeps hinting that she's got some grand plan that'll keep us all employed for years. But every time we ask her for specifics, she clams up." He scanned the crowd to see where she was. "She's a bit unhinged, you know."

"No kidding."

"Everyone in theater is, if they're any good. In Jo's case, it's genetic."

Mo glanced at his watch. "Maybe I'll have that pizza after all. Then I've got to get going. My girlfriend's down with the flu, and I want to make sure she's all right."

"Girlfriend?" John voice registered slight disappointment.

It finally occurred to Mo that John had been cruising him. He repeated the word more emphatically. "We've been together for two years now."

John took Mo's arm and led him through the crowd to the food tables. There had been five kinds of pizza; nothing was left but anchovy. Mo tucked in.

"You like anchovies!?"

"Mm-hmm." He talked through a mouthful. "Best topping there is."

"And I was telling you *Jo's* crazy."

Mo poured himself a draft. "Good beer, too. What did you mean about Jo's craziness being genetic?"

"Her mother produces on Broadway. Marianna Marshall."

Mo's face was a blank. "I couldn't name a Broadway producer if I had to."

"Don't say that too loud. In this crowd, real New York producers are just a thin cut below God. If not higher."

"Pardon my blasphemy."

"Jo's mother is supposed to be the most pushy, unpleasant bitch in the business. Jo'll be like her, too, some day. You can see it. I feel kind of sorry for Mark."

"Marrying into a Broadway family can't hurt his career, I imagine."

"You said it. Jo pretty much gets her way around the department. Even the profs give in to her. Such is the magic of the theater."

John picked up a slice of pizza, started to pick the anchovies off it, then thought better of it and put it back. "I'm overweight. Anyway, no matter how screwy Jo gets, she gets away with it. They're actually letting her do her thesis on theater ghosts."

"Yeah, I know. She told me all about it the other day. I was thinking that's what she wants to get me in on, but if there's something else. . . ." He glanced at John, grinned, and took the last slice. "Why would she want me involved in a theater company? I don't know a footlight from a flashlight."

"You'll be directing on Broadway in no time."

"I'm serious."

"So am I. You think this is about talent?"

"Look, I'm asking seriously." He made a broad gesture that took in the whole room. "This isn't anything like the atmosphere I'm used to."

"The History Department doesn't have parties?"

"Not good ones. Not even very big ones. We're historians."

"Well, all I can do is guess, but Joanna's instincts about people are usually pretty reliable. She sees something in you."

"You make it sound like I have a metal plate in my head or something."

"Do you?"

Mo was finding John mildly annoying, but he laughed. "No, just rocks."

John poured himself a second draft, then put the hose to his mouth and drank some more. "If you're serious about wanting to know, why don't you ask her? She won't tell you the truth, but she'll flatter the hell out of you."

"Flattery, I get at home."

The young actor in the cowboy outfit made his way through the crowd and joined them. John introduced them, then the kid whispered something in John's ear. Then he left again, almost as quickly as he'd come. John put on a wide grin. "It looks like this is my lucky night."

Mo looked after the kid. "He's—?"

"He's just a boy who can't say no." He scanned the crowd to see where his date had gone. "Listen, it's been great meeting you. My guess is we'll be seeing each other again. Like I said, Jo nearly always gets her way." He went off to find his boytoy, leaving Mo alone with the empty pizza boxes.

Mo thought briefly about finding Joanna or Mark again, but there seemed to be even more people at the party now. Someone called out that more pizza was on its way. Everyone seemed to be pairing off, and it made him slightly uncomfortable. This was all . . . well, not the usual thing for him. He decided to leave quietly.

Half a dozen jostles, bumps and frisks later, he was at the side door of the theater, looking out at a snow-covered campus. It didn't seem to be coming down all that heavily, but it was steady; and everything was white. Academic Tower loomed high overhead; the floodlights that lit it lit the falling snow, too. Mo hated cold weather, but he trudged out into it and headed home.

It was a half-hour walk. There were buses, but after the noise and press of the party, the relative quiet of the snowy world seemed preferable. He heard his footsteps crunch in the snow, four inches of it, and he hoped it wouldn't get much deeper. Winter.

When he got home, Tonya was sitting up in bed, reading. He brushed the snow off his shoulders and smiled. "Hi. You're feeling better?"

"A bit. At least I'm not coughing."

He crossed the room and kissed her on the cheek. "It's coming down pretty badly out there."

"So I see."

"I walked home from the theater."

"Why? For heaven's sake, Mo, I don't want you getting as sick as I've been."

"I won't. I just needed to think. It was an odd night."

"Odd good or odd bad?"

"I'm not sure. There's this woman, Joanna Marshall—the one I told you about the other day?"

"The one with the ghosts?"

"Right. She seems to have me in mind for some kind of, I don't know, for some kind of a job or something, with some theater company she wants to start."

"That doesn't make any sense." Suddenly, violently, she coughed.

He got her a glass of water. "You okay?"

She nodded her head and drained the glass.

"Anyway, she seems to see something in me, I'm damned if I know what."

"You're cute."

"No, I'm not."

"Are."

"Anyway, I don't think it's that."

"Then . . . ?"

"Like I said, I really don't know. But I can't imagine myself working in the theater. It's just not anything I've ever thought of doing."

"Don't, then." She coughed again, worse than before. When it finally passed, she said she needed to get some sleep. Mo kissed her again, switched off the light and left the room.

In a drawer of his desk, in a locked metal box, was a folder of old, badly faded photographs. He got it out, unlocked it with a key on his chain and carefully removed the one on top, the oldest of them. It was cracked and yellowed, and the image had bleached to a pale grey. It was a photograph of his great-grandfather, so badly faded that the man's features were barely discernible. But the pain in them was quite clear, quite evident. It was taken by a member of the white crowd on the day he was lynched. His body hung from a huge oak tree. A grinning mob posed in front of him, making various gestures for the camera's sake.

Mo had studied it a thousand times. It was all that was left of the man. "What," he whispered to himself, "can she want with me?"

That night Joanna dreamed again. There was that theater, old, garish and enormous, its façade set about with monsters and demons. Against her better judgment she approached it, then stepped inside. It was pitch black, and the only sound was the echo of her footsteps. Something clawed at her face. She screamed and wakened.

Mark woke, alarmed, and sat up in bed. "Jo!"

She was sobbing hysterically. "It happened again, Mark. Something was tearing at my eyes this time."

"Something?"

"I couldn't see what. It was dark."

He reached for the lamp on the nightstand and switched it on. "Jo!"

Her face was torn—the part of it around her eyes. Blood flowed.

Self-consciously she covered the gashes with her hands. "Don't look at me!"

"Let me see."

Gently he moved her arms aside. There were a dozen or more cuts, not deep, but the thin flesh was torn and blood was flowing. It poured down her chest and stained the bed sheets.

"I'll call 911."

"No!"

"Jo, your face is cut to ribbons."

"I can't have anyone see me like this. What would they say?"

"For God's sake, you sound like an actress. Some of those cuts may be deep enough to need stitches."

"I said no, Mark."

It was exasperating. "I'll get some disinfectant from the bathroom." He let out a deep sigh and got out of bed.

"Not iodine."

"Jo, for God's sake."

"I can't walk around with that stuff on my face. I can't let people see."

"Do you think they won't see anyway? You're cut to shreds."

"It's the weekend. These will have healed by Monday."

There was no chance of that, but he didn't see any point arguing with her. "I think there's some hydrogen peroxide." He pulled on his shorts and headed for the bathroom. Joanna sat in bed, crying.

A moment later he was back with the peroxide and some cotton balls. Gently, carefully, he dabbed it onto the cuts. Joanna flinched at the sting of it but didn't make any fuss.

"Sit still. Your tears are keeping the blood from coagulating."

"It's not like I'm doing it on purpose, Mark."

"No. I was just saying." The first cotton ball was red with blood; he switched to a fresh one. "There, that should do it, I hope. It looks like the bleeding's pretty much slowing down."

She covered her face again. Then, slowly, she moved her hands and looked at him. He was careful not to react. Joanna got out of bed and crossed to the mirror. Even in the dim light from the nightstand she could see how bad it was. "Mark, why on earth is this happening to me?"

He didn't have an answer. The obvious one was that somehow, for some reason, she was doing these things to herself. But to say so would only have upset her or, worse, started another of their fights. Instead of answering, he waited for her to sit on the bed again, beside him, and put an arm around her. She rested her head on his shoulder.

But suddenly, violently, she pulled away from him. "For God's sake, Mark, why don't you do something to stop this?"

"Because I don't know what 'this' is."

"What am I supposed to do?"

"Dreams mean something. Maybe you should think about seeing a counselor. The ones on campus are—"

"I am not crazy!" She shrieked it at him. "I am not crazy, goddamn it!"

"I'm not saying you are, Jo. But something's causing this. It's got to be something inside you. A good therapist could—"

"Will you stop saying that! There's nothing wrong with

me." She calmed a bit and lowered her voice. "If you keep saying things like that—Mark, the place is real. The theater I keep dreaming about. I know it is."

He tried putting his arm around her again, and again she pulled away. "It's a dream, Jo. That's all."

"No."

He wanted to hold her. And he knew she wouldn't let him.

The gossip around the department was that Mark had made the smartest kind of match: marriage into a family of Broadway producers. Joanna would almost certainly be producing herself, one day, and she and Mark would make the kind of husband-wife creative team press agents love. Terrific career move.

But that wasn't his motive. He genuinely loved her. Increasingly, he was afraid for her. Why was she doing this to herself, and how could he help? And how on earth could he do anything at all for her, when she wouldn't let him?

The following week there was another uncharacteristic warm spell. Joanna had more dreams, but they weren't quite so upsetting. The cuts around her eyes had healed more quickly than Mark had expected them to, without leaving any noticeable scars. She had covered them by wearing dark glasses most of the week; the sunny weather made them seem more plausible.

She and Mark, enjoying this period of relative harmony, decided to have a midwinter picnic on the lawn of Academic Tower. The air was just warm and fresh enough to promise springtime. They ate without talking much; there were plenty of people to watch.

The picnic turned out to be a bad move. Though the snow had melted, the ground was uncomfortably damp; but they tried to make the best of it. Worse, Academic Tower was just next to the theater. Half the Theater Department came walking by and mooched food. Any hopes of a few quiet moments between the two of them were in vain.

John Bartlett came ambling by, saw them and sat down uninvited. "Afternoon. Great weather, huh?"

"Hi, John." Mark was enough of a politician to smile and pretend he was glad to see him. They were theater people.

Joanna, on the other hand, frowned at John and asked him if he'd had a chance to look over her designs for their next show, *Macbeth*, yet. "The show goes into rehearsal next week, and Bill's getting nervous." Bill was the student director; this was his first mainstage production.

"Bill always gets nervous." He helped himself to a handful of chocolate cake. "He's a director. It's what they do."

"They also scalp designers who don't have sets and props ready."

"Don't worry, Jo, everything's on schedule."

Mark laughed. "You two. The average director is a lot more understanding than the average producer's daughter." John snickered, but Mark went on, "Or the average stagehand."

John decided to change the subject. "I'm heading over to the department. Either of you need anything?"

Mark glanced at Joanna, then shook his head. "Nope. Thanks, though."

Joanna made her voice cold. "I worked for days on those designs. You should be at work already."

"The show doesn't open for nearly a month, Jo. Will you relax?" He helped himself to more cake.

Mark decided it was time to try and soothe her overwrought nerves. "Joanna, you've been getting crankier and crankier. With everybody. These dreams are getting to you."

"How could they not? I mean—"

John decided discretion was the better part of valor, stood up, dusted off his trousers and headed off to the department.

Joanna, angry at him for whatever reason, glared at his back. "Besides, everybody's giving me more than enough reason to be cranky."

"All he did was take a piece of cake. You didn't think we could eat it all ourselves, did you?"

"He could have asked."

"It was right there in the open."

"Stop contradicting me all the time, Mark."

Within minutes they were having another argument.

Stage Fright

* * *

Dinnertime at the Z. Mark offered to buy John a burger. John, suspicious, agreed but kept his guard up; you never knew what people might want. They found a table at the back of the joint, as far from the jukebox as possible, and he asked Mark pointedly, "What's bugging Jo? She's been even more difficult than usual."

"I don't think I want to talk about it."

"Yes, you do. That's why you're buying my dinner."

Mark looked at his burger and fries and decided he wasn't hungry after all. "You saw how she was this afternoon. She's been getting harder and harder to deal with."

"From what I hear, it runs in the family. Like mother, like daughter."

"I've never even met her mother. But I hear the same thing."

"Do you love her, Mark?"

"What kind of question is that?"

"It seems to me it's perfectly to the point. You have to know what most of the department thinks. Do you love her?"

Mark picked up his burger, started to take a bite, then put it down again. "I don't know. I don't know how much more of this I can take. I haven't told her so, but I'm beginning to have second thoughts about our engagement."

"That bad?" John reached across the table and took a few fries off Mark's plate.

"She's getting more and more impossible, John. I really don't know how much more I can take."

"You're repeating yourself." John put on a sunny smile. "Look on the bright side. At least she isn't gaining weight."

"I'm serious, John. She's been having these nightmares. Every night she wakes up all upset, and she takes it out on me. I haven't had a full night's sleep in weeks."

"What kind of nightmares?"

"About a theater full of blood and death."

"I can relate." John shrugged. "The show we're working on is having a lot of trouble. *Macbeth*, for Christ's sake. That's probably why. Shakespeare always gives *me* the willies."

"What kind of trouble could there be with *Macbeth*? Not enough ham?"

John laughed and took a swallow of crummy Z draft.

"No, John, I really don't think that's it. This was going on back when she was still on *Oklahoma!*." Mark gestured at the empty pitcher on the table between them. "Should I get another one?"

"No, I have to get home and do some leisurely cramming. Besides, *Oklahoma!*'s the kind of show that gives nightmares to everyone past the age of ten."

Mark raised his glass, said cheers and drained the last of it. "Thanks for listening."

"I'm a good listener. Everybody knows I always have the best gossip."

Mark narrowed his eyes. "You wouldn't."

"No. Of course not. You can trust me."

"If she found out I was talking about this with anybody, she'd—" He looked down at the tabletop. "I don't know what she'd do, but it wouldn't be pleasant."

"She's her mother's daughter, all right."

Marianna Marshall was famous, or infamous, as the most tyrannical producer on Broadway—a place filled with tyrants. She was also supposed to be smart, something not all producers were.

Mark didn't like the sound of it. The prospect of in-law trouble on top of everything else . . . "No, it's not that. Well, maybe it is. Hell, I don't know. But if she keeps having these dreams, and if she keeps taking them out on me . . ." This was the first time he'd talked about it with anyone. It left him uncomfortable enough to change the subject. "They're saying it's going to get cold again tomorrow."

"Good, I'll have an excuse to stay home." He put on a big grin. "Professors don't like it when I tell them it's just because of a hangover."

"God, John, don't stay home. *Woolf*'s opening Friday night and the set's only half finished."

"It'll be ready. It's simple enough. Trust me."

Impulsively Mark blurted it out. "John, she's been hurting herself in her sleep. Cutting herself, choking herself . . ."

"You're kidding."

He shook his head. "I've never had to deal with anything like this before." He looked directly into John's eyes, then quickly looked away. "I'm scared shitless." It came through in his voice.

"I can tell. Is there anything I can do?"

"Not unless you know a way to get her to an analyst. I've tried suggesting it, but she keeps getting defensive, saying I think she's crazy."

"Do you?"

"Christ, I don't know what I think. I just know I have to find a way to put an end to this."

" 'This' being . . . ?"

"I don't know. I love her, John, at least I think I do. But I don't know if I can marry her." He reached for his burger again and saw that his hand was shaking. "God, what can I do?"

"I wish I knew."

"Not half as much as I do."

The stage of the Fulton theater was quite bare. *The Turn of the Screw* had come and gone, to almost total indifference on the part of both critics and audience. Vince Gallardo stood center stage, looking about, trying to remember why anyone had thought the show would be a good idea.

The acoustics in the theater were good; his footsteps, even his breathing carried clearly to the back row. The next show wasn't due to open for nearly a month.

He heard someone coming and turned to see Joanna. She was dressed for winter, corduroy slacks, boots and a bulky sweater. And large dark glasses. "Joanna, hi."

"They told me upstairs I could find you down here. How have you been?"

"Just fine. You?"

She shrugged. "So the show bombed, huh?"

"It happens."

"Tell me about it. Growing up, I watched one after another of my mother's shows whimper into stillness."

His mood was somewhere between rueful and wistful; he

was grateful to have company who seemed to be in the same frame of mind. "Why do we keep doing it?"

"It's what I keep talking about—the irrational that drives art."

He laughed. "This was *The Turn of the Screw*. We had plenty of ghosts."

"Have you ever wondered what it would be like if we could coax one of the theater ghosts—one of the real ones, I mean—to take part in a show?"

"I've seen too many actors who came off dead. Ghosts would almost be redundant."

She laughed and put an arm around his shoulder. "You know what I mean. Anyway, you promised to take me up to the archives today."

"Sure." He took another look around the stage. "Why do these places always seem so cavernous when you're onstage and so small when you're in the audience?"

"More irrationality? Now about those archives . . . ?"

He led her up that back staircase to the offices, where she'd left her coat and bag. She got her laptop out of its carrying case and said, "Let's go." A side door off the reception area led to still another flight of stairs. These were much steeper and narrower than the others; when they twisted and turned, Joanna had to turn her body sideways to make it up. They climbed to the very top of the building.

The room was enormous, filled with heavy cardboard file boxes, all of them labeled, most of them apparently cross-indexed. There was dust, and the air was oppressive with it; there were cobwebs. There were four windows, side by side, overlooking the river and thick with grime. She could barely see out.

Vince let her climb the steps first; she waited for him to join her. She took his hand to help him up the last few steps "You have this room, and you had to build a set for a ghost story?"

"The unions insisted." He found himself liking Joanna more and more. Her sense of humor melded well with his own.

She slapped the top of one of the file boxes and a cloud of dust rose. Vince coughed.

Stage Fright

"Who keeps all this current?"

"One of the secretaries files all of the clippings in a fresh box. When it's full, we haul it up here and dump it. I doubt if anyone's looked at this stuff for years, maybe decades."

"Are they in any order?"

"Roughly, I think. The oldest ones should be way in the back. I can send one of the interns up, if you need help moving them."

"That'd be great, thanks."

"I'll probably come up myself, every hour or two, just to see if you need anything."

"Thanks, Vince."

"Believe it or not, someone used to live up here. Samuel Fulton, the guy who built the theater. He was a descendant of Robert, and he was pretty well off. This was his penthouse."

"And you keep it full of dust in his honor?"

He laughed. "It used to be 'lavishly appointed,' as they say. They say he used to bring chorus girls up here for private . . . auditions, I guess you'd call them"

"They've been called other things."

"Somewhere around here, I think there are photos of the 'penthouse' as it was back then. Quite opulent. It was the time of wealth in Pittsburgh, all those steel barons and coal magnates." He rubbed some grime off one of the windows and looked down at the city and the river. "A long time ago, huh?"

Joanna walked in a circle around the room and ran a finger through a layer of dust on a file box. "Do you suppose this is some of his mortal remains?"

He chuckled and glanced at his watch. "Listen, I'm due at a meeting. I'll see you in a while. If you need anything, give a shout." He went back downstairs, to all appearances in a better mood than when they'd met.

Jo exhaled deeply and looked around. It was impossible to tell for sure, but it looked like there had to be a hundred and fifty boxes, maybe more. Somehow, she hadn't been expecting so many. If she'd stopped and thought about the theater's age . . .

She began inspecting the labels. They seemed to be organized more or less chronologically, which wasn't much help.

When had that actress died? When had her ghost first appeared? What had she done? It was too much to hope there might be a box labeled FULTON THEATER GHOST. But she rubbed her hands together, took a long, deep breath and began working her way through them, checking the labels one at a time and starting with the oldest ones.

There were press clippings for shows long forgotten and actors long dead. One sheaf of stories, bound in a thick folder, covered the building of the theater, "a new jewel in the glittering crown that is Pittsburgh." There were faded photos of the place under construction, with Samuel Fulton and the architect, William Beatty, standing proudly in front of it. Three men died in construction accidents.

Then came the gala opening. President McKinley himself was expected to attend; it seemed he was a personal friend of both Fulton and Beatty. But at the last moment some emergency arose, and he stayed in Washington. So he missed a review called *Lovely Ladies Are Like Flowers*, the theater's first attraction. There were no reviews of the show, no information about it of any kind, at least not in that box.

Lillian Russell came to town. The *Floradora* review toured through, with its line of notorious showgirls who were actually brazen enough to expose their ankles. And almost at once there were complaints from church groups about immorality onstage—and backstage. Rumors began circulating almost at once, at least among the churches, that Samuel Fulton's "penthouse" was actually a love nest, where he took innocent young showgirls and robbed them of the flower of their youth.

A few minutes later she heard someone coming up the steps. A head of bright red hair appeared, then a pale bespectacled face, then a slim body. The kid looked like he ought to be in high school, not a college student interning with the Arts Foundation; he was wearing jeans, sneakers and a T-shirt. Jo couldn't quite conceal her surprise. "Hi, I'm Joanna Marshall. Welcome to my nightmare."

The kid seemed mildly confused. "You're Joanna Marshall?"

"Yes. Did you think I was kidding?"

"Yes. No. I mean—" He blushed, the most marvelous

Stage Fright 63

shade of crimson. "I've heard of you. Vince asked me to come up here and help you. I'm Jim Plunkett."

"Hi, Jim. Come on. It looks like I've got a lot of work ahead of me. You don't mind helping?"

"It's got to be better than making copies and going out for coffee."

"Did Vince tell you what I'm looking for?"

He sat on one of the boxes. "Just that you're researching the early history of the theater. Is there something specific you're after?"

She explained her interest in the alleged ghost.

"Wow, that's cool. I never would have thought of it. But that's a great topic of research."

"Here, I'm working my way through this first box. Why don't you take the next one and see what you can find?"

"Actually, I have some stuff to do downstairs. I just wanted to check on you. But I'll be back up as soon as I can, okay?"

"Sure. Thanks."

"Do you need anything now?"

"Just some help finding what I want." She smiled a sarcastic smile. "I don't suppose you're a psychic, are you?"

"Nope, just a drama student."

"Really? Not at West Penn—I'd know you."

"No, at Morgan-Wilmer. They keep telling us we have the best drama school in the region."

She wrinkled her nose. "They say that about every department there. Snotty school. If I were you, I'd take it with a grain of salt."

He laughed. "I figured that out freshman year."

He headed for the stairs, then seemed to have another thought. "I'm going to be going out for coffee in a few minutes. Can I get you anything?"

"Thanks, Jim, but I don't think so. Is that really how they keep you busy?"

"Like I said, making copies and going for coffee. A fine theatrical internship, huh?"

She laughed. "I'll see you later, okay?"

"Sure." He headed back down to the real world.

Joanna found herself feeling a bit sleepy, and she wished

she'd asked Jim to get her some coffee after all. She got to her feet and yawned, then walked to the windows. A city in winter stretched out below her. There was traffic; the afternoon rush hour was beginning. People were wrapping themselves tightly against what seemed to be a stiff wind.

Back to it. She found herself going through the box more quickly now, even though some of the individual items caught her attention. Lillian Russell sprained her ankle on the Fulton stage and missed three shows. Harrigan and Hart came touring through, and there was scandal involving an underage boy. Some things, she found herself thinking, never change.

Gradually, without wanting to and without realizing it was happening, Joanna drowsed off, slumped over the box.

When she opened her eyes again, the place was different. It was night. Everything was clean, downright immaculate in fact. Pale blue damask covered the walls; there were gaslights, and the damask seemed to shimmer in their glow. The room was filled with plush furniture, upholstered in a deep wine red velvet, and heavy drapes matched the furniture. There was a divan, a love seat, a sofa, all in an ornate Italian provincial style. A writing desk occupied one corner, its leaf open; a brightly polished brass oil lamp burned brightly on it. Next to it a bottle of champagne was cooling in a silver bucket. And at the far end of the room there was a bed; its covers matched the red furniture.

A man came in, followed by a young girl. He was in a tight dinner jacket and black tie. His eyes, jet black, seemed to look about the room like a nervous animal's. His hair was brilliantined. From the cut of his clothes, Joanna knew what she was seeing was at least a hundred years old.

The girl was younger than she'd seemed at first sight, fifteen, maybe sixteen years old at most. But she was heavily made up, which made it hard to be sure. She was wearing a showgirl's costume, pink tights, sequins, feathers. Her hair was piled high on her head. And she looked as nervous as he did, though not in the same way.

The man was Samuel Fulton; Jo was certain of it. He was younger than in the news photographs she'd seen, but it was unmistakably him. At the same instant she recognized him,

Stage Fright

she realized, in her dream, she must be dreaming. Or . . . having a vision?

Fulton popped the cork on the champagne bottle. From nowhere, it seemed, he produced a pair of crystal flutes and filled them. The girl took hers, held it to her nose and giggled.

Joanna couldn't hear them. They moved in a silent world. Sometimes they seemed almost to be in slow-motion; other times they appeared to be slightly speeded-up; still others there was a jerkiness to their movements, like actors in a silent movie. It was only too obvious to her what was going on. Theatrical impresarios from Keith to Albee to Ziegfeld and beyond were notorious for it. *Do you want to be a star, my dear? Come up to my room and we'll talk it over.* Jo had even heard rumors that her own mother did much the same thing but with chorus boys. Not that she blamed her. . . .

The girl got drunk quickly—quickly and apparently happily. Then Fulton produced a silk rope and tied it playfully around her wrists. She giggled. But when he jerked it tight, a look of alarm crossed her face.

He threw her violently onto the bed and tied her down. In that same dreamlike silence, she cried out. Fulton tore at her clothes. She struggled, but the rope on her wrists wouldn't come loose. When she screamed again, Fulton slapped her violently.

Startled, alarmed at what she was seeing, Jo took a step toward them. She tried to yell, "Stop!" but no voice came out of her mouth. She watched as Fulton beat the girl more and more brutally. There were bruises on her arms, legs, stomach, throat, but not on her face. He was a shrewd enough showman not to damage what his male patrons came to see.

Again the girl tried to scream, and again he pummeled her, more viciously than before. Finally, whether from fear or pain, she lapsed into unconsciousness. Fulton, quickly, deftly, finished undressing her and had sex with her.

Joanna woke to find Jim Plunkett and Vince Gallardo standing over her, shaking her. "Joanna! What happened? Are you all right?"

She blinked and gaped at them. From the window she saw daylight. "What happened?"

"We need you to tell us. You were screaming."

Jim took her hand and felt her pulse. It was normal, or nearly so. He held a paper cup of water to her lips.

Slowly, she sat up.

Vince tried to make it into a joke. "Did you see the Fulton Theater Ghost?"

"Yes." Her face and manner told them she was perfectly serious. "I think I may have. At any rate, I have a good inkling what might have happened to her."

"But—"

"Jim, can you get me some coffee, please?" She laughed a bit. "Sorry. I was hoping I might find something more productive for you to do."

"It's okay."

"Really strong and really black, okay?"

He disappeared down the stairs.

Once Jim was gone, Vince put a hand on top of hers. "Now I want you to tell me what happened here."

"Relax, Vince. It was nothing the foundation could be liable for."

He relaxed slightly. "Then—?"

"As I said, I think I have an idea what might have happened to the girl who died here. It didn't happen down in the theater proper. It was up here."

He looked around. "Let me guess. She died from inhaling too much dust. Joanna, you fell asleep and had a bad dream, that's all."

"This was no nightmare, Vince. Believe me, I know from nightmares."

Jim came back up the steps, carrying a large cup. "Here. At your service, Madame."

She took it and drank. For a moment or so no one said anything. Then, at exactly the same moment, Vince and Jim noticed something. There were bruises and welts beginning to appear all over her arms and throat. She drank her coffee, and it seemed to give her strength. She got to her feet, stretched and let out a loud sigh.

Stage Fright

Then she noticed the bruises on her hands. They seemed to be getting darker and more purple with each moment. Startled, she put her arms quickly behind her back.

"We saw." Vince was stone serious. "Who was up here with you?"

"No one."

"Joanna, I have to ask. Please."

"I'm telling you, Vince, I was up here all alone. I fell asleep and had a dream, like you said. That's all there is to it."

"You need to have those bruises looked at."

"So, look at them."

"Joanna, please, I—"

"It's okay, Vince. I'll be fine. But I think I've done enough work here for today. I have a good start."

There seemed no point pressing her. Vince led her and Jim back downstairs to the reception area, and he helped her into her coat. "Did you even find any definite proof that anyone died here?"

"Definite enough for me." She thanked them both, wrapped her scarf around her throat and left.

Jim looked at Vince, puzzled by it all. "Her mother's a Broadway producer, you know."

"I know. Believe me, I know. Why don't you take off, okay? And don't mention this to anyone."

"Thanks." He reached for his coat. "Who do you think I could tell?"

"Nobody who'd believe it, I guess." They said goodnight, Jim left and Vince headed back to his office. He had to get out a press release about the chairman's wife's next charity event. There couldn't have been anyone in the loft with Joanna. There couldn't.

THREE

At the top of the grand staircase at the west end of the lobby of the Imperial Opera House, on a pedestal that had once been pure white but was now a faded yellow, stood a sculpture of Medusa. Unlike its base, it still looked fresh and new; it was carved from black marble, veined with blues and purples, and not even a century of dust had darkened it further.

Most of the gods and demons in the opera house were of their time, fantastic nightmare creatures rendered with the style and logic of a nineteenth century fairy-tale. Not Medusa. She had the classical lines and pristine beauty of a faun by Praxiteles or a nymph by Phidias. There was a grace to the curve of her brow, a delicacy to the bend of her wrist, a charm to the way she craned her neck and looked directly down the staircase. And most of the others resented her, not just for her looks.

When she was alive, when she had movement and life—when one of the Imperial's ghosts inhabited her—her movements were lithe and supple, as if she was one of the Three Graces instead of a half-human monster. But the snakes that were her hair writhed and seethed with venom. And her gaze could turn anyone ascending the stairs and foolish enough to *look at her into stone harder and more permanent even, than the black marble she was made of.*

But despite her awful nature, she thought of herself as kind, even benevolent. After all, the ones she turned to stone were not killed and eaten by the other monsters. What she did, she did out of love. She thought of herself as kind, and that thought, she knew, made her much more human than the others.

For the moment she was cold and unmoving. Her marble eyes saw nothing but black eternity. But somehow, though she had no brain and no nerves, she knew that would change.

Cost analysis wasn't going well.

Tonya Harper sat at a table in the main campus library, going over some lessons for the third time. The stuff wouldn't register. She found herself wondering whether she was really cut out for business administration after all. At least the books were big; there was plenty of space in the margins for doodling. She did plenty: houses, clowns, flowers. . . .

Someone came up behind her and put his hands on her shoulders. "Mo?" She looked down; the hands were white.

"No, not Mo, whoever that is."

She turned and looked. It was John Bartlett. He bent down and kissed her on the cheek, then pulled out the chair next to her and sat down. "Hi, sugar."

"John. You scared me for a second."

"Sorry. I saw you sitting here, looking miserable, and like a faithful St. Bernard I just had to come to the rescue."

"If I only had a dog treat."

He laughed. "So how you been? I haven't seen you for eighty or ninety years."

"And you look it."

"Don't be unpleasant."

She closed her textbook, firmly and emphatically. "I'm wondering more and more why I decided to get into this field. I'm just not cut out for it."

"Why'd you go into it, then?"

"Oh, you know. My parents kept telling me to learn

something practical, get ahead in the world. The stuff parents always say but most kids have sense enough not to listen to."

"Everybody in America hates their job, Tonya. Why shouldn't you?"

"Everybody?" She shifted in her chair, to face him. "You think all those rich white CEOs and CFOs and COOs and suchlike hate their jobs?"

He leaned close and told her, in a mock-confidential whisper, "They don't actually have jobs, they just collect money. Instead of jobs, they have country club memberships."

"Yeah, and there are big signs on the door that say 'Whites Only.'"

He shrugged. "Why be so narrow? 'White, Straight, Christian Males and Their Trophy Wives Only.'"

She looked glum. "The Sixties were a waste of time, weren't they?"

"I don't know, old lady. They were way before my time."

She slapped at him playfully, and he ducked it.

"Anyway, who's this Mo you mistook me for?"

"Wow, we really haven't seen each other in a while. Mo's my fiancé."

"You're engaged to one of the Three Stooges?"

She slapped him again, and this time it landed. "You met him at a party once. Remember? You said he was cute."

"I say every guy I see is cute. Remind me."

There was a minor fracas at the checkout desk. One of the librarians raised her voice at a male student, who gave every sign of being high. The third time she told him to leave, he finally did. Everyone within earshot watched, startled. Libraries and librarians were supposed to be quiet.

When silence finally set in again, Tonya pushed her book pointedly away, across the table. "Mo's working on his MA in history. He's on the short side—"

"I should have known you'd pick a guy you could push around."

"If you're not careful, the next slap is really going to hurt."

"Sorry, ma'am."

"He's a year younger than me, but he looks even younger than that, like he's about eighteen."

"Nope, I don't remember." He felt a bit shamefaced, and it showed. "He sounds like somebody I'd remember."

"If I recall the condition you were in that night, it would be amazing if you remembered anything about it."

The stoned kid stumbled back into the library, made an unflattering comment about the librarian's mother, then lurched out again. John suggested they head over to the Z for a beer. "It doesn't look like you're getting much studying done."

She frowned at the book on the table. "I was, till you showed up. Let's go anyway." She made a sour face. "Business administration. What was I thinking?" She gathered up her things and they headed outside.

Suddenly John snapped his fingers, like a man who'd just had an idea. "Wait a minute. There's been a guy named Mo hanging around the Theater Department lately. Can that be him?"

She nodded. "Yeah, I think it probably is. He's doing his thesis on the old minstrel shows."

"I was right, then."

She looked at him. "About what?"

"He's cute."

"Keep your distance, John. He's mine. And when I'm cornered, I fight dirty."

He laughed. "Fair warning. Last time I saw you, you were still seeing that guy from the Astronomy Department."

"God, that was ages ago." She made a sour face. "What a loser. He knew everything about the moon except what to do under it."

The Z was nearly empty, for some reason. They pretty much had the place to themselves. John made a show of unplugging the jukebox, and they took a seat at a side window. He got a pitcher of beer and an order of onion rings.

"Not fries?" She took one and bit into it. "I thought the Z's fries were famous."

"Famously greasy. I'm trying to lose weight."

"You mean you think these aren't? You could wring these out and use what you get in your transmission."

John tasted one. "You're right." He looked doubtfully at the basket of rings, then took a handful. "Oh well, waste not, want not." He grinned like a guilty devil. "Tell me about Mo."

"Oh, there's not a lot to tell. He's smart, he's funny, he's determined to make a name as a historian . . . and he loves me."

"Sounds like he's got his head on straight."

She nodded. "When I had the flu last month, he nursed me and mothered me like I never thought any guy could."

"And he's straight!"

"Shut up. Yes, he's straight. And boy, is he good at it."

"Why can't I get a motherly type?"

The conversation drifted to smalltalk, gossip about mutual friends and such. Finally John got around to asking her what she planned on doing when she got her degree.

"You're asking me? I don't have the slightest idea."

"Do you know anything about theater?"

"I saw *Jack and the Beanstalk* when I was a kid."

"I'm serious, Tonya."

"So am I. It was great." She took another onion ring and then a deep drink of beer. "Of course, the beanstalk was a lot more convincing than the actors were."

He laughed. "You should see the production of *Who's Afraid of Virginia Woolf?* we're doing now."

"Where's your department loyalty?"

"It lies bleeding, center stage."

"Anyway, why do you care what I know about theater?"

"Well," he took another handful of rings, "some of us are planning to start our own company. We could use a business manager."

"That wouldn't be me, John. I don't know the first thing about how to run a theater."

"You think anybody else does? It's always by the seat of everybody's pants. That's why most companies go belly-up within a year or two. But, see, that's why I think you'd be good."

"So I could take care of running it into the ground for you?"

He scowled at her. "Don't be silly. You're as practical as anybody I know. You wouldn't be impressed by all the talk of 'art' and 'genius' and so on. You could help us keep our feet on the ground."

Stage Fright

"Honey, if you want to have your feet on the ground, get a job at Kmart."

"I'm serious, Tonya. Think about it, okay?"

"How definite is this thing?"

"Well . . ." He looked slightly shamefaced. "We're still only at the talking stage."

She scowled back at him. "And you're talking about having your feet on the ground."

"We're serious about doing it, Tonya, at least, most of us are. And having you involved . . . that would make it all seem more concrete, more doable."

She poured herself a second glass of beer. "Who else is in on this thing?"

"Mark Barry. Good friend of mine. He's a director. The fact that *Woolf* isn't a complete disaster is his doing. And his fiancée, Joanna Marshall. She's going to be the artistic director and producer." He picked up the last of the onion rings, stared at it as if it might be poison, and put it back in the basket. "She's good, too. And her mother's a Broadway producer. So we'd have that connection."

"Really? A real Broadway producer?"

"Yep." He picked it up again and ate it with a manner that suggested he was committing an act of vengeance. "I hear she's a major bitch, but she's in New York and we're here."

"Well, why didn't you say so before? So there's actually some prospect this thing might float?"

He licked the crumbs off his lips. "You want to know about things floating, ask a physicist. All I know is, we're all good, and we're more and more serious about doing this and making it work."

Tonya glanced at her watch. "I have a Political Economics class to get to." She pulled on her coat, scowled at John and said, "I'll think about it, okay?"

"Promise?"

She looked doubtful. "Sure. Nobody else is offering me a job."

She headed out, leaving John to pour himself the last of the beer. Some loud fratboys came in, arguing about "cunt." He drank quickly and got out.

* * *

Mark was having actor trouble. The two leads of his show— both of them unsuitable, both of them forced on him by his professors, were having an affair so blatant he wondered why they didn't just go into porn. The other two actors were clueless, one of them aggressively so, the other one, Annie Moore, sullenly so. And they were all late for tech rehearsal. A crew of stagehands and lighting technicians was in place, waiting. No cast.

Joanna walked casually into the auditorium where he was pacing angrily. They kissed, and she dropped heavily into a chair.

Her face and throat were covered with bruises and cuts. She had refused to get them treated, refused to talk about them with Mark or anyone else, refused, in fact, to acknowledge they were there. Her own dreams were less frequent— they were only coming once or twice a week. But every time she went downtown to explore the archives of the Fulton Theater, she came home battered. It was impossible for Mark not to want to know what was happening to her, not that it did him any good.

"Hi." He smiled slightly through his black mood. "Have you come to help me kill my cast? You can give me an airtight alibi."

She sighed. He'd been complaining about his actors for weeks. "Just make the best of it. Everybody knows you didn't have any say in casting. No one will blame you."

"Everyone will blame me. I'm the director."

"I think this one gets filed under, 'You can't make a silk purse out of a sow's ear.'"

"These four remind me of a part of a pig's anatomy, all right, but it isn't the ear."

Just at that moment the two leads came in, holding hands like junior high school kids on a first date. "Hi, Mark. Ho, Jo." Their mood couldn't have been breezier. Joanna decided to settle back and enjoy what was coming. Mark was doing a slow burn; it would turn into a fast one soon enough.

But to her surprise he held his anger inside and settled for mild irony. He smiled broadly at the two of them. "Only half an hour late. You're getting better."

The leading man looked around. "Where are the others?"

"They've been taking cues from the two of you. There's no sign of them."

The leading lady looked at her watch. "They'll be here."

"Eventually. I guess."

There would be no entertainment. Joanna got up to go. "I'm heading downtown." She pulled on her coat and gloves. "I've got another appointment at the Fulton."

Mark wanted to say something, or ask something, or . . . he didn't know what. The situation was so strange, and she seemed so unconcerned by it. Instead of saying anything, he gave her a tight hug. He knew exactly where the worst bruises were; she winced slightly with pain. Knowing he was hurting her gave him, unexpectedly, a rush of pleasure. She needed it; nothing else had worked. He tried to tell himself that was all there was to it, that the actual inflicting of pain wasn't what gave him the buzz.

Even more to his surprise, Joanna leaned into him and pressed against him even harder than usual. Then she swept grandly out of the hall, every inch the future producer, and left him to his cast, such as it was.

The Fulton penthouse was dark; it was just after sunset, and Joanna had not bothered to turn on any lights. The glow from the city streets below gave what illumination there was. The archives, dauntingly large as they were, were giving her information, and she was quite absorbed in what she was finding. She went back to her work, had to squint, decided it was time to light the place.

The rumors about Samuel Fulton's "love nest," as reported in various press outlets, grew thicker and more persistent with each passing year. Young showgirls, 'starlets,' even the occasional chorus boy was taken there for what was called, in the parlance of the times, "illicit pleasure." There were drugs— marijuana, which to Joanna's surprise was legal in that time; opium; cocaine; even heroin. And there was sadomasochistic play, some of it vicious. Occasionally there were accidents; Fulton's playmates or, depending on your point of view, victims, had to be taken to local hospitals.

She heard footsteps coming up the stairs. It was Jim Plunkett, smiling happily; she hadn't seen him all day. "Hey, Joanna!"

"Jim, hi."

"How's it going?" He reached the top step and leaned against a box.

"Pretty well. I'm starting to find the kind of stuff I'm looking for."

"The ghost?"

"No, not yet. Hit the light switch over there, will you?" She got up and walked to the window. The city was lighting up more and more for the night. "But I'm on its trail, I think. Or *her* trail. Anyway, bad things happened up here. It's funny this should be where they store the archives isn't it?" She turned back to the view outside. "Say what you will about Pittsburgh, it is a pretty city."

"I've never noticed. The prospect of staying here—of actually living here—I'm still not quite resigned to it."

"Then look someplace else, when you go job hunting."

"Oh—haven't you heard? The foundation's hiring me. I'll be doing PR."

This surprised her. "Working with Vince?"

"Vince is being downsized. I'll be taking over what he does. I guess they know they can get me cheaper. It's pretty shitty for him, but—" He shrugged as if to say, what can I do? "Next week's his last."

"That's too bad. I like Vince a lot."

"Yeah." It didn't seem to concern him much. "Listen, everyone's leaving for the day. Are you going to be all right up here?"

She nodded. "I'll be taking off pretty soon myself. I just want to get through the rest of this box."

"Well, I'll see you again, okay? It'll be nice working with you." He switched on the lights for her and headed cheerily back downstairs.

Stage Fright

Night was falling quickly. Joanna went to the light switch and turned them off again. She decided she wanted darkness.

From her bag she took a joint. Good Columbian; John Bartlett had scored it for her. She lit up and inhaled deeply. Yeah, the stuff was strong, all right. If anyone caught her, it would be . . . she decided the right word was *awkward*. But Fulton and his little concubines used drugs. She wanted to see them again, and dope seemed as reasonable a way to try it as any she could think of. Dope, plus the haunted atmosphere had worked every time. . . .

Outside, the sky began to cloud up, surprisingly quickly. It would be a dark, overcast night. She hadn't heard a weather forecast and hoped there wasn't another storm heading in; winter had been unpleasant enough already.

Meditation might help. She sat on the floor in the lotus position, closed her eyes and began to chant softly. Nonsense syllables—she was making them up—but they were soft and warm and after a few moments they began to lull her to sleep.

Fulton came in, switched on the lights in the opulently decorated room, then went to the window and drew the heavy drapes shut. A few steps behind him was another young girl. To Joanna she looked even younger than the first one she'd seen, weeks earlier. This one was already undressed; she held one hand to her crotch, the other over her breasts, not that they were very developed.

"Come in, Christina."

"It's Christine," the girl said. She was looking around in a way that suggested she'd never seen such a room before. Joanna wondered if this was the girl who would die and haunt the Fulton.

Her host smiled a gracious smile. "Christine, then."

She went to the bar, as if she'd never seen so much liquor in one place. Fascinated, she reached out for one of the bottles.

Fulton caught her hand and stopped her. "Leave the bourbon alone. Have you ever tasted champagne?"

Same routine as before. It worked for him, it got them to do what he wanted. Why would he vary it?

He poured two glasses, crossed to her and very gently took the hand over her groin and placed the glass in it. She seemed not to know how to react. "Thank you, sir."

"Call me Sam. All the girls do."

She tasted the champagne and made a sour face. Unless he forced her, she wouldn't get drunk for him. But it didn't faze him; he crossed to the burner and lit the opium. Then, for good measure, he lit a marijuana cigarette, handed it to her and told her it made her look grown up and sophisticated.

"Really, Sam?" She was delighted.

"Really, Christina."

She smoked; the drugs had their effect. He made small talk for a few moments. Then he moved behind her and put his arms around her. The girl didn't resist at all. His left hand slid down the front of her body and began to fondle.

She giggled. "Please don't. It's wrong for someone to touch you there."

"Is that what they taught you?"

She nodded and took another drag on the reefer.

"Christina," he cooed into her ear, "they were wrong. Doesn't this feel good to you?"

Again she nodded.

Suddenly his arms wrapped around her and held her tightly. She struggled, but he was way too strong for her. In a moment, she was tied down to the bed. In another, he had his whip.

He lashed her viciously. She writhed; Joanna couldn't tell if it was with pleasure or pain or some combination of the two. The girl cried out, and the sound of her sobs seemed to make Fulton even more excited. He whipped her harder and harder, and each time she yelled he became even more brutal.

There was something wrong with the light from the window. Joanna crossed to it, not taking her eyes of the bed and the whipping. Outside, it was preternaturally dark. She realized that she was seeing old Pittsburgh, the Pittsburgh that had long since ceased to exist, and that bellowing smoke from the steel mills had made everything black.

In the street below, horse-drawn trolley cars moved up and down Sixth Street. She could barely make them out through

Stage Fright

the smog. Even more faintly, she saw lights on the river. A stern-wheeler was making its way slowly along the watercourse; red lanterns made a bright line along its sides. Nothing else was visible at all distinctly.

Old Pittsburgh. She was there, she was seeing it.

Fulton beat the girl. Her cries were mere whimpers now, faint, barely audible. Joanna looked and saw that the girl Christine was hardly moving. Would she die? Would she haunt this place? Joanna had to see, had to *know*. There was no sound in the room but the lash, the girl's cries and the hiss of the gaslight.

Then through the drugs Joanna realized that what she was seeing was murder, or something near it. This was not right. She had come here to read about the ghost, not to witness its making.

"Sir?" She did not speak too loudly.

Fulton ignored her.

"Mr. Fulton?"

He stopped the beating and looked at her. He was quite aroused; it showed.

"Please, Mr. Fulton, you're killing her."

Slowly he smiled. Then he gestured toward the bed.

It took Joanna a moment to realize he was inviting her to change places with the girl.

Christine, or Christina as Fulton kept calling her, was covered with gashes. Blood soaked the bed. Wanting to stop it, not thinking about the consequences for herself, Joanna crossed to the bed and began to undress. Fulton untied the girl and eased Joanna into her place. Gently he tied the ropes around her wrists and ankles. Then with a sudden jolt he tightened the knots.

They were too tight. She felt circulation stopping in her hands and feet. Then she felt the whip.

Whether it was because she knew that taking the young girl's place was the right thing to do, or because she had a predilection for pain, the tears streaming down her face gradually stopped, to be replaced by a wide, sweet smile.

She would have to ask Mark to explore this kind of pleasure with her. She only hoped he would.

* * *

Mo's search for information on minstrel shows hadn't yielded enough results to flesh out a thesis yet, though he was confident he'd find what he needed. As embarrassing as that chapter of the past had been, it could hardly have been hidden completely.

On a friend's suggestion, and partly to kill time one afternoon, he tried the architecture library. Not knowing much about the field, he had to rely on the librarian's help. There were plenty of books about theater design, but very few with any substantial information about the shows that had been presented.

On the table in front of him was a stack of oversized books, all of them ornately bound, all of them filled with old engravings and antique photographs. All fascinating; none helpful.

Near the bottom of the stack was a particularly large, heavy volume from 1942 titled *Fantastic Theater Design in the American Northeast, 1880–1940*. The author was William Beatty. Mo almost set it aside on the assumption it would be as unhelpful as the rest. But then, curious, he began to flip the pages idly, and the garish, sometimes grotesque buildings caught his eye. There was a thick section of oversize illustrations, then a text section containing detailed information on the theaters.

There had been theaters with every possible historical or mythological theme, Egyptian, Greek, Aztec. . . . And there were theaters called "atmospherics," where the forces of nature were simulated. Projected clouds floated across their ceilings, which were painted sky blue; later, lights were dimmed, and stars were projected there. Despite the fact that it wasn't what he was looking for, Mo found it all fascinating.

One old photograph in particular caught his attention. It was not the oldest theater in the volume, nor the largest, but it had a mad, skewed opulence that he found almost irresistible. The caption read: IMPERIAL OPERA HOUSE, BOURBON, OHIO. 1890.

The building was, as the book's title suggested, fantastic, a bizarre mix of architectural styles impossible to categorize. An even more bizarre mix of ornamental styles seemed to be pulling the place in four or five different directions, Art Nouveau, Greek Revival, Egyptian Revival, Gothic Revival and others less easy to put names to. He didn't know the terms for all this, but Mo studied the plate, fascinated. Who could have built such a grand monstrosity, and why?

Some of the theaters had multiple photos or drawings, some showing the interiors. Not this one. But the plate referred him to the appropriate page in the text. After examining the old photo for the dozenth time and making no sense of what he was seeing, he flipped the pages and found the entry.

> The Imperial Opera House in Bourbon, Pennsylvania, was erected in 1890 by Pittsburgh theatrical impresario Samuel Fulton, who considered it his greatest achievement. It was designed and built by his usual collaborator, William Beatty.

Mo assumed this must be the same Beatty who wrote the book, modestly not referring to himself in the first person. But... "Bourbon, Pennsylvania"? The caption on the photo said "Bourbon, Ohio." Sloppy.

> In use until the 1930s, the Imperial served as an opera house, of course, and subsequently as a legitimate theater, a vaudeville house, a burlesque house, and ultimately a cinema palace before being closed permanently.
>
> The theater seemed cursed and, according to some sources, haunted from its very inception. Numerous construction workers died during the building, many more than was usual for such a venture. Over the succeeding decades, several actors died onstage during performances. In 1936, the great crystal chandelier in the auditorium fell into the orchestra, mirroring an incident in French writer Gaston Leroux's fantastic novel *The Phantom of the Opera*. This marked the death knell for the Imperial.
>
> It was long rumored in the region that the unnatural amount of ill luck that plagued the theater was due to the

fact that it had been built on the site of a former slave warehouse and auction site. No verification of this has ever been forthcoming.

That was the end of the entry. And it was the thing that particularly caught Mo's attention. It didn't exactly deal with minstrel shows, but this was an interesting bit of history that could enliven his paper. If he could verify that minstrel shows had actually played the Imperial, which they almost certainly must have, at some time or other . . .

Almost as soon as that thought occurred to him, he thought of Joanna and her search for theatrical ghosts. Here was an old place thought to be haunted. He'd have to tell her about it.

But . . . Bourbon, Pennsylvania. Or Bourbon, Ohio. He had never heard of such a place. Where might it be? With Fulton involved, it would likely be someplace near Pittsburgh. But where?

He left the architecture wing and headed to the main reference room. The atlas of Pennsylvania he consulted showed no Bourbon anywhere in the state. Same with Ohio. The librarian helped him find several older reference books, but none of them had a Bourbon either.

A mystery. Maybe he and Joanna could work on it together, to see what they could find.

Joanna was not looking good, not at all. Her face was bruised; so were her arms. She walked with a slight limp. She kept telling people it was all due to a series of unfortunate accidents. "What can I say? I'm a klutz."

Mark suspected otherwise. He could not quite convince himself that her bruises were actually appearing right before his eyes; that was not possible, it must be a trick played on him by the dim lighting in their bedroom. As for all the other injuries, the ones that seemed to occur when she went downtown to research her thesis . . . there didn't seem anything for him to do but suspect the worst. And so they fought, only he never quite found the nerve to accuse her of what he was thinking.

Stage Fright 83

Mo found her backstage at the campus theater, the day after his trip to the library. She looked like hell. He smiled and told her how great she was looking.

"Thanks, Mo. If I have to deal with one more prima donna director, though . . ."

"Maybe you should only work with Mark."

"Good God, no. There are enough fights around here as it is."

"You're not getting along?"

"Never mind. It's nice to see you here, Mo. I had a suspicion the theater might get under your skin. I have a sixth sense about things like that."

"Don't kid yourself." He laughed. "The only thing under my skin is the tattoo on my shoulder. I just came across something I thought you might find interesting."

"Unless it's a new director, I probably won't. Shakespeare wasn't kidding when he said the whole world could be reduced to the space of a theater. Look at this."

She held out a sketch. It showed three houses, Greek or maybe Roman, in a row on a street.

Mo inspected it. "Very elegant. I like it. Are you doing a Greek tragedy or something?"

"Nope, another damn musical. *A Funny Thing Happened on the Way to the Forum.*"

He looked from the sketch to her. "You're kidding. There's a show called that?"

"Tell me, Mr. Settles, how do you like our planet?"

"It's that well known, huh?"

She nodded, with the manner of a teacher correcting a dull student.

"Sorry." He smiled at her, more than a little shamefaced. "I grew up in the ghetto. We never done seed no forums."

"Stop it. Anyway, what did you find?"

"Oh." He rummaged through his backpack. "I know it's in here someplace. I thought of you as soon as I saw it."

"I hope it's an undetectable poison. With instructions."

"No, it's about a theater." He started emptying the backpack, spreading its contents out on the floor.

"Really, Mo, you're as bad as an aging actress."

"Here." He found a Xerox of the page from *Fantastic Theater Design* and held it out to her. "Did you know Samuel Fulton had another haunted theater?"

"You're kidding." She took the page and skimmed it. "I had no idea. There's no mention of it in any of the archives downtown."

"There's something of a mystery about the place. Read it."

She did, quickly. "It must have been torn down ages ago, right?"

"Jo, I know it sounds weird, but I can't find any indication outside this book that the place ever existed at all. Or even that a place called Bourbon, in either Pennsylvania or Ohio, ever existed."

She reread the copy. "But this is a photo. Unless someone was playing a really odd joke, the place must have been real."

"I don't know. I mean, yeah, it must have been. The book's from the forties. This picture can't have been gimmicked up with software or anything. And I don't think the kind of special effects stuff they had back then could make this look so real."

She inspected it for a third time. "You're right, it doesn't look retouched. But . . . Bourbon!"

"There are lots of other French place names around here. North Versailles, Dubois, Fort Duquesne, a lot of others. This was French territory at one point. So it's not as absurd as it sounds, I guess. But it's not on any map I've been able to find. I was kind of hoping you might have found something about the place in those old archives you've been searching through."

She studied it. "No, not a thing."

"Do you at least know something about Fulton? And what's his name, the architect?" The name came to him. "Beatty."

Joanna gestured him to a seat, then took one herself. "You remember me asking you once if you believe in ghosts?"

"As I recall it, that was the first thing you ever said to me."

"Well, do you?"

Something made him reluctant to answer. He pointed at the Xerox in her hand. "What do ghosts have to do with that?"

Stage Fright

"Think, Mo. Fulton had two theaters, the Fulton and the Imperial. Both rumored to be haunted. And both were places where terrible things happened."

He narrowed his eyes; he didn't like where this was going at all. "What terrible things happened at the one downtown?"

"Well." She took a deep breath. "I haven't told anyone else about this. Can I count on you to keep it to yourself?"

"Sure." He nodded.

"Fulton was into S&M. Pretty severe stuff. I mean, he really hurt people. He'd take naïve little chorus girls up to his penthouse, and . . ." Something made her reluctant to get too explicit. "And boys, too, sometimes."

"You found news stories about that?"

"Not exactly, no."

"It doesn't sound like anything that would have made its way into the press, back then. Not even about a millionaire debaucher. We must keep up America's image."

"No, but I know that's what he did."

"How can you know that, Jo? Without finding it in print somewhere?"

She held out her bruised arms.

He looked from her bruised face to her arms, then back up again. "What are you saying?"

"Mo. I've seen him. And his victims. Well, some of them. He used drugs on them. Weed, even opium. When they couldn't resist, he—"

"I don't believe it."

"You must have read enough history to know what the ruling class in this country has always been like. Fulton was one of them. Money from steel, money from coal. . . . Money means the power to do what you want and get away with it."

"But—but—"

"I think he killed one of the girls. I think she's the ghost."

"*I* think this doesn't make any sense, Jo."

"There's a ghost. That, I've found stories about. It's the background stuff—the backstory—that I'm seeing for myself."

"And Samuel Fulton beats you."

She nodded.

"And you let him?"

Again, she nodded. "I want to know. I want to see everything that happened. Besides . . ." She looked away from him, then back, with a sly grin on her face. "It's kind of a turn-on."

"You're into that?"

"I guess so. I never was before, but . . ." Her grin grew wider.

"Jo, this is crazy. Did he work his perversions at the Imperial, then, too? Why is *it* haunted?"

"Maybe it's those slaves."

He stood up. "That isn't funny, Jo."

"I'm not trying to be funny. I'm just guessing, that's all. But you read what the book says. Anything could have happened there. In a country run by men like Fulton, *anything*."

He put on a skeptical expression. "Ghosts."

"Yes. Why not?"

"Look, I don't have time to talk about this anymore. Let's get together soon. I'm going to see what I can find out about Bourbon. If the place ever really existed, there has to be a record of it somewhere. A passing mention, something, anything. If it's there, I'll find it."

"Let me help."

"Historical research is a lonely kind of enterprise. But why don't you see if you can find anything about the Imperial down in the Fulton archives?" He stood up to go. "Whoever would have thought our two theses would turn out to be related?"

"Are you sure you don't have a bit more time to talk about this? You've got me fascinated."

He glanced at his watch. "I'm due to meet Tonya for lunch, over at the business school."

"You're dating an MBA candidate?"

"Mm-hmm."

"That comes as even more of a shock than the stuff about Fulton."

"Tonya's in business because her parents made her. She hates it."

"She may come in useful, then. I don't suppose you know if she's ever taken any courses in theater management, do you?"

Stage Fright

"Not that she's ever mentioned. She wants to make money."

"That, Mr. Settles, is below the belt. Does the business school even offer any course in arts management?"

"God knows. Look, I really have to run, okay? Let's stay in touch."

He headed out of the theater. *A Funny Thing Happened on the Way to the Forum.* What the hell kind of title was that?

"John, she's seeing someone else. I know it."

Mark and John had stopped at a campus bar for drinks after a long day's rehearsal. Mark was quite depressed, unable to keep his mind off his relationship problems.

"I don't think she'd do that, Mark."

"She's doing it. I keep finding these marks all over her body. Bruises, cuts. Some of them have even scarred over."

"I never would have guessed she has a taste for . . ." John groped for a euphemism but couldn't think of a good one. "For kink. At least nothing that heavy."

"She never used to be. She always liked her sex to be . . . well, sexual. Now it's all she wants. But I'm not into it. She keeps asking me to . . ." He downed his drink and looked away from John. "But I can't do that kind of thing."

John wasn't at all certain what to say. He sipped his cocktail and waited for Mark to go on.

But Mark had talked enough. There was an uncomfortable silence between them. Mark ordered another round. "You won't tell her we talked about this? I mean, if she knew I—"

"Relax, Mark."

"How are things going with you and Jim?"

They had been dating. It was hard to tell which one had been more surprised when they realized they were attracted to each other. "Tim. Okay, I guess. The closer we get, the more aware I am of how young he is, though."

"He's, what, nineteen?"

"Yeah. A whole generation younger than me."

"Five years. No big deal."

"He likes S&M, too. He really gets into it. You should let down your inhibitions and try it."

Mark shook his head. "I have. It just doesn't feel right to me."

"If it feels right to Jo, you should make the effort anyway. That's how relationships work."

"I just can't figure out who she's seeing. Every guy we know is either gay or in a relationship."

"Maybe it's someone you don't know."

Mark drained his glass. He was getting drunk, and he was feeling good about it. "She keeps telling me it's ghosts. I don't know whether to laugh or be angry." He took a deep swallow and ordered a third drink.

John said he'd had enough, thanks. "Ghosts, huh? We've been doing too much Shakespeare."

"I guess a brazen lie is better than a halfhearted one. But Jesus fucking Christ." He made a fist and started to pound the bar but caught himself. "How can she expect me to believe a thing like that? How can she expect our . . . relationship to survive that?"

"You'd be amazed what a relationship can survive. If you could hear the music Tim listens to. . . ."

This finally broke Mark's mood, at least a bit. He laughed and thanked John for listening. Some mutual friends came in and joined them, and they made pleasant gossip about everyone they knew who wasn't there.

John enjoyed the company more than Mark. Even though Mark had said he'd talked enough, it was clear he wanted to vent. Oh well, another time.

It was almost a month later when Mo finally found out about Bourbon.

The history department was having a party; one of its professors had just snagged a job at Princeton, which was more than enough excuse for a celebration. Most of the faculty was there, nearly all the grad students, and more than a few of the brighter undergrads. A large room had been rented at one of the hotels near campus.

There were impromptu skits, illustrating papers the lucky faculty member had written. He was a medievalist, with a

Stage Fright

specialty in church history, so volunteer actors were "poisoned" by Borgia popes; witches and sorcerers were burned in the public square before St. Peter's; and Pope Stephen VI dug up the corpse of his predecessor Pope Formosus and put the body on trial for heresy. Grotesquely comic as it all was, no one paid much attention. There were better pleasures to be had.

Liquor was flowing freely, weed was being smoked, several more questionable substances were being snorted, smoked and what have you. There was loud music—since these were historians, it was "alternative"—the light was low, and people were making out in odd parts of the room.

Mo and Tonya were at one of the food tables, trying to find something decent to snack on. She wasn't enjoying herself. "I shouldn't have let you talk me into this."

But Mo was quite in his element. "Have a drink and relax, will you?"

"Every conversation I've had has ended up about somebody's damn fool history thesis."

"It's not that bad."

"Isn't it? I've already been lectured about the political economy of the Mayan empire, backroom politics under Franklin Pierce, the effects of the opium trade on higher education in Singapore.... I've never been so bored in my life."

"Try and enjoy yourself."

"I am trying. But you won't let me leave."

"Tonya, please."

"Some guy cornered me a while ago and told me all about economic decline in early twentieth century West Virginia. The punch line was that there used to be a town someplace down there called Bourbon. Isn't that a laugh riot? When I wouldn't have a drink of bourbon with him in honor of the place, he tried to grope me. Mo, I'm getting out of here."

He sighed. "All right. But . . . who was that?"

"That who?"

"The one who knew about Bourbon."

"Just take a look around. Everyone here knows more about bourbon than they ought to. If women hit on men as obnoxiously as men do women, there'd never be another party."

"Tonya, who was it?"

She made a vague gesture toward the opposite corner. "He never told me his name. He was over there someplace. I'll see you at home." She kissed him on the cheek and left.

He stared where she had gestured. It could have been anyone in the room, anyone. But . . . economic decline in early twentieth century West Virginia. There couldn't be more than one historian with a research topic like that. He wouldn't be hard to track down. He hoped.

But Bourbon, West Virginia? Now there were three states with towns of that name. There had been French influence in the region, but that seemed so unlikely.

Next morning he headed back to the library and unshelved every historical atlas he could find. And again there was nothing. No Bourbon in West Virginia, no more than there had been one in Ohio or Pennsylvania.

He spent an hour making inquiries around the department. Finally a political economics prof was able to put him onto the right student, a guy named Frank Martino.

Mo approached him that afternoon, introduced himself and explained that he was trying to track down an old theater in a place called either Bourbon, Ohio or Bourbon, Pennsylvania. "That town in West Virginia that you mentioned to Tonya is as close as I've been able to come."

Martino was pretty badly hungover. He was blond and blue-eyed; Mo had been expecting someone more Italian-looking. "Tonya's your girl? I didn't know, man. I really didn't mean anything by—"

"Relax. She'll get over it. But when she mentioned that place you told her about . . ."

Martino rubbed his eyes and yawned. "I need to stop drinking so much."

"You and everyone else on campus."

"Anyway, Bourbon was up in the northern panhandle of the state, up past Weirton." He yawned again. "You know, right up where West Virginia, Ohio and Pennsylvania come together. Where the Ohio River flows out of Pennsylvania and then forms the border between the two other states."

"So the three of them touch there?" Interesting—that could

account for the fact that no one seemed certain which state Bourbon belonged to.

Martino nodded. "There were a lot of border disputes back then, I guess. Like, you know, how the Mason-Dixon Line was drawn to settle the border dispute between Pennsylvania and Virginia."

"Thanks, Frank."

It was something to go on, at least. He went back to the library and poured over the maps still again. And found nothing.

After giving it some thought, he decided to talk to Joanna about this. Maybe she'd come across something that could help explain it all.

She was at the theater, working on some sketches for *The Trojan Women*. Ruined cities, stacks of bodies. When Mo showed up, she was clearly grateful for the break. "There's never been any excuse I can think of for doing Greek plays."

He put on an embarrassed grin. "They're Greek to me."

"If there was any justice, they'd stay that way. What's up?"

"Well, I've found something. Or I may have. I think." He took a seat. "Possibly."

"Do you have a point?"

He told her about the three Bourbons, and explained how he thought they might really have been one.

"Fine, Mo. But since we don't know where any of them were, what good does it do us?"

"I think they were all the same place. Or may have been. And I think they were located—or I should say, it looks like it may have been someplace up northwest of here, where the Ohio River crosses the border and flows between West Virginia and Ohio." He explained why.

"But Mo, even if that's true, why isn't the place on any of the old maps?"

He shrugged. "Have you managed to find out anything more about the Imperial?"

"Nope." She rolled her sketches up. "Let's get some lunch. But I have found that Samuel Fulton owned a whole string of theaters around the region. And at least a few of them had, er, unsavory reputations. So the Imperial would fit that."

"What are you doing Saturday afternoon?"

"I don't know. Mark might have some plans. Why?"

"I was thinking we might take a ride up there and see if we can find anything. Maybe some of the locals might remember something about the old place."

She scowled. "Why don't we just chase after a wild goose? I can't see that there's any reason to think the Imperial was really there."

"That photograph, remember?"

"The theater was real, sure, but who knows where it might have been?"

"You said you want ghosts, Jo. This is as close as we've come so far. I mean, if you're not doing anything else, we could—"

"I'll tell you what—let's do it."

"Fine. Noon-ish?"

She nodded. "I'll see you then."

That night, Mark was out drinking with some friends. Joanna had put in a long day, and she decided to hit the sack early. She mixed herself a strong highball, downed it quickly and crawled into bed. The forecast was for warm sunny weather on Saturday. Their little outing should be fun, even if they didn't find anything—and she didn't think they would.

There were more of her dreams. She saw the ghostly theater, its face swarming with demons and monsters. The more human of them beckoned to her. "Come. Join us. We are waiting."

Then, somehow, she found herself in Fulton's loft at the downtown theater. He was there with the girl Christine. She headed for the liquor, as Joanna had seen her do before. And Fulton caught her arm to stop her.

But the scene was slightly different this time. Fulton turned his face to Joanna and said to her, directly and menacingly, "Leave Bourbon alone." At first she thought he'd said, "Leave the bourbon alone." But then his words became clear.

He led Christine to the bed, as he always did. But before the savagery could start, Joanna woke up.

Stage Fright

He had warned her.

All her dreams had been warnings, of a sort, but this one had been aimed directly at her.

And all her dreams had been personal, she realized; all of them had focused on her. But now... But this one... Fulton's words had been a challenge, and she knew she had to meet it. Her mother's daughter could not back down.

She sat up in bed, switched on the light and went to make herself another nightcap. Unconsciously she avoided the bourbon.

It was one of those late winter/early spring days when the air is cold but the brilliant sunlight promises renewal. The air was crisp and dry, in that early spring way. Mo was at the wheel of a battered '83 Chevy pickup, and the tires kicked up dust as he drove the country road.

Jo rode in the passenger seat, studying a copy of an old map. "I can't make heads or tails of this. Nothing looks the way it should." She looked at him. "And there's no Bourbon on it." She had a second map, a modern one, and she switched her attention to it.

"I know. The roads have probably changed. So has a lot else. We're just going to have to hope something looks familiar, some landmark or road or whatever, so we can get oriented." He hit a pothole; the jolt shook them both up.

"Careful, Mo. You're carrying precious cargo."

"The old map's just a copy. Don't worry."

"I did *not* mean the map. I didn't think there were any dirt roads left." She was feeling irritable. "They're something from the nineteen twenties."

"What do you think we just hit? The Teapot Dome?"

"Just drive." She wrapped her coat more tightly around herself. "Doesn't this thing have a heater?"

"Are you kidding? We're lucky it has a motor."

It was midafternoon. They had started their expedition that morning by hitting a few of the bigger towns in Beaver County, northwest of Pittsburgh. First Mars, then Butler—they were both too far from the Ohio border for anyone to know much about the place where the three states met—and then, to Mo's amusement and Joanna's obvious annoyance, a town called Big Beaver.

They had hit a few diners and bars—which had a surprising number of customers for so early in the day—but no one had been able to help them with their inquiries. Jo said she thought they were just being small-town suspicious, not wanting to be helpful to strangers. Finally, frustrated, they stopped at a gas station and got still another current map of the county, then set out in the general direction, hoping vaguely they'd find something, anything, so the day wouldn't be wasted.

Jo scanned the map. "We should be on 65. It parallels the river, more or less, heading north."

"I thought it went off on its own way."

"Eventually, yes. But it'll get us in the right region, anyway. Turn left here."

If nothing else, though, spending that much time together, under not-quite-ideal circumstances, had made it clear they really were cut out to be friends. After a lot of general talk—mutual friends, undergrad teachers they'd both had—the talk got more personal. Joanna went on about her conviction that the world, or at least the human part of it, is driven by irrational forces. Mo talked about his belief that the past never really dies, and that people dead a century or more can still affect us today. Before too long they decided their hang-ups were the same, or at least enough alike for them to be quite simpatico.

Route 65 was a four-lane highway when they hit it. Before too many miles, it narrowed to two. The Ohio River, wide, dark and muddy, flowed swiftly to their left. There were trees all around, except where the road passed through cuts in the hills. At one place there had been a rock fall; one lane was closed, and traffic slowed.

For a time they rode without talking, in that comfortable silence that sometimes happens between friends. Then Jo noticed that the Ohio was pulling away from them, heading west now instead of north.

"What do we do?" Mo yawned widely. "Is there anything on the map?"

"Nothing that goes just where we want." She shaded her eyes and took a careful look. "It looks like there are some dirt roads over there, following the river."

"I'll get off the highway at the next exit and we'll see if we can't—"

"More dirt roads. Just what my sacroiliac needs."

There was an exit before too long. Mo headed west. The sun was beginning to sink, and they had to lower the visors to protect their eyes.

The dirt road was even worse than the ones they'd used earlier. Bumps, potholes . . . Mo had to slow to twenty, and even to fifteen in places. The trees around them were thicker. Finally the road came to the river and began to parallel it. It was wider here, and it seemed to be flowing even more quickly.

Jo scowled at it. "I don't like the look of that."

Mo shrugged. "Early spring rains. What can you expect?"

At one point a rabbit darted in front of the truck. Mo had to swerve to avoid it, and they nearly ended up in a ditch.

For the next three miles, Joanna clutched the door handle and didn't let go.

"Are you all right, Jo?"

"I guess so. I'm just not used to things like that happening. I'm a city girl, through and through."

"Then what are we doing here?"

"I don't know, exactly. The thrill of the unknown. The excitement of discovery." She grinned at him. "Like *Star Trek*."

"Or *Psycho*. You know what happens to city folk when they venture out into the country."

"If the Imperial's there, finding it would be an important contribution to cultural history." She scowled, yet she was pleased at the sound of her voice as she said this. "A feather in both our caps."

"What if it's not there? Those feathers could easily be from a wild goose. You said it yourself."

"It's there. I know it."

She said it firmly, with conviction, and it startled him. "How can you be so sure?"

But Joanna dodged the question. "Besides, if it's in anything like good repair, it'll fit nicely into my plan."

He slowed the truck to a stop. "Okay, you've mentioned that before." He stared directly at her. "I want to know about this plan. And I want to know what it has to do with me."

"You didn't have to stop for that."

"I didn't. I have to take a leak."

He got out and disappeared behind some bushes. After him, she shouted, "Be careful, Mo. There might be cobras or something in there."

She heard him laughing, and he called back, "You really are a city girl, aren't you?"

A minute later he was back. "There. I needed that." He grinned widely. "Now, about your plan."

"Let's get moving. It's getting late."

Mo started the truck and they headed off along the road again. Joanna made a show of checking the maps again. But Mo wasn't to be put off this time; he asked again, quite insistently.

"Okay, fine." She let out an exaggerated sigh, just like an actress. "Give me your word you won't tell anyone about this, though."

"Sure."

"Not even Mark knows what I have in mind."

"It takes a heap o' lovin' to make a home like that."

"Stop it."

She explained. They all wanted to start their own theater company. That was almost a given in their set. The big question was, how do you make it successful? Jo's idea was to find a big, elaborate, historic old theater, get funds to renovate it, and use the publicity from that to launch the place.

But that wasn't all. The theater gave them a connection with history. They would capitalize on that, too. Put on historical plays and pageants, then count on schools from all around the region to bus in loads of kids—at, say, five dollars apiece, maybe ten—and use that money to keep the place afloat while they did the plays they really cared about at night. Properly promoted, the place could turn into a "destination" and even draw tourists.

When she finished explaining all this, she added with a triumphant smile, "That's why I want you in on this—a historian to write our pageants. Or at least to advise us on them, give us input to make sure everything's historically sound. And the Imperial—if it's really there—might be just the place for all this."

It took him a moment to absorb it all. "But Jo, renovating a place like that would cost a fortune."

"I know it. I've been sending out feelers already. All three states have arts councils *and* history foundations. With the right spin, we could get all the money we need and then some."

"You need connections to get that kind of money."

"My mother's a respected Broadway producer. You'd be amazed what doors her name can open."

Suddenly he liked the sound of it. "Oh!"

"Yes. Exactly." She couldn't have been more pleased with herself. "You're the only one I've talked to about this. Do keep it to yourself, for now. But when the time comes . . . Have you lined up a job yet?"

"Nope. I was hoping for a fellowship at West Penn, but it looks like that's not going to happen."

"Then welcome aboard."

He was still turning it all over in his mind. "If we can find the place, that is. And if it's in a good enough state of repair to make it worthwhile renovating."

"It is." She turned mysterious. "I've seen it."

He looked up the road ahead, but there was nothing but dirt and river. "What are you talking about?"

"I've seen it. A lot of times. I already know what it'll look like. It'll need a new roof—that's almost a given—but other than that, it's in fine shape. Old, dirty and dilapidated, but more than worth salvaging."

"How can you know that?"

She put on a cryptic face. "I can dream, can't I?"

"Dream on. But if we can make some money out of it . . ." He put on an impish grin. "Why the hell not?"

The road narrowed. Technically, it seemed, it still had two lanes, but if anything larger than a Volkswagen Beetle passed them, things would be tight. The trees and vegetation became markedly thicker, thick enough to make the road dark. Mo decided they must be getting near the river.

But he began to have second thoughts about Joanna's "plan." "You really think this road can handle a lot of school bus traffic?"

"That can be dealt with. There has to be another road somewhere. Or we can get this one widened. Or—"

"And do you really see the carriage trade from Pittsburgh coming up here?"

"Drawing people is a matter of the right spin, that's all. Besides, we won't just be drawing from Pittsburgh. We're about equidistant from there, Cleveland, Erie, Wheeling and Akron. . . . With the right advertising, you can promote pretty much anything. . . ."

"That's what Ford said about the Edsel. And remember New Coke?"

Then abruptly the trees and vegetation stopped. They found themselves in the midst of a huge, barren field, nothing but bare dirt. Here and there a few trees and shrubs still stood but they were dead things, black, barren, their branches scraping the sky. The nearest sign of anything like life was a line of green on the horizon to the north.

"Take another look at the map, will you?" Mo was beginning to think he'd had enough of this outing. "This can't be taking us to the river."

Joanna shaded her eyes. "Then what's that?"

Ahead of them in the middle distance, the road came to an abrupt end. And there was the Ohio. Mo squinted and managed to make out some details. He stepped on the gas. "There's something wrong, then. There should be a lot of trees growing along the riverbank." He looked at her doubtfully. "Shouldn't there?"

"And I thought *I* was a city kid."

In a few minutes they reached the river. Mo stopped the truck about ten feet from the bank; the road simply . . . vanished. The Ohio was wider and darker than at Pittsburgh, more so than either of them had ever seen it. Joanna made a joke that even the river seemed to find getting out of Pittsburgh a liberating experience.

"Jo, there's something wrong here. This isn't right. There

should be trees, shrubs, grass, something. There isn't even a stray rabbit."

"What would a rabbit be doing here?"

"If it's a March Hare, it could be planning to start a theater company."

"Be quiet. What's that down there?"

About fifty yards downriver there was an island. It was as barren as everything else in sight. But at the north end of it there was a huge, ramshackle old building. Jo took a few steps in its direction. Then she seemed to freeze. "That's it, Mo."

"That's what? That ruin?"

"That is the Imperial Opera House. I know it."

"Then we've been wasting our time. Come on, let's go."

"No."

She seemed almost to go into a trance and started to walk toward it. Irritated, Mo followed. "Joanna, it's on an island. It's no good for your 'plan.'"

She walked. "I have to see it."

"Joanna, for God's sake!"

Deciding to make the best of it, so they could get the hell out before the afternoon light failed completely, he caught up with her. "There's no way to get out there. Or did you bring your water wings?"

"This will work."

"Will you be serious?" He was beginning to understand some of what Mark must go through with her. Joanna Marshall was a headstrong, determined young woman—maybe irrationally so.

Just as they reached a spot on the bank opposite the island, a huge black cloudbank covered the sun. The world turned dark and markedly cooler. "Jo, this is a sign. The universe doesn't want us here."

"Don't be silly."

She gazed at it. And yes, it was real. The place she'd seen in dream after dream. All about its façade, its roof, its side walls, even its rear one, were those fantastic animals she'd seen in her dreams, time and time again. In her dreams they moved, they stalked her, they inflicted pain, exactly like the ghost of Samuel Fulton. They were still now. The building was black. Was it made that way, or had decades of dirt and soot blackened it? None of the sculptures was facing directly toward her. But she whispered, "They know we're here."

Mo found her mood alarming. "They? They who?"

"Can't you see? This place has been waiting for me."

"You sound like a character in a bad movie."

Suddenly she snapped out of it. "Or a bad play, I guess. Sorry. How do we get over there?"

"We don't. We get back into the truck and go back to Pittsburgh and talk wistfully about what a good idea it was while it lasted."

"It still is." She took a step to the very edge of the riverbank. "This is the place. We can make it work." She turned to Mo and put on a wide smile. "If we renovate it, they will come."

"And how do you think they'll get out there? Free aqualungs to all season ticket holders?"

"Come on."

"Come on? Where?"

"We're going out there."

"I can't swim."

"There has to be a way."

"Being a producer's daughter doesn't mean you can walk on water, you know."

"That's what you think."

She walked farther along the shore, to see as much of the island as she could. There was a sign lying in the dirt, its paint faded and barely legible. Mo picked it up, brushed it off and made out—just barely—the words BOURBON, PENN. Then he checked his map. "It looks like we're just at the place where the three states meet. Just ahead of us"—he pointed—"that must be the state line, with Ohio beyond. Then, on the other side of the river to the south, that must be West Virginia." It was all barren, all empty. The only indications a human being had ever set foot there were the sign and the ruined theater.

"There's a boat." Joanna shaded her eyes to make certain she was seeing right.

"Where? I don't see anything?"

"There, right at the south tip of the island."

He looked, and she was right. A small rowboat was there, pulled up on the shore.

"Someone's here, Mo."

"That boat could have been there for fifty years."

"Then how could whoever owned it have gotten back to shore?"

He shrugged. "Maybe it was a swimmer. Maybe it was Mark Spitz."

"It looks fairly new."

Suddenly from behind them they heard a voice. "That island is mine."

They turned and looked. Some twenty yards up the road behind them, a young woman was walking toward them. She was tall, graceful, wearing a light cotton dress and no shoes. But there was something that seemed . . . not right about her. She had the most unnaturally pale skin, and bright yellow-red hair. Mo realized an instant before Joanna that she was an albino—and an African American.

For an instant Mo and Joanna glanced at one another. Then Mo smiled and called out, "Hello! We didn't think there was anyone around here."

"There isn't." The woman smiled briefly; then her face lost any trace of emotion. She had a marked African accent. "That island is mine."

Joanna put on a professional smile and took a few steps toward her. "Hello, there." She extended her hand. "I'm Joanna Marshall, and this is Mo Settles."

The woman reached them. She did not return their smiles or take their hands. "My name is Portia."

"This is such an interesting place." Mo groped for small talk.

But Portia was having none of that. "This is my place. You should leave."

"Your place?" Joanna wasn't quite sure how to deal with this situation, but a superior air had nearly always worked for her in the past. "You're not keeping it up very well. Couldn't you plant some spring flowers?"

"People like you have made this place what it is. But it has always been mine, and it always will be."

"Of course."

Mo decided it wasn't a good idea to let them bicker. If nothing else, it occurred to him that Portia might really *be* the owner. "It looks like someone's out on your island right now."

"I know about her. Her name is Helen. She pays me. And now and then she feeds my little pets on the island."

"Pets? What are you talking about?"

Suddenly the clouds cleared the sun; the three of them were bathed in blinding light. Portia's eyes were dark brown, almost jet black. Jo realized; she was not quite a true albino. She peered directly at Jo, as if she was seeing her for the first time. She reached out and rather violently took hold of Jo's arm, and she pulled up the sleeve of her sweatshirt. Seeing the bruises there, she let out an exultant cry. "Aha! You already know!"

Portia was surprisingly strong. Jo tried to pull free of her, but she couldn't manage to. Mo took hold of Portia's arm and removed it. Jo rubbed her own arm; Portia's grip had been tight enough to hurt. It left a bruise.

Oddly, Portia laughed. "Your whole body is covered with such. From them." She pointed to the opera house.

Mo was completely lost. "Listen, Miss—er, Portia, we're hoping we might renovate the old theater out there. There could be a lot of money in it."

"I got all the money I need." Her African lilt sounded even stronger.

"You can have more."

Portia laughed and spit on the ground. "You don't know what you're talkin' about."

"Probably not." He glanced at Jo. "But we want to try."

"Nobody done tried here for seventy, eighty years. People have more sense."

Joanna had listened to this long enough. "You actually have a deed to all this?"

Portia turned coy. "Don't need one."

"Well, if you don't have a deed, you can hardly claim to own the place."

"I own it. By right."

The sun was low enough in the sky to be shining straight

into their eyes. Joanna positioned herself with her back to it. Mo shaded his face. "You said you know who took that boat out there?"

"Whore. She's a whore. Who else would be there?"

Joanna decided to try a more imperious tone. "Perhaps you don't understand. We're hoping to renovate the opera house and start a theater company here."

"That's what I said." Portia laughed long and hard.

"Listen, Portia"—Jo put just a hint of sarcasm into her voice—"we're going to make this place live again. And we're going to do it whether you like it or not. If you don't have any valid legal claim to this place, one you can prove, then you're wasting our time. That's all."

"I got to go now." Portia didn't sound at all intimidated. "The sun is bad for me. Skin burns." She turned and started to walk back up the road. Then slowly she looked back over her shoulder, smiled and said almost wistfully, "Lots of people burn here."

She walked on. Trying one last time to be friendly, Mo called, "It was nice meeting you."

Under her breath Joanna said, "It was no such thing. What was that you said before about March Hares?"

"Okay, so we met one of the locals and she's crazy." He turned to look at the island again. The sun blinded him, and he turned quickly away. "That doesn't mean we have to go nuts, too."

"Not crazy, Mo, just irrational."

"Why would a whore go out there?"

She shrugged. "Privacy? Atmosphere? Come on, let's see some more. I wish we had a boat."

She headed farther along the riverbank, with Mo following. He decided not to try and hide the fact that Joanna's "plan" seemed screwier and screwier to him. "Maybe we could build a pontoon bridge. Or rent water skis."

Joanna pointed to something at the bottom of the bank. "Look, old stone pilings. There used to be a bridge. I'll bet there was another one at the opposite side of the island, to bring people from over there, too."

"Look, Jo, it's time for us to get going. The sun will be

down soon, and I really don't want to be here after dark, okay?"

"Are you superstitious?"

"Don't be foolish. It was hard enough finding our way here in broad daylight. If we get stranded here after sunset . . ."

"You've seen too many cheap horror films."

"You've seen too many plays."

"Touché!" She looked around. "You're probably right, though. Let's get going. We'll be able to find the place again with no trouble."

He headed for the truck. "I take it you think you're going to get me back here again?"

She put on a sweet, ironic smile and flittered her eyelashes, like a Southern belle in a corny old play. "How can you argue with the Marshall Plan?"

"Believe me, it isn't hard. Get in."

"Listen, Mo, I have to, uh, I have to . . ."

He looked around. "Where? There's no place that isn't open."

"When we get up the road a piece. Stop at the first clump of bushes you see, will you?"

"Sure."

He started the truck and they drove for a while without saying much. When the vegetation was thick enough, he pulled to the side of the road and let the engine idle. Jo got out and headed behind the largest of the shrubs. Relieving herself, she noticed her body—noticed that all the bruises that had covered it were gone. Healed. Even the one Portia had made.

When they were under way again, Jo was quite uncharacteristically silent. Mo kept trying to make small talk, but she was almost completely unresponsive. Coming to the island and the Imperial Opera House had healed her. It wasn't possible, but it had happened.

There was a difference in her, and everyone noticed it. John found her easier to work with on their remaining projects for the semester. Her professors in the department found her less domineering; she even gave up her idea of a thesis on ghosts and persuaded them to accept the body of her design work, plus some extra projects she did specially, as her thesis. The people at the Pittsburgh Arts Foundation noticed her interest in the Fulton Theater ghost diminish.

Mark felt a palpable improvement in their relationship, no more eerie dreams, no more disagreeable behavior, no more seemingly unmotivated fights, and no more of her supposed cheating. Part of it, he imagined, was that he had finally caved in and started S&M play with her—light, no marks on her body, but she really seemed to get into it. He didn't, much, but what the hell.

Yes, Joanna Marshall was a changed woman, no longer the bitch everyone had called her and an actual pleasure to work with. It never occurred to anyone that that change might be for the worse.

Her first move was to form the nonprofit Bourbon Island Arts & Development Corporation, with herself as president, Mark as vice president, Mo as secretary and Tonya as treasurer. At first they were reluctant, but when she told them she was ninety percent certain she'd be able to pay them salaries within three months, they went along. What did they have to lose?

Then late in March she called a meeting of all her friends and colleagues who had expressed interest in founding a theater company with her over the years. Mark was there, of course, and John, and seven other grad students. Mo and Tonya came; neither had been able to find a more promising job. John brought his boyfriend Tim, who decided that if he could get real work with a professional company, college could wait. And Jo managed to track down Vince Gallardo. If they were to make a go of this, they'd need a good PR person. Vince was still unemployed and, better yet, he already had relationships with all the major press outlets in the region.

After everyone had a chance to meet one another and break the ice, she began with a history of the Imperial Opera House, or as much of it as she'd been able to track down. Samuel Fulton, William Beatty, the rumors the place was haunted . . . She ended this part of the talk with the weird fact that no one had been able to determine which state owned the island.

"But if we work this right, that can be to our advantage," she told them. "It's a huge old building. Mo's seen it. And I want all the rest of you to see it as soon as we can arrange a trip. I've already sent out feelers—through my mother's office—to the arts councils in the three states and to all three state historical preservation boards."

John asked, "What kind of feelers?"

"Preliminary grant requests, for seed money. Just enough to get a company started and pay us enough to keep us all solvent. The first check," she told them cheerily, "arrived this morning."

She held it up so they could see, and there were the expected murmurs and giggles of approval as they strained to make out the dollar amount.

It was more than any of them had imagined. Yes, there would be salaries, only for the four administrators at first, but soon enough for everyone. And there was a good prospect of even more. "Once we get the National Endowment for the Arts behind us, that'll make a total of seven funding agencies. And there are city arts councils, too; I haven't even begun to explore the possibilities there. All we need to do is start planning our first season."

Mark wondered out loud if Jo wasn't being a bit premature in that kind of optimism. "What about the physical work of getting the place restored?"

She produced letters from all of the various state agencies, expressing a desire to help renovate the Imperial and turn it into a viable arts venue for the twenty-first century. That was the end of that discussion.

That night, Mark and Jo fought again, for the first time in weeks.

"Why did you let me make a fool of myself like that? Why didn't you tell me what you'd been up to? And why the hell didn't you tell me you already had a check?"

She shrugged. "You didn't ask."

"Should the vice president of the Bourbon Island Arts & Development Corporation have to ask?"

It escalated from there. And he slept on the couch. As he fell asleep, he was wondering whether Jo had really changed as much as everyone thought.

Stage Fright 107

* * *

The loft at the Fulton Theater was as it always was, filled with boxes and dust, windows streaked with soot. Jo decided she ought to go back one last time, if only to thank the foundation for letting her do all her research and to clean up some of the clutter she'd made as she plowed through the archives.

Jim Plunkett escorted her up to the attic, as usual. "I hear you're really starting that new company."

She smiled and nodded, pleased that word was getting around.

"I saw the grant proposal you submitted. And I hear you've done a lot more elsewhere."

"We're not only promoting ourselves as an arts organization. We think, if we do everything right, the Imperial can serve as an engine for economic and social development for the entire region."

"You've got the language down right, anyway. Will you be needing someone to handle PR for you?"

"That post is already taken, I'm afraid."

"Oh." After a moment's glum response, he remembered to smile and go on buttering her up. "Well, if things get as big as you seem to think they will, you'll always need more."

He left her alone in Fulton's loft. Their exchange pleased her more than not. Arts people were always ready to jump onto the next wagon; and buzz is half the key to success. If someone as frankly ambitious as Jim Plunkett was that anxious to get in on this, it was a very positive sign.

She took a deep breath, made herself relax and looked around the loft. The windows had never been washed, not even on the inside. She had wanted to bring a bottle of Windex and clean them, but somehow she always got distracted from the thought, and they stayed dirty.

It was a bright spring day, and the street below was busy. There was traffic, both motor and foot, and a lot of recreational boats were out on the Allegheny. She spit on a fingertip, wiped a clean streak on the glass, then rubbed her finger clean on her jeans.

This would likely be the last time she'd be visiting Samuel

Fulton's private loft. The last time she'd watch his . . . extra-professional activities. There had been so many, over the months. Girls, boys, all hurt, all willing. And no matter how vicious his treatment, there were always more of them. It didn't quite make sense to her, not really, but he had money and power, and that was probably explanation enough.

She had been using too many drugs. But . . . one last time couldn't hurt, could it? It was only hash. She lit up.

Time and again, Joanna had wondered how it was she was seeing these things, when no one else seemed to. Did she have some sort of connection to Fulton? Was there something about her, in and of herself? There didn't seem any convenient way to explain it. But drugs did it. Even Fulton's drugs, in her dreams, which couldn't possibly have been real but affected her none the less, in the same way his whips and handcuffs did.

The room was his room again, not the foundation's attic. The light was dying. Fulton entered.

This time he was alone. Joanna waited and waited for his toy of the evening, but no one followed him. Then she realized he was watching her and smiling.

Briskly he crossed the room to her. Quickly, nimbly he undid her clothes. When she was naked, he looked her up and down and smiled approvingly.

She went to the bed. One last time, why not, it couldn't make much difference, and it felt so good. She held her hands out compliantly.

But this time Fulton did not want brutal sex, he wanted lovemaking. He undressed, and she closed her eyes and pretended his body was not that of a middle-aged man. He kissed her, fondled her, crawled on top of her and fucked her long and hard. No drugs, no opium, but it was the most intense thing she'd ever felt.

When they both were finished, Fulton rolled to one side and took her hand. He had never spoken to her much before, not directly. But into her ear he whispered, "My sweet Joanna, you will not come here again, will you?" Before she could answer he went on. "It does not matter. You and I shall meet again. And it will be richer and more rewarding than this. Richer and more rewarding than anything you have ever

Stage Fright

known, or ever thought you could. This place is nothing but a place for vaudeville. Where you are going now, you will find the greatest theater of all."

He was gone. She was alone.

She heard Jim Plunkett's footsteps on the staircase and reached quickly for her clothes. But he got to the loft too quickly. "Joanna!"

Naked, lying on the floor but still moist from making love with Fulton, she glared at him. "Don't say anything about this. Do you understand?"

"But what—?"

"You never saw me like this. Period. If you ever want to work in the theater again, you'll forget this."

He stared at her, uncertain what to think or say. Slowly she got back into her things. When she was lacing up her shoes she smiled an artificial smile and said, "You're a good boy, Jim. You know how to behave."

And so the Imperial's occupants waited. For once there was *no cause for impatience among them. Soon enough, their home would see life again. And blood.*

PART TWO

FOUR

It was late afternoon, a glaringly bright, unseasonably warm spring day. Helen stood a hundred yards downriver from the island, where the barren land ended and the vegetation began, and watched it glumly. There were people again. More people than before. On Portia's island.

Behind her a man in late middle age stood, impatient. "You said we could go out there."

"There's people there."

"Where we gonna go, then?" He smelled of whiskey. And he was older than a lot of her clients, but not by any means all of them. Helen knew she was no longer young herself, and she had to make do with the business that came her way.

"I don't know." She shaded her eyes and looked again. "They're going inside the Imperial. They'll learn soon enough." She turned to him and smiled. "We could do it here, maybe."

"Here? In these bushes? What do you think I am, a sixteen-year-old boy? Don't you have a place?"

"No." She paused tentatively. "Do you?"

"No. I live with my daughter. Why am I telling you this?"

"You want to do it or don't you?"

He turned to go. Helen caught his arm. "You wait. The bushes are thicker over there. We can do it there."

"No."

"You want to get off, don't you?" She fondled her breasts for his benefit.

He looked around and licked his lips. "You give good head?"

"Real good. All my clients say so."

He looked around cautiously. "You sure nobody will see us in the bushes?"

"There's nobody to see."

He gazed uncertainly up the river at the island. The people there would never see him with his whore in the bushes, and there was no one else around. "What else do you do?"

"Name it."

Shyly he asked, "Water sports?"

Helen nodded. Her client stepped into the thickest growth, and she followed. Forty bucks was forty bucks.

"That!" Mark shouted. "You want us to work in that!"

A hired minibus with eight members of the company, driven by Mark and "navigated" by Joanna, approached the river at Bourbon Island. There was a second bus, with Mo in charge; Joanna hadn't seen it for more than an hour. She hoped they'd gotten there without drifting off the right road. But "her" bus had had its troubles. They had driven over half of Beaver County trying to find the place. The bus wasn't air-conditioned; except for Jo, everyone was in a foul mood.

Then finally they managed to find Bourbon. As their bus approached it, they saw the other one parked by the side of a dirt road. Then the island and the theater itself came into clear view.

"That monstrosity?" Mark saw no reason to try and hide his scorn. "That's not a theater, it's a goddamned nightmare!"

"Don't be redundant. It is," Jo corrected him patiently, "the future temple of your art. No, of *our* art." She said this loudly enough for everyone to hear. "And our livelihood."

Stage Fright

John Bartlett shaded his eyes. "Until a good stiff wind comes along and blows it over. Jo, you can't be serious."

"I can be, and I am. The engineers all say it's still structurally sound."

Tim chirped, "I think it's kind of neat."

But the closer they got, the more annoyed Mark grew. "You do mean engineers? I mean, you didn't just have a couple of set designers look at the place?"

"What's that at the top?" Tim was getting more and more enthusiastic. Mark wished the kid would be quiet. But he answered his own question. "It's a pyramid! And a sphinx!"

"If you like that, wait till you see the rest." Despite all the negativity, Jo was enjoying herself. Yes, the place was strange, she announced cheerily, but it would grow on them.

"Like warts, or skin cancer." Mark grunted, and leaned back in his seat. "I can't believe this."

Ahead of them, three people were waiting beside the other bus. Jo recognized Tonya as one of them. Then, out on the island itself, she saw some of the others. Her bus pulled up beside the first one, and Mark cut the engine. Jo stepped out first.

"Tonya, hi."

"Hi, Joanna."

"You didn't go out with the others?"

"I don't do water."

An assistant set designer named Julie Watts and a costume designer named Tom Giambatese seconded this.

"Well, fine for now, but sooner or later you'll have to."

"That's what you think."

Behind Jo, her party got off the bus. The day seemed even more unpleasantly hot than before; Jo decided it must be humidity from the river or something.

Tim was grinning like a schoolboy which, she reminded herself, he was. "Look at all the monsters. This place is so cool."

"There are more inside."

"I like dragons. Are there any dragons?"

"You'll see." Her eyes twinkled. He was nineteen.

Out on the island, Mo waved to them and shouted. "I'll have the boat over in just a sec."

One of the corporation's first purchases had been a large launch. The expense was more than justified; they'd be back and forth a lot, naturally; and the construction crews could use it, too. Ohio and West Virginia had agreed to build bridges. Pennsylvania decided it already had enough bad roads and declined to chip in at first; then one-upmanship kicked in and they decided to do it after all. But until they were built, a boat was a necessity. An Ohio bureaucrat complained that no arts organization had ever needed one before, but he grudgingly agreed it was a legitimate use of grant money, necessary for the project. It was a good-sized thing; it could hold as many as fifteen people without becoming unstable.

Mark's mood was growing darker by the minute. He pulled Jo aside. "You can not be serious about this. Look at the place. And we're in the middle of nowhere."

"As long as your definition of *nowhere* includes three states—and three metropolitan areas within an hour's drive."

"Doesn't the fact that nobody owns it and nobody wants it tell you anything?"

"Mark, it thrived for decades after it was built. People came here from all over the region. Vince has done some research, and from what he's found, this place was a major draw."

"Why is the shore on both sides of it so barren? There isn't so much as a dandelion growing."

She shrugged and laughed. "If you want dandelions, we'll plant some, okay?"

He grunted, turned his back and walked away from her.

Mo untied the launch, started the engine and steered it to shore. Joanna's party had grouped themselves into twos and threes and were chatting, some about the Imperial, some not. When he tied up on shore, at a little dock that had been built for them, he crossed quickly to Joanna. She lowered her voice and asked him how the people he'd brought liked the place.

"Mixed, Jo. Some of them see possibilities, some just see ruins. Jack Bilicic, that guy you said is going to be the facility manager, is running around like a kid in a toy shop. Vince Gallardo loves everything about it."

"Good."

Stage Fright   117

"And that actress, the dumb blonde?"

She nodded and laughed. One of the first people she had recruited for the Imperial's rep company was Annie Moore, the girl who'd given Mark so much trouble in *Who's Afraid of Virginia Woolf?* She had done it on purpose; Mark was being more than usually difficult, about nearly everything.

"Well, she keeps saying she thought this was the Imperial Theater from Broadway. Once, she actually asked how they got it down here."

"You're kidding."

"Nope."

So things in Jo's little world of theater were, more or less, as usual. "Let's get this group over there, okay? Has there been any sign of . . . you know who?"

He knew. She meant Portia, who had shown up every time they'd visited the site, and Helen, who was there more often than seemed quite likely, usually with customers. The first time they'd encountered Helen, some deep evangelical streak in Mo came to the surface. "I'm not sure how I feel about prostitutes doing business here."

"One prostitute." Jo corrected him.

"Even so."

She smirked at him. "You really are new to the theater, aren't you?"

"You know I am, but—" He realized what she was saying and caught himself.

As for Portia, she nearly always seemed to be there, making veiled threats of one sort or another, reasserting her claim to the island and generally making a pest of herself. Once they actually found her on the island, but there was no boat in sight. She might have swum there, but it seemed unlikely. How could she . . . ?

But Mo told Joanna there hadn't been any sign of either of them. "All's clear on that front, at least."

"Good." She took a long look around, as if she was certain she'd see either Helen or Portia; then she rubbed her hands together briskly. "I'll get everybody into the boat."

"Jo?"

"Hm?"

"Listen, Tonya's kind of freaked out by this place. By the fact we'll be on an island, I mean."

"She'll get over it."

"I'm not so sure. She won't talk about it, but her mom told me one of her sisters drowned when she was little."

"Mo, she'll adjust. She'll be fine when the bridges are up. Trust me."

"I just hope you're right."

Joanna busied herself getting everyone into the launch. At the last moment Julie Watts changed her mind and decided to come along. Mo took his seat at the wheel and they pushed off; in less than a minute they were at the island. Mo didn't slow enough and the boat hit land with a severe jolt. "Sorry. Is everyone all right? I haven't gotten the hang of this yet."

They all grumbled, but they were okay. One by one they stepped ashore, climbed the riverbank and began to look around.

The Imperial was larger than any of them had expected, larger than it looked from shore, a huge, towering building. Jo announced it would look a lot better once it had been sandblasted, or at least a lot less unfriendly. Tim said he loved it the way it was. Slowly, by ones, twos and threes, they began to drift off and explore.

Mark stayed behind with Jo. "Is it safe? I mean, the engineers really did say it's safe for people to go prowling around the place?"

Joanna nodded. "Like I said before, a big chunk of the ceiling collapsed—from the weight of the chandelier, they say—but they're sure the rest of it's sound enough to stay up. Everything else is rock solid."

"Where do we work?" He looked doubtful.

"The crew will be putting up some temporary office space for us, first thing." She pointed. "Down there at the end of the island, where that little shack is now. But once the theater's ready, there'll be plenty of office space on the upper floors. There's even a residential suite. Samuel Fulton used to live here, on and off." She looked at Mark from the corner of her eye, and he didn't look at all happy. "He did at all his theaters. Rode around like a circuit preacher." She put on a stiff smile. "I'm taking his old office for my own."

Mark walked in a wide semicircle, trying to take the whole island in. "What do we do when the river rises?"

"We could do *The Frogs*." She made a sarcastic face.

"I'm serious, Jo. A flood, or even just high water from heavy rain, could close the place down."

"Relax, Mark. We're going to be fine. The bridges will be good and solid."

"But—"

"Everyone at the state historical societies understands the situation. They've checked, and floods high enough to cut into our business are rare."

"But not unknown."

"And we have to assume the highway departments know what they're doing."

"Are you kidding? Have you ever driven the Pennsylvania Turnpike?"

She barked at him. "Will you stop focusing on all the negative stuff, Mark? Look at this place. We have our own company, we have funding, and by the end of the summer we'll have a magnificent showplace. How many directors fresh out of grad school get a chance like this?"

What she was saying made sense, but there was still something . . . not right, something he couldn't put a finger on. "That's assuming anyone can ever find their way here." He turned snide, as usual when he found himself losing an argument. "Maybe we can give a free set of dishes to any customers who can actually find this place."

"Right. The state highway departments will forget to put up road signs. Terrific reasoning, Mark." She walked off toward the theater, then looked back over her shoulder. "Are you coming?"

"No thanks, I'll wait here. There'll be plenty of time to see it after they've propped it up."

Jo walked quickly to the theater and went inside. Everyone seemed to be fascinated by the place, for better or worse, which she took as a good sign. When it was all restored, the public would love it, too. Or hate it. But it would get talked about.

She found Vince Gallardo at one end of the lobby, staring up at the sculpture of the gorgon. "Hi, Jo."

She pointed up at the statue. "Like it?"

"Not exactly. It reminds me of my sixth grade nun." He turned to face her. "But you were right—this place is fantastic. A publicist's dream. I won't have any trouble at all planting stories about the place."

"That's what I thought."

"Have you thought about doing horror plays here? I mean, *Dracula*, *Frankenstein*, Grand Guignol. . . . The setting would be perfect. And the stories I could write!"

"I've had the exact same thought. At least around Halloween, it would be perfect. I mean, if all those little rinky-dink 'haunted houses' can make money, we should be able to clean up."

"Right. And even just offering tours of this place should bring in a lot of extra cash."

"I like the way you think, Vince." She kissed him lightly on the cheek and headed off into the main auditorium.

John Bartlett, Tim Myers and Jack Bilicic were there, on the stage. The monsters on the walls and the proscenium looked down on them, seemingly impassively. John was playing with the keys of the old theater organ, at the right edge of the stage; it let out a mild wheeze now and then but no actual music. Just as Jo came in, Tim launched into an aria from *Phantom of the Opera*. The others winced and pretended not to hear.

Jo crossed the auditorium to the fallen chandelier. A lot of the crystal prisms were shattered; splinters of glass covered the floor all around it. Seeing her at the chandelier, Tim sang even louder. John hurried across the stage and put a hand over his mouth.

Tim pulled free of him. "What's the matter?"

"Andrew Lloyd Webber is the matter."

"What do you mean?" He pouted. "You said you like the way I sing."

John lowered his voice. "That was when you were singing Cole Porter."

Jo called out to them, "Calm down, you two. The acoustics in here are terrific—way better than I would have expected."

Tim made a smug face at John. "See?"

Stage Fright

But John wasn't impressed. "She said she could hear you clearly, not that she liked what she was hearing."

Jack was upstage, staring up into the flyspace. "This equipment's all in pretty bad shape."

Jo joined them on the stage. "I think that's a given, Jack. We're planning to replace it all, anyway. And computerize the whole facility."

"I can't program." He looked concerned.

"Don't worry, that'll be the designers' job."

A group of four people came in, led by Mo. He was showing them around knowledgeably, pointing out various features and decorations around the building. He led them up to the foot of the stage.

Julie Watts, the assistant set designer, was one of them. "Joanna, this place is cavernous."

"They knew how to build real palaces back then, huh?"

"No, that's not what I mean. The stage—it's bigger than any I've ever seen. Bigger than the ones at those big old movie houses back in town. Building sets for this place will cost a fortune."

It hadn't occurred to her before. But, designer that she was herself, she couldn't very well admit it. "There are things we can do, shortcuts we can take. We'll be fine, Julie."

Suddenly there came an ear-piercing scream, a woman's voice crying out hysterically. It echoed through the huge space; one of the organ pipes vibrated slightly in sympathy with it. But the echoes made it impossible to tell where it came from. It was followed by a second scream, then a third.

They rushed out into the lobby, with Joanna leading. There was still another agonized cry, then everything fell silent. As they stood there, looking around and trying to guess who they'd heard and where she might be, Mark rushed in from outside. "What's wrong?"

John stepped up to him. "We don't know. We heard someone screaming, but . . ." He spread his hands wide apart in a what-can-we-do gesture.

"Well, whoever it was was in trouble. We need to find her." Mark took charge like the director he was. "Let's pair off and search the place."

They quickly formed themselves into twos and headed off in different directions. Mark took Julie and went into the auditorium, even though everyone told him they'd just come from there and it wasn't where the screams originated. Mo and Joanna headed up to the mezzanine. The others split and went wherever it seemed no one else was going.

Tonya and Tom waited by the buses on shore. The heat was getting worse, none of them had brought bottled water, and they had pretty much run out of small talk. Tonya, in particular, kept looking out to the island, hoping she'd see everyone coming back. No luck.

Tom climbed into one of the buses. "At least there's shade in here."

Tonya walked to the edge of the river and waved at the people she could see on the island. None of them saw her.

Then Tom noticed someone walking up the road toward them. A terribly pale woman with bright red hair. As she got closer, Tonya noticed her, too. "That must be that Portia Mo told me about."

"What about her?"

"She's crazy. Says she owns all this."

"She can have it."

When he found the energy to get to his feet and rejoin Tonya, Portia was almost there. They smiled at her. She did not smile back. She was odd looking, and Tom knew it, but for some reason he found her hot.

"You are new here." Portia looked from one of them to the next. It was a pronouncement, not a question.

"I guess you could put it that way." Tonya kept her smile on despite Portia's unfriendliness.

"I told the others. I warned them."

Tom sized her up; yeah, something about her was really turning him on. "Warned them? About what?"

"I told them that island is a place of death. They would not listen to me."

Tonya picked up on Tom's reaction and decided that, for someone with albinism, Portia wasn't at all unattractive—and

Stage Fright   123

therefore no one she wanted around. "What exactly is 'a place of death' supposed to mean?"

Portia shrugged. "Isn't it obvious?"

"No, it isn't."

"Ever since the first deaths, none of the others have mattered to me."

Tom sensed the tension between Tonya and Portia and decided to get between them. "We own this place, you know. You're trespassing. You should leave."

"This land is mine by right." She pointed vaguely. "That is my island. The blood there is on my hands." After a moment she added, a bit weakly, "My brothers' blood."

"Of course," Tonya snapped. "Now, why don't you just move along before there's any trouble, all right?"

"Are you serious, woman? There will be nothing but trouble. Requiring me to leave will not change that. My spirit will still be here, in this place that I own."

"Well, then, there's no reason for your body to hang around, is there?"

Portia let out a long, loud laugh. Again she pointed in the direction of the island. "There is already death. There will be more." She turned abruptly and walked away, back up the road.

The two of them were left standing there, staring at one another, wondering what to make of her. Tom muttered, "What on earth was that?"

"Mo and Jo keep running into her whenever they're here." Tonya glanced back at the island; there was no one in sight. "Mo told me she was crazy, but wow, she's really off the rails."

Tom whistled. "Crazy would be the word. But I'm going back inside. She wasn't nearly a good enough diversion. Wake me up when everyone gets back okay?"

Then, from the island, they heard the screams.

Jack Bilicic and Tim went down the stairs to the basement.

It was an enormous space, with light from above barely penetrating. The floor was covered with dirt and littered with rubbish of various kinds, discarded newspapers, cardboard boxes, broken glass. . . . From his back pocket Jack produced a flashlight. Tim looked at him, surprised, and he shrugged. "A good facility manager is always prepared."

They walked ahead, through the debris, being careful not to step on anything. There was no sound but their footsteps. The place had long since been turned into a storage area; it was littered with debris, old statues and fragments of plaster moldings and such. There was dust everywhere, and most of what they could see was covered with cobwebs. Jack looked for any sign of recent footprints; there were none. He found himself smiling. "It's like an old horror movie or something, isn't it?"

Every few seconds Tim looked back over his shoulder nervously. "Jack, there's nobody down here. Let's go back upstairs."

"Quiet." Jack stopped walking and listened. "I think I can hear someone crying."

"I don't hear anything."

"You're younger than me. Aren't you supposed to have better hearing?"

"Let's go upstairs."

"Go on, if you want to."

Unhappily, not wanting to seem more nervous than he already did, Tim followed him.

They passed from one large room to the next, and the beam from Jack's flashlight was the only illumination. There were enormous storage crates; numerous pieces of lounge furniture—couches, settees—were covered with dirty drop cloths. A big old mirror, twenty feet long and covered with grime, stretched along a wall. When the beam hit it and reflected dimly back, Tim jumped and took hold of Jack's arm.

Jack decided he was enjoying Tim's discomfort. "When I was a kid," he said softly, "we used to go and play in this big old abandoned house at the end of our neighborhood. We always thought it was haunted."

"Do you have to talk about that now?"

Jack smiled and went on. "We used to go after dark and see who could stay the longest without getting scared and running outside."

"Never mind that—was it really haunted?"

"We never knew. There were always noises coming from

Stage Fright

whatever part of the place we weren't in. We thought there might be an escaped convict or mental patient there, if there weren't ghosts."

Tim put a hand on his arm again. "Are you trying to scare me?"

"No."

"Well, you are. Why don't you talk about an amusement park or something?"

"Calm down, Tim. You've seen too many slasher movies, that's all."

"Did you see *The Colors of Hell*? It scared the shit out of me."

From ahead of them in the darkness came a low moan, followed by a series of deep sobs.

Jack stopped talking and walked faster. Tim, reluctantly, kept up with him. Marble demons loomed up around them—a dragon, sharp teeth bared; a human skeleton made of some smooth, shiny black stone, glistening even through the dirt. Tim told himself there was nothing to be afraid of. They were only statues. The sounds were from the building settling or whatever.

Then from behind a bronze Egyptian sphinx something jumped out at them. It was a ghostly white figure, face contorted with pain or fear. Then in the light beam they saw it was Annie Moore. Her features were distorted with horror, streaked with tears. She tried to speak, or to scream, but nothing came from her mouth. Jack lowered the beam a bit, and she was soaked in blood. And they saw that both her arms were gone—it looked like they had been torn off, one at the shoulder, one at the elbow. Blood flowed heavily; it glistened bright red in the light.

As soon as he realized what was happening, Jack reached out a hand to touch Annie's shoulder. "Annie."

Tim doubled up and vomited.

And suddenly she let out an ear-piercing yell and tore past them, heading for the room they'd just come from.

Jack, not having time to think or react, looked from Annie to Tim. "Are you all right, Tim?" He took a step to follow Annie.

"Don't leave me here!"

"Come on, then."

"I can't. I'm afraid."

There was a trail of Annie's blood, clearly visible in the dirt on the floor. Jack scanned the place she'd jumped out from, but there was no sign of her arms, or of anything obvious that might have happened.

Jack took Tim by the hand. "Come on, Tim."

Tim had gone numb. He let Jack pull him, and as quickly as he could, Jack headed after Annie. It wasn't hard to see where she had gone. Her blood told. Jack hoped she'd gone to the steps, but the trail led first to the foot of them, then off to another part of the basement.

She was in an empty room, no furniture, no marble, just dirt on the floor. Blood was still pouring from the stumps where her arms had been. When the flashlight hit her she turned, wild-eyed, and tried to say something. But only incoherent muttering came out. Then she collapsed.

"Annie?" Jack took a step toward her.

She was perfectly still.

"Annie?" He moved still closer, then turned to Tim. "For God's sake, Tim, I think she's dead. Run upstairs and get Mark."

"I don't have a light."

"Here." He held it out.

But Tim recoiled from him. "You'll be in the dark."

"I'm not afraid. I remember the way."

"For God's sake, Jack, something tore her arms off."

"She had an accident or something, that's all. Go up and get the others. I'll be fine."

"But—"

"Go!" He bellowed it.

Tim ran to the foot of the stairs and shouted up to the lobby. "Mark! Mark!" Anxiously he looked back where he had come from.

There was no answer from above. He climbed halfway up the stairs to the lobby and called again; and again no one answered. Looking doubtfully back down to the darkness, he climbed to the lobby. There was no one in sight. He switched off the flashlight and shouted as loud as he could.

Stage Fright

Thankfully, voices answered him from various parts of the Imperial. People assembled quickly; Mark was among the first of them.

Shaking from the shock, Tim told them what had happened. "We've got to get down there. Jack's down there with her."

"Who?"

Confusion registered in his face; he didn't know what to say. She was dead. What was the point of guarding her? He shook his head. "Come on."

Just as they reached the top of the staircase, there was another loud scream. This time the voice was male. Mark was certain it was Jack.

They hurried down stairs. Tim led them, a bit uncertainly, through the maze of rooms. None of them said much. Mo took it all in, trying to remember the layout. Mark was right behind him, determined to make certain nothing bad could have happened. Jo, designer that she was, paid more attention to the sculptures and the décor, what she could see of them.

Then they reached the room. Tim's light fell on Annie's body, lying exactly as he had told them. The arms were gone, the face twisted with fright or pain or some awful combination of both.

There was no sign of Jack.

Everyone gasped or cried out at the sight of Annie's body. Joanna crossed the room ahead of everyone else and got down on a knee next to it. Then she looked back over her shoulder at the others. "For the love of God, what can have happened?"

But John ignored the question and shouted, "Where's Jack?"

Everyone looked around stupidly.

John caught Tim by the front of his shirt and shook him. "Where is he? You said you left him here."

Mark pushed between them. "Calm down, John. He just went off somewhere else, that's all. We'll find him."

Stupidly, Tim added, "He said he wasn't scared."

"And you left him down here alone?" John lunged at him again, but he ducked.

Mark caught him again. "John, will you for Christ's sake calm down? He's around somewhere. He has to be. We'll find him."

Jo had her cell phone out. She was dialing 911. The operator asked, "What city, please?"

"We're on Bourbon Island."

"Bourbon Island? There's no Bourbon Island in our area."

She had been careful to dial the area code for Pennsylvania. "We're on Bourbon Island, Pennsylvania," she said insistently. "We have to be in your area. There's been a death."

"Who is the victim?"

Jo explained patiently. The operator asked her to hold for a moment. When she came back on, she repeated, "There is no Bourbon Island in our area. There is no Bourbon, Pennsylvania on our map."

There was no point arguing. Jo tried Ohio, then West Virginia 911, and got pretty much the same response. As far as any of them knew, there was no such place as Bourbon.

"Jo," John asked her angrily, "What kind of place is this? What have you gotten us into?"

Still again Mark took hold of his arm and tried to calm him down. He had never shown signs of being such a hothead before. Mark decided it must be the grotesque surroundings affecting him somehow. The theater was getting to everyone.

He decided it was time for him to take charge. He told everyone to go back upstairs to the lobby. Tim was wearing a sweatshirt; he took it off and covered the top part of Annie's body with it. When they were all assembled near the front entrance, Mark told them he was taking the launch back to shore. He'd find the nearest municipality on the Pennsylvania side and bring the police. Everyone was to remain calm till he got back; he hoped it wouldn't be long. "And no one," he added with heavy emphasis, "is to go down to the basement till I get back."

"What about Jack?" Tim was still shaken by what had happened.

"Jack just went off on his own someplace, that's all. We'll find him, or he'll find his way back up here."

"But we heard him scream—"

"Look, Tim, nothing could have happened to him. He's okay, wherever he is. If he's still missing when I get back, the police will find him."

Stage Fright

Tim was unhappy but he decided there was no point arguing.

Mark took Mo aside and asked him to take charge of things till he got back; he kept his voice low so Jo wouldn't hear.

Then he asked John to drive the launch for him and bring it back to the island.

The people on shore asked him what was wrong.

"There's been an accident, that's all. Stay here, okay?"

Tom offered to go with him for the police, but Mark said he'd rather do it alone. He got behind the wheel of one of the minibuses and headed off in what he hoped was the right direction. Just as he reached the edge of the barren land, he saw a young woman staring at him from behind some shrubs. She was, he realized, an African American albino; her bright yellow-red hair gave her away even though she was obviously trying to hide.

On the island, the others were left staring at one another. Jo headed off to a corner, got out her phone and made another call.

Mo followed her. "What's up?"

"Shh. I'm talking to New York."

He waited till she was finished, then asked again.

"I put in a call to Marvin Mittelberger, my mother's lawyer. He's what they call high-powered."

"Can he get us the police and an ambulance?"

"I'm guessing he can get us pretty much anything."

"Good. I have a feeling we'll need him. Jo, should we reconsider this?"

"You mean the project? No!" She seemed to be offended at the mere suggestion.

"But—I mean, how are we going to exist out here? You heard what the 911 people told you—officially, there's no such place as this."

"Marvin will take care of that."

"And it isn't just emergency service we'll need. One of the power companies will have to run lines out here. And one of the water companies, and—"

"Mo, that's all been thought of already."

He narrowed his eyes. "Joanna, exactly how much have you done? I mean, that you haven't told us about?"

"There's a design/architecture firm. Beatty, Priori, and Cook. The Beatty is the great-grandson of William Beatty, who built this place." She smiled. "His name's William, too."

"Somehow, I don't find that reassuring."

"Their engineers have gone over the place thoroughly. Except for that collapsed ceiling in the auditorium, everything's sound. They think the chandelier was too heavy for the structure." She made a slight shrug, as if to say there was nothing to be concerned about.

"And do they know there's something here that rips people's arms off?"

"Look. Annie Moore was dumb. And I mean really dumb. She got into some kind of trouble. Caught her arms on a dragon's teeth or something."

"Are you serious? Jo, they were torn off."

"You didn't know her, Mo. Believe me, she was stupid enough to do it."

She made a pretense of wanting to talk to John. Mo was left alone in the corner, feeling more and more doubtful. There was something bad about the place, something that didn't make any rational sense. Having the woman in charge refuse to acknowledge it was even worse. He found himself wishing idly that he'd taken a job a Wal-Mart or someplace.

An hour later Mark was back. He had a deputy with him from the Beaver County sheriff's office. The deputy did not look happy to be there. John saw them drive up, took the launch back to shore and ferried them both to the island.

Joanna approached the officer at once and introduced herself. "I'm in charge here."

"I'm Deputy Dahlgren." He looked at Mark, then back at her. "This gentleman told me he's in charge."

"He's not." That was the end of that discussion, apparently. "I'm the head of the Bourbon Island Arts & Development Corporation. He told you what happened?"

The deputy nodded. "Where's the body?"

She explained it was still in the basement.

"And the other one? The man who went missing?"

"We haven't seen him."

He sighed; this was clearly not a job he wanted. Then for the first time he took a good look at the building. "Ugly old place, isn't it?"

"They don't come uglier." Mark glared at Joanna in an I-told-you-so way.

Deputy Dahlgren looked from one of them to the other and sighed again. "Show me where it happened."

The deputy's appearance seemed to dispel some of the tension everyone was feeling. She introduced Dahlgren to everyone who wasn't off someplace else. Tim actually smiled when Jo introduced him.

"Tim here was one of the ones that saw her downstairs, just before she died."

"And who was the other one?"

"Jack Bilicic." She avoided looking at him. "He's the one who disappeared."

"People do not 'disappear,' Miss Marshall."

"Ms."

He snorted. "Ms., then. Like Mr. Barry, here, said, he went off someplace down in the basement and got lost. Let's get down there."

They walked to the staircase and descended. Mark asked, "Have there been many disappearances, er, I mean accidents here?"

"To be honest with you, I've never heard of this place at all. I mean, there are old stories—folk tales, I guess, but I never even knew this place was really here." He looked around, as if he was trying to convince himself it *was* really there. "I remember something about a crazy old whore."

"Helen," Jo said, not helpfully.

"Till today, I mean. People avoid this place. Used to be a town here, but it disappeared a long time ago. It covered both riverbanks and spread into all three states."

Mark couldn't resist. "Disappeared?"

Dahlgren shot him a dirty look. "Stopped existing, if you like. Everyone moved out. I remember my grandmother telling me stories about something bad happening here, but she never really said what. She used to say when they abandoned the town, they sowed the earth with salt."

"So it's a ghost town?" Mark smiled as he asked. "And no one ever comes to this area?"

"Well, I can't exactly say it's a ghost town, no." Dahlgren looked at the building again and made a sour face. "There'd have to be a town, for that. Do you see one? They tore the place down before they left. I guess to use all the building materials wherever they were going, I don't know."

Mark led the way through the basement labyrinth. Enjoying himself, he repeated with exaggerated emphasis, "Not even a ghost town. Imagine."

Joanna had listened to enough of this. And she didn't want anyone else hearing it; they were nervous enough. "It's a good thing they didn't have to pay today's prices for salt, then. Let us show you the girl's body."

"Besides," Dahlgren added—he really seemed to be enjoying himself, "this whole area was used for long-wall mining back in the thirties and forties. I'm not sure how stable this ground is. If it starts subsiding . . ."

"It is hasn't subsided by now, it's not going to." She led them inside the Imperial.

Dahlgren kept looking around, and he seemed more and more disapproving. Finally he asked her, "So you're the one heading this place now?"

She nodded, pleased that he understood.

"Well, what the hell do you think you're doing? You honestly think you're going to get people to come and see movies in this ugly place?"

"Plays," she said, not trying to hide her annoyance. "We're going to do plays here."

"Nobody goes to plays."

"All three states are behind us."

"Oh." He stifled a laugh.

More than a bit pissed at him, Joanna strode ahead. He fumbled with his flashlight, then he and Mark followed her through the maze of dark rooms. There wasn't much more talk.

When they finally reached Annie's mutilated corpse and uncovered it, he whistled. "Jesus."

Stage Fright   133

"No, deputy, her name was Annie Moore."

"Where are the arms?"

"I don't know. Maybe Tim does." She called up the stairs for him.

After a moment, he and John joined them in the basement. Tim was obviously nervous. He told them he had no idea what might have happened to her, or where her arms might be. "I was hoping you'd know. I've never seen anything like this." Upset at having to see her again, he took John's hand.

Dahlgren noticed the hand holding and smirked. "Where did it happen, then?"

"Back that way." Tim pointed, hoping the cop wouldn't ask him to go back there.

But he did. "It looks like there's a trail of blood, but you better show me."

Reluctantly, staying close to John for security, Tim led them all back to the place where he and Jack had first seen her. There was nothing there that might have given any indication what had happened. Dahlgren checked the floor and the walls carefully, but except for blood—still sticky—there was nothing of any use. And no sign of Annie's arms.

"Could she have come from somewhere else?"

"I guess." Tim was looking more and more uncomfortable. "She came from behind that sphinx."

Dahlgren pointed his light there. And there was a hole in the wall. Tim said he and Jack hadn't noticed it before, what with Annie's appearance and all.

"There's another room back here." The deputy pushed his head into the space. "Looks like it might have been deliberately hidden behind this statue. Now, what happened to this other guy, Jack—?"

"Bilicic." Joanna decided it was time to take charge of this.

Tim added, "He stayed down here with her body while I went up to get everyone."

"Then where'd he go?"

"I don't know."

They all looked at one another; the question seemed to bring the horror of Annie's death into even sharper relief.

Dahlgren took a deep breath. "There's this one hidden

room. There may be more." He looked back into the concealed room again. "Or . . . has anyone noticed any signs of anyone else here, someone who doesn't belong but must be hiding?"

They looked at each other again; no one had. Mark couldn't resist a touch of sarcasm. "The Phantom of the Opera House."

Joanna interrupted this. "I've been over all the building plans with my engineers. There are no hidden rooms."

Dahlgren gestured at the one they'd found. "You didn't know about this?

"No. But—"

"Then how can you be sure there aren't more?"

"My engineers—"

"Listen, Miss Marshall—"

Joanna stiffened a bit but didn't say anything.

"—I'll be frank with you. When this gentleman showed up at headquarters, none of us took him seriously. I came out here expecting to find he was a crackpot or a jokester or something. I mean, no one comes here. Do you understand that? But now that I've seen the body—" He seemed to notice something just inside the entrance to the hidden room. "What's this?"

Everyone craned to look over his shoulder as he bent down.

"More blood."

Mark pushed himself in front of Joanna. "This is still fresh, and still warm. Why isn't it drying, like the rest?"

"Maybe it's not hers."

"Then whose—?"

The deputy didn't wait for him to finish his question. "That missing man." Then he turned back to Joanna. "This is a crime scene. You'll have to get all your people out of here."

"But—"

He began making out a report. "All except you; I'll need you for a statement. Ferry them back over to shore. I'll be calling for a CSI team. They'll need statements from you, too, and from that young man"—he gestured at Tim—"and anyone else who saw or heard anything."

"That would be everybody. Deputy Dahlgren, I—"

Stage Fright

"You're to have everyone wait on shore till they get here, understand?"

She was tempted to argue. The day hadn't gone anything like what she'd planned. But she thought better of it. She asked Mark, John and Tim to round everyone up, and the whole party came together at the front entrance She stayed in the basement and gave Dahlgren a full account, step by step, of the day's events. When he was satisfied he'd gotten everything he could from her, he let her rejoin the others.

Mo seemed to have emerged as the leader of the group in the lobby. Everyone was accounted for but Jack. Joanna explained that they were to go to shore and wait, and the group started filtering outside and toward the launch. None of them seemed any too happy about the way their first visit to the Imperial had gone—or what it might foreshadow.

Jo, Mo and Mark were the last to exit. Jo called down the stairs to Deputy Dahlgren, "You will let us know what happens, won't you? And when we can get back in here? The restoration crew is supposed to start work Monday."

"I don't know if that will be possible. We'll be sure to keep you informed, Miss Marshall."

"Thank you so much. And when you find Jack—?"

"We'll get him checked out to make sure he's okay. Then you can come and get him." For her benefit, he added, "If he's alive, that is." He pulled out his cell phone but waited for them to leave the building before he dialed.

When Jo got outside, half the group had already climbed into the launch. John started the engine, gunned it, waved to Jo and Mark, then cast off for the Pennsylvania shore.

"Well." Mark exhaled deeply. "The Bourbon Island Arts & Development Corporation isn't exactly off to a rousing start, is it?"

"Don't rub it in." Jo made it clear she was in no mood for him. She walked to a nearby rock and sat down.

The sun was sinking; it was that bright orange it sometimes turns in late afternoon. The long shadows seemed appropriate.

Mo walked to the edge of the water. "I wish you two would stop bickering all the time. This is all so new to me, so strange. I have so much to adjust to, and it's hard enough without getting stuck between the two of you when you fight."

Mark looked a bit shamefaced. "Sorry, Mo. We're engaged. Soon enough, we'll be married. We're supposed to fight."

"Maybe you could try channeling all the energy into sex." He smiled, then realized from their expressions that he'd said the wrong thing. "Or something."

John brought the empty launch back, and they all got in. A few minutes later they were waiting on the shore with everyone else.

But Mark's mood got the better of him. "Jo, has it occurred to you that there's no place out here for us to live?"

John chipped in. "If you call this living."

"Both of you, be quiet."

But John went on. "I mean, look, Jo, we can't exactly commute from Pittsburgh every day. And we sure can't expect actors to."

"The Ohio Arts Council has approved funding for some housing to be erected. Enough for all of us, if need be, with some extra rooms for whatever extra actors and crew we need for our shows. It's going to go at the south end of the island, where that little shack is."

"I don't like the sound of that." Mark scowled at her. "It sounds like they're putting up a tenement or something."

"We live in an apartment now, Mark. This one will be newer and better equipped."

"And built on ground plowed with salt."

"Shut up."

A few minutes later a police launch came down the river. On the side was stenciled BEAVER COUNTY P.D. There were a half dozen passengers, only two in uniform. Jo watched as they landed at Bourbon Island and headed up to the Imperial, where Deputy Dahlgren was waiting for them. The two uniforms set about stringing POLICE LINE tape around the front of the building; the others followed Dahlgren inside.

Everyone in the party seemed to be in a bad mood that was getting worse. Julie Watts complained she was hungry, and everyone else took it up. "We didn't expect to be here all day."

Stage Fright 137

Several of them needed a bathroom, too. Joanna's suggestion that they use the bushes—"What else can we do?"—didn't exactly go over well.

Joanna paced impatiently. "They were supposed to get statements from us."

"They have to know what happened, first. See the crime scene and the body, I mean." Mo was trying to be the voice of calm and reason, but he was finding it harder and harder.

Tonya told him, "You watch too much TV."

John squawked, "Well, if they don't talk to us soon, I think we just ought to leave. I haven't been so hungry in my life. I'm about ready to eat my cigarettes."

Just at that moment, a pair of men came out of the theater, got into their launch and headed for Joanna and the rest. They introduced themselves as Detectives O'Day and Murphy; their suits didn't fit. Jo introduced everyone; the interviews went smoothly and quickly, all except for Jo herself and Tim, who took longer and were questioned in more detail; and forty minutes later the two minibuses were on their way back to Pittsburgh.

Joanna had them pull in at the first diner they came to. Otherwise, there would have been a mutiny. It was a place called Esther's, a ramshackle little greasy spoon with a sign that said WORLD'S BEST PIES. In a mood to fight about something, Jo decided to have a slice of the blueberry. It was delicious, but that didn't really help her mood. Determined to find something to complain about, she muttered, "This pie has too many blueberries in it."

Under his breath, Mark said, "Listen, we all know you're the producer. But don't you think you're overdoing the professional bitch thing just a bit?"

She looked to John for support, but he avoided her eyes. "You *have* been a bit much all day, Jo."

She turned sullen and finished the pie without saying anything else.

They only took one wrong turn on the way back to Pittsburgh. When they arrived, it was just nine P.M.

* * *

Jo didn't hear anything from the Beaver County P.D. the next day. She was about to call them for a status report that afternoon when her phone rang.

"Marvin! Well, it's just about time you got back to me."

"Sorry, Jo. What's up?"

She explained what had happened at the Imperial.

He listened, sometimes having her pause so he could make notes. "Do you have a number for this sheriff's office?"

She gave it to him. "Ask for Deputy Dahlgren."

"You're kidding." He laughed, she wasn't sure at what. "Well, at least it isn't Barney Fife."

"They seem to know what they're doing. I guess."

"Listen, Jo, about that retainer. Am I going to be the corporation's counsel, or what?"

"Do you want the job?"

"Never ask a lawyer such a naïve question. Besides, your mother pretty much told me to give you any help I can."

"You mean we can bill this to her?"

"Part of it, maybe. I'll see what I can do."

"You're an angel, Marvin. And you're hired. I'll send another check off today."

He laughed again; obviously he was in a much better frame of mind than she was. "So you really think you can make this thing fly?"

"We have the arts mafias of three states behind us."

He whistled. "Your mother could take lessons from you."

"People keep telling me I'm turning into her."

"'Every woman becomes like her mother. That's her tragedy. No man does. That's his.'"

"Shut up."

"Yes, Madam Producer."

"Call me that again, you'll be fixing jaywalking tickets for tourists on Times Square."

A few minutes later, she was in the shower. Marvin would deal with the police and let her know what was happening. Meantime, she had a new show to design, her last for the university. Later, while she was blow-drying her hair, Mark came in, smiled at her nakedness and kissed her. "A shower—that's

Stage Fright   139

a great idea." He quickly got undressed. "Why don't you get back in here with me?"

She reached in and slapped him firmly on the backside.

"Ow—that hurt!"

"It was meant to. I'm still pissed at the way you behaved yesterday."

"Sorry, Jo. It was just all so—so—you know."

"Yes, I know. But why take it out on me?" She slapped him again, even harder. It wasn't easy for her to be certain, but she had the impression he liked it. It was what she'd been waiting for, or hoping for. She got into the shower with him after all. And spanked him still again. To her immense satisfaction, he really got into it. They had the best sex they'd had in months.

When they were finished, he looked at the time and said he had to rush to rehearsal.

"Fuck it, Mark. Let's play some more. I have a hairbrush I could use."

He got to rehearsal half an hour late. Two of his cast still weren't there. He wondered if they had hairbrushes, too.

The next night, Jo was home alone. Mark was off working with his cast. Her designs for the new show had come together pretty quickly. She was feeling more than a bit restless. There had been no word from Beaver County, not directly and not through Marvin. When she'd called Marvin's office that afternoon, he was out, and she left a message.

She glanced at the clock. 8:20. It was going to be a long night. She decided she needed a drink.

It was a cool evening, with a bright full moon. Her favorite watering hole—the one where most of the department were regulars—was a place called Fitzgerald's, a few blocks west of the campus. It was a basic neighborhood bar, no ferns or stained glass, TV over the bar tuned to TCM and not ESPN, nothing that could attract yuppies or jocks. She strode in like a producer's daughter, soon to be a producer herself, and took a seat at the bar.

The bartender knew her usual and poured it without asking as soon as he saw her. "Evening, Jo."

"Hi, Billy." She put a twenty on the bar and looked around.

In a booth at the far end of the room, apparently hiding, was Tim. She took her drink and joined him. "Tim. I don't think I've seen you in here before."

He looked up. It took him a moment to recognize her; he was halfway drunk. "Jo. Hi."

"Aren't you underage?"

"Fake IDs aren't that hard to come by. I only hope al-Qaeda doesn't know what every college freshman in the country does."

She sat down. "Where's John?"

"Who knows?" He shrugged.

"Trouble at home?"

Tim nodded. "I think he blames me for what happened to Jack. Couldn't you tell?"

"We don't even *know* what happened."

"Tell him that. I mean, Jo . . ." He looked at her, then turned his eyes away. "What happened to Annie . . . I mean, I've never seen anything like that before. If you could have seen the look in her eyes."

"I know."

"No, you don't." He raised his voice, then looked shamefaced. "Sorry. We've been fighting since we got home. I'm spoiling for more, that's all."

"It's okay. I have a stormy relationship, myself."

He looked at her. "You and Mark?" He seemed to have no idea what everyone else in the department knew.

Jo nodded at him. "We love each other. I guess. I mean, when things are good, it feels like love is supposed to feel. I guess. But . . ."

Tim was looking confused; she realized he was the wrong one to be talking with about this. Too young to get it. Or maybe too young and too drunk. She and Tim had never really gotten to know each other. "How many have you had?"

"Three." He held up four fingers.

"I'll catch up with you before you know it."

Stage Fright 141

He laughed as if what she'd said was a lot funnier than it was. "John wants me to get my nipples pierced."

Not knowing what else to say to this, she just said, "Oh."

"Yeah. Oh."

"If you don't want to do it, don't."

"I'm in love with him."

"Even so. They're your nipples."

"Yeah, but—"

"Tim, just because you're in a relationship doesn't mean you have to—Oh, shit, never mind."

"Is Mark pierced?"

"No. I wish he was."

Tim looked at her as if he'd never seen her before. "I mean, I really like S&M. But lately John's been way too rough. Is everybody into that?"

She tried to smile, but it wasn't convincing, not even to her. "For my taste, not nearly enough. But this isn't really what's bothering you, is it?" She drained her drink and went to the bar for another one.

When she got back to the booth, he was getting up, reaching for his jacket. "Leaving? I thought we might talk for a while. Get to know each other."

"John says there's not that much to me."

"Oh." She was in no mood to play marriage counselor. "That's too bad. Maybe you should—" She was about to tell him to find someone he was more compatible with. But that was too uncomfortable. Now that things were going a bit better between her and Mark, or seemed to be . . . what if someone had given him that advice? "Where are you going?"

"I don't know. Do you know any dealers?"

"I know where we can score some weed."

"I need something harder than that."

She downed her second drink. "Come on. So do I."

Her behavior was confusing him. "You're the one in charge, I guess."

"'Uneasy lies the head that wears the crown.'"

"Huh?"

"Line from an old play. Come on."

The bartender, Billy, had some stuff for sale. Acid—windowpane. When she asked him why he didn't have anything else, he shrugged. "Cops." Neither Jo or Tim had done the stuff before, but what the hell.

Academic Tower was floodlit brilliantly, as it almost always was at night, and the lawn was wet with evening dew. Twenty minutes later they were lying on it, side by side, looking up at the full moon as if it was the strangest thing they'd ever seen.

Tim seemed not to know how to deal with what he was seeing. "There's stuff on the moon."

"Yeah."

"It's ugly."

"Yeah. It looks like it's on fire with something reddish green or something." Jo giggled like a kid.

"No, it's purple. Did they find them?"

"Did who find what?" She kept her eyes on the moon, not Tim.

"The cops. Her arms."

"I don't know. Haven't heard from the cops."

"Let's go look for them."

"For what?"

"Her arms."

Jo sat up and looked at him. He was grinning like a grade school kid with a birthday cake. She giggled. "Where are they?"

"At the Imperial."

"Where are we?"

He looked around. "Here."

"That's what I thought. I have the keys to the minibuses."

He got to his feet. "We'll get lost."

"We already are. Let's go look for them."

"Huh?"

"What do you want to do, then, wait here for Godot?"

"Huh?"

"It was your idea. Let's go."

The minibuses were parked behind the department. Jo unlocked one, started the engine and pulled into traffic. "Why are all the headlights so loud?"

"We're on a trip."

This seemed to satisfy her. "How do you get there?"

"Where?"

"That's what I thought."

Somehow, she managed to find the highway to Beaver County. And somehow, she managed to find the turnoff to get to Bourbon. The acid was beginning to wear off, and she managed to realize this was the first time she'd gone to the Imperial and hadn't gotten lost. It didn't seem right.

"I don't like working on an island." Tim's tone turned oddly wistful.

"A lot of people seem to be nervous about it."

"My mother never let me learn to swim. My father drowned in the Mississippi."

"Oh. I'm sorry, Tim."

"Then two years ago my mother killed herself."

"Good God, I'm so sorry. Who took care of you?"

"They put me in a foster home. So I took care of myself, mostly."

Then gradually the trees and bushes along the road gave way to barren earth. They were in Bourbon, Pennsylvania, all right. In the moonlight ahead of them they could see the river, the island and the opera house.

She parked the bus. For the longest time the two of them just sat there, in the front seat, staring at it. Even in blazing moonlight the theater looked black. The statues on the cornice were dark outlines against a slightly brighter sky. The river sparkled with the moon's light. It was a warm night, and there were crickets chirping and frogs ribbeting.

"It's pretty." Tim giggled.

"You want another hit?"

"You have more?" The idea seemed to delight him.

She nodded, pleased with herself. "Here."

They ate the acid. The moonlight turned to fire; the call of the frogs and crickets turned into classical music.

After fifteen minutes of sitting and tripping, Tim got out of the minibus. "Come on."

"Come on where?"

"We're looking for her legs, remember?"

"Arms."

"Limbs. What the fuck."

"Where are they?"

He pointed vaguely in the direction of the island.

"Tim?" She opened her door, stepped out and stretched.

"Huh?"

"You're cute."

He giggled. "Thanks."

"You want to cheat on John?"

He looked around, puzzled. "There's nobody here."

"Oh. Never mind."

They walked to the edge of the river. Tim stumbled and almost fell down the bank. Jo helped him to his feet, then put her arms around him. Oblivious, he laughed again. "What river is this?"

Jo couldn't decide whether to be annoyed with him. "Why?"

"I want to know what river I almost drowned in."

"You did not almost drown."

"I can't swim."

"Oh." There was no point coming on to him anymore; she was the one who got him stoned. "There's the launch."

He stumbled again; this time he hit the ground three feet from the edge. "Ten, nine, eight, seven, six, five, four, three, two, one, blastoff!"

"What are you doing?"

"You said launch."

She took him by the arm and got him to his feet. "Come on. We're going out there."

"Why?"

"It was your idea, remember? We're looking for Annie's arms."

She took his hand and led him to the dock. The launch was bobbing slightly, but Jo got in right away. Tim stayed on the dock, staring at her unhappily. "We can't go there."

"This was your idea."

"The river's made out of molten lava." In his eyes it was. Then it turned to something like melted red Jell-O.

Jo looked. The river was made of flowers. "That's okay. We'll be in the boat."

"I can't swim."

"I won't push you in. Oh wait—we need lights."

"We didn't bring any."

"There's some in the van." She went and got two large flashlights, the kind used for road emergencies, and rejoined him.

Suddenly Tim moved very close to her. "You're pretty. You're really pretty."

It caught her completely off guard. "No one's ever told me that before."

"Not even Mark?"

"No."

He laughed. "Then maybe you're not. But I think you are."

Jo looked around furtively. "Let's make love on the island."

"That's sick."

They both sat down in the launch and Jo pushed off. Then she realized she hadn't brought the keys for it. But there was a pair of oars. Clumsily she got them into the water and began to row toward Bourbon Island.

A pair of bats appeared out of nowhere and circled the launch a few times. Jo tried to swat at them with one of the oars, but she had no chance of hitting them. Seemingly oblivious to her and Tim, or maybe uninterested, they flew off.

"I hate bats." Tim watched them fly off with relief.

"They're harmless."

"They have rabies."

The launch hit the island with a bump. Tim got out first and tied the line to the dock. Jo dropped one of the oars in the water, and Tim rushed to fish it out before it got away from them.

Then they got their flashlights and, without switching them on, stood at the bottom of the bank, looking up at the theater. It was larger, blacker, yet more welcoming then Jo had ever seen it. "I like it here at night."

A light flickered on in the shack at the end of the island. Puzzled, Tim and Jo went to see who might be there. Jo pulled the door open and there was Helen, stark naked, with a boy who looked about fifteen. They had an oil lamp; Jo switched on her light.

The boy looked at her in alarm. "I told you I heard someone." He scrambled to get into his clothes. But he was still excited. It showed.

But Helen wasn't thrown by their presence. "What are you doing here?"

"This is our island." Jo turned into her managerial self. "We've told you that before, Helen. Remember? You'll have to find someplace else to take your . . . customers."

Casually, Helen picked up her bra and put it on. "Don't *you* remember what I told you?"

"What you told us doesn't matter. Bourbon Island is ours now, and you have to stop coming here."

Helen's boy looked frightened. Tim watched him as he got into his clothes—jeans, polo shirt, sneakers—and the kid looked like he wanted to cry. Some impulse made him tell the boy, "You don't have to prove anything like this."

"Fuck you."

That was that, it seemed.

A minute later they were both dressed. Jo told Tim to turn on his light, then watched them both carefully. "Where's your boat?"

"On the Ohio side."

"Take it and go. Now."

Helen laughed at her. "You think we want to be here when the ghosts in the theater tear you to pieces? We're going. Come on, Johnny."

Johnny, completely out of his depth, followed her compliantly.

Jo followed them to the Ohio-side bank, watched them get into her old rowboat and leave. Under her breath Jo muttered, "Damn crazy whore."

There was a night mist coming up off the river. The beams from their flashlights showed vividly though it. Tim was coming down from his trip, and suddenly he didn't want to be there. For the briefest instant he thought he saw another flash of light, this time inside the Imperial. "Jo, I don't like this. Let's go home."

"There's nothing to worry about."

"That must be what Annie thought."

Stage Fright   147

She headed up the grade to the theater. "Annie had some kind of weird accident, that's all. A fluke, but nothing more than that."

"What kind of accident could rip her arms off like that?"

"Just stop it, Tim. Come on."

"And what about Jack? Where is he?"

"Something spooked him. He left. Probably swam to shore. He may still be hitchhiking back to Pittsburgh."

He stopped walking and pointed his light directly into her face. "You really believe that?"

"Of course. There's no other explanation. When you've eliminated the impossible, whatever remains, however improbable, must be the solution."

The quote was lost on him; it showed. "Jo, I was with him. He wasn't acting like he wanted to leave."

"Not even after you found Annie?"

This made him hesitate. "She found us."

They were at the front entrance. The mist was growing thicker. Police tape was strung across the front door: POLICE LINE—DO NOT CROSS. Jo stepped casually across it.

Tim didn't. "We shouldn't."

She took him by the hand and pulled him; reluctantly, he stepped across.

Inside, the theater seemed more vast than ever. The beams from their lights barely lit the walls. The lobby seemed to stretch into eternity.

Jo pointed her light at the stairs to the basement. "Let's go," she said softly.

"No." He was absolutely frozen.

"There's nothing to be afraid of."

"Then why are you whispering?"

"We're in a theater. Talking loudly is rude." She smiled, but he was in no mood for a joke.

Jo walked toward the steps. Tim stayed, pointedly, where he was.

"Jo, this isn't right. What if the police come back and find us?"

"At night? Be serious."

"What if there's someone down there?"

"Will you come on?"

"I've seen enough slasher movies to know better. The dumb heroine goes down to the basement even though she knows there's a killer there. And she never comes up again."

"There is no killer down there, Timothy."

"See what I mean?"

She was at the top of the steps. She stared down into the darkness. Loudly she called, "Any mad killers down there?"

"Please, Jo, this isn't funny. You heard what that prostitute said."

"That half-crazy, half-retarded whore? Yeah, let's let her make all our decisions for us."

"Jo," he said loudly and firmly. "I am not going down there."

She stiffened, then made herself relax. "Fine. Wait here, then. I'll go alone."

"Don't!"

"Are you afraid of the dark, Tim?"

"No, I'm afraid of what might happen in it. Can't you hear?"

There were whispers in the air around them, very faint ones, some identifiably human, some not.

From the corner of his eye Tim saw something move. He turned quickly and pointed his light in that direction. There was nothing there but a statue, an old thing made of some black stone, a lion. Impulsively and without thinking, he took a step toward it. "This wasn't here the other day."

"Of course it was. Do you think we're in *The Wiz*?"

"I've never seen *The Wiz*. All I know is, there was no lion here the other day."

From somewhere below there came the sound of a deep growl. This time it was unmistakable. Joanna tried to hide her discomfort. "There are old mines under the river. The cop said so. They must make noises, that's all."

"Right. I'm telling you, Jo, I'm not going down to that basement. Not at night. Not ever."

"Sooner or later, you'll have to."

"That's what you think."

She sighed. This was so frustrating. First all the horrors of that awful afternoon; now Tim, acting as if he really believed there was something supernatural going on. "All right, fine. Wait here."

"Jo, don't go downstairs. Please."

"I'm not." She smiled faintly. "I want to go *up*stairs for a few minutes. There's something I want to see."

"What?"

"Never mind. Do you think there are killers upstairs, too?"

"I don't know. But I don't like it here. I want to go."

"Just relax. I won't be long."

Slowly she climbed the stairs to the mezzanine. Weakly, Tim said, "Jo, I wish you wouldn't." She ignored him and kept climbing.

Then there was a second flight of stairs, a private one hidden behind a door painted with a trompe l'oeil landscape, a fantastic, bizarre one. The steps were covered with dust, and with her own footprints. She had been there on earlier visits, before the . . . unpleasantness.

At the top of the steps was a small empty office. Beyond it was a large, rather magnificent one. Huge mirrors, caked with dirt now, covered the walls. There were elaborate plaster moldings, angels, devils, nymphs; a few of them still had traces of gilt. And in one corner, battered, covered with decades of filth, was an oversize bed. There were no covers, just a filthy, half-rotten mattress and box spring. This had been Samuel Fulton's "office." There could not be any doubt.

Jo stood at the doorway that connected the two rooms, sweeping the large one with the beam from her light. She sensed she wasn't alone, but there was no actual sign of anyone. There were the remains of a corpse on the bed, cut into pieces; bits of rope were still tied to the wrists and ankles. Then finally she realized someone was standing just behind her.

Alarmed, she turned. It was Fulton. He seemed not to recognize her. She started to speak. "Mr.—"

Suddenly, quite violently, he raised a hand and struck her across the face. And she screamed, quite loudly.

Her scream reached Tim, who was waiting anxiously in the lobby. His eyes widened, and he looked up the staircase to where he'd last seen her.

"Jo?"

There was no answer.

"Joanna?" He called more loudly.

And there was only more stillness.

Without thinking, he put a foot on the bottom step. Then he caught himself. No way was he going up there. Not after what happened to Annie. And Jack. And now . . . No. He would not let what happened to them—whatever it was—happen to him. He backed cautiously to where he'd been standing.

Around him in the dark there was movement. He could sense it, just barely, faint swift sounds, blurs at the corner of his vision. But when he pointed his light in that direction, there was nothing but sculpture and paintings on the walls.

And then there was music in the air. Organ music. Through the fog of the drugs he'd taken, Tim realized that someone was playing the organ in the auditorium. And the sounds it made were clear, crisp and vibrant, not like the ugly wheezing sounds it had made before. No one could be playing it. It didn't work; it hadn't been played, or properly maintained, in decades. Yet someone was playing it.

There were voices, hundreds of them, quiet ones, subdued. Like the music, they were coming from inside the theater. He looked in that direction. There was light there; he could see it clearly, in the cracks around the doors.

It was impossible for him to contain his curiosity. After all, he told himself, this isn't really like a slasher movie, not with the sounds of lots of people—and organ music. Besides, the lobby was not so wide that he couldn't make a dash for it and run outside if he needed to.

Cautiously he approached the nearest door. A lamp above it flickered on; dimly it read AISLE 2. He put a hand on the door handle and pulled it slowly open.

The auditorium was full; there was a capacity audience, men, women, all of them in chic evening clothes from the twenties. Some of them sat quietly in their seats; others moved about, socializing, hobnobbing with one another, clearly trying to be seen. A woman sat at the keyboard of the organ and played energetically.

The place was whole. There was no gaping hole in the

Stage Fright

roof, and the crystal chandelier was hanging where it ought to be, lit brilliantly by hundreds of tiny electric lights. And there were sconces along the walls, with more lights. All the paintings and sculptures around the hall were fresh and new. The proscenium, with its monsters, glistened like it had just been finished. The Imperial Opera House had been restored quite wonderfully.

Or so he thought. Then he found himself wondering if what he was seeing wasn't the future but the past, whether he was seeing the theater at the height of its glory and success.

The lights dimmed; the curtain went up; the show was on. But it did not seem to be a play, just a series of tableaus. The first one showed a group of African Americans, all naked, huddled together. Two white men with bullwhips lashed them till their flesh tore and blood flowed. The organist played mad music.

In the next one, a black women suckling a baby was set upon by one of the white men. He tore her infant from her arms and dashed its brains out on a nearby stone.

There were more—rape, torture, lynching. An elderly black man, clutching a book to his chest, was tied to a stake and burned alive. Then the curtain came down again. But the lights did not come up. Instead, a tightly focused spotlight hit the organist. And Tim saw for the first time that she was Portia, the mad albino woman. She turned to him and smiled, a wide, leering, evil grin.

This was not happening. He tried to tell himself it was the drugs, nothing more.

Someone caught hold of him from behind.

The lights went out; the crowd was gone; the theater was in ruins again, and his flashlight gave the only light.

Terrified, he turned, ready to fight.

But it was Joanna. By his light he saw that the left side of her face was badly bruised and cut; blood was flowing.

"Jo!"

"Let's go now, Tim." Her voice was a coarse whisper.

"What happened to you?"

"I can't tell you. He wouldn't like it."

"He? Who are you talking about?"

She got a firm grip on his arm and pulled him out to the lobby. "Come on. It's time we went home."

"Jo, did you see what was happening in there?"

"Nothing happened, Tim. Not to you, not to me. There is nothing supernatural here. Understand? We should never have taken the acid, that's all."

"This wasn't a trip, Jo. I saw it all."

"No."

Outside the theater, the sphinxes and minotaurs and chimeras watched them go. They walked slowly down the path to the dock, looking cautiously around as they went, as if they'd never seen this land before. They got quietly into their boat and rowed away to the Pennsylvania shore. And all the time, the theater's denizens watched. No, it was too soon to take them, for now. They would be back; there would be more of them.

And inside, the Imperial Opera House resonated with the pained laughter of the dead.

FIVE

"Marvin, where the hell have you been? I've been trying to get hold of you for days."

Jo was on the phone with the company's lawyer. Things were not going well. She was on the island, watching the renovation crews do their early work. Mostly, so far, it consisted solely of shuttling materials out to the island. No actual reconstruction had begun yet.

"Sorry, Jo. I've been working on some stuff for your mother."

"That's not good enough. Things down here are spinning out of control."

It had been two weeks since Annie died and Jack disappeared. There was still no sign of either him or of her arms or of a killer, if there was one. And the police . . . well, the police had not been much use.

"Spinning out of control? Isn't that a bit strong, Jo?"

"Marvin, listen, I—"

"Your mother's always been the drama queen in the family."

"Marvin, if you don't shut up and listen to me, I swear I'll fly up there and beat the living daylights out of you. Just shut up and listen."

"Sorry, Jo." He didn't try to disguise the fact that he was finding this awfully amusing.

"First, Annie Moore's family is threatening a lawsuit."

"Let them threaten."

"Second, the police are doing nothing to help."

"You mean the police from—what's the name of that county again?"

"Beaver."

He laughed. "And you expect me to take this seriously."

"Marvin!"

"Okay, fine, what are they saying?"

"It's the same rubbish we've encountered since this thing began. They claim there's no proof that Bourbon Island is actually a part of Pennsylvania. Therefore, it can't be in their jurisdiction. Therefore, they're not doing a damned thing. We tried the Pennsylvania State Police and got the same thing."

"So, call Ohio."

"We did. And West Virginia. They won't touch us."

Marvin whistled. "Jesus. I can't say I've ever come up against anything like this before."

"No. And the weird thing is, other agencies are all falling over themselves trying to help us. From all three states. The theater will bring people to the region, and that means money. And prestige, or what passes for it in West Virginia. But the minute there's any trouble, or even the least hint of difficulty, or even a tinge of controversy... They're all being extra careful not to say or do anything that might actually commit their state to anything. We can't even get them to decide which state is responsible for our public utilities."

"You could always go back to using limelight."

"This isn't funny, Marvin."

"No, of course not." He couldn't stop laughing. "Now listen, in some ways, this can work to your advantage. If all three states deny jurisdiction for the killing, then the family can't very well sue, because the courts in all three states will deny jurisdiction, too."

"I hadn't thought of that."

"So you can lay your worries about the Moore family to rest, at least for now. And I wouldn't press too hard to get the issue of jurisdiction settled. What's happening with the roads and bridges?"

"Well." She stopped and lit a cigarette. "There, at least, we seem to be okay. There's no question that the roads in each state are actually in that state. They're dragging their feet—"

"State bureaucracies."

"But it looks like it'll happen. If you know of any way to goose them along, though—I mean, we *are* planning to open this fall."

"I'll see what I can do. There have to be a few state legislators who like the arts. Would you have a problem putting their wives on the board, or some such?"

"If they can get our bridges built, they can swing from the chandelier."

"Good. I'll get moving on it."

"Thanks. Oh, and Marvin?"

"Hm?"

"What has my mother said about all this?"

The question surprised and dismayed him; he had no intention of getting caught between them. "You know your mother."

"Yes, I do. That's why I'm concerned. If she starts complaining to the wrong people, it could—it could—hell, I don't know what it could do, but I can't have her giving this project any unfavorable buzz."

"Why would she do that?"

"Don't be a fool, Marvin."

"I'm a lawyer. I can't help it."

"Just talk to her, will you?"

"Jo, I work for her, not the other way around, remember? There's no reason why she'd let me tell her who to talk to or what to say."

"Just try. Oh, and there's some problem about the building permits we need."

He laughed again.

She was beginning to be really annoyed with him. "What's funny?"

"Nothing, Jo. I mean, it puts you in the same boat as with

the police. None of the states acknowledges that you need a permit from them?"

"Exactly."

"Fine, then you don't need them."

"And we can count on that?"

"For now, at least."

"You're our lawyer, Marvin. Talking with you is supposed to reassure me. You're not doing that."

"Be sensible, Jo. Just get everything from them in writing. When the money and people start coming in, they'll probably change their tune. I'm guessing you'll have all three of them scrambling for their share of the pie. But as long as you have everything on paper—'no, that island isn't in our state'—they won't be able to make any retroactive trouble."

"You're sure?"

"As sure as I can be. Like I said, I've never really encountered a situation like this before. I doubt if anyone has."

"Fine. Get back to me soon. I'll talk to you then."

She clicked off her cell phone, put it in her bag and looked around the island. There were a dozen or so workers, carrying sacks of concrete, bundles of tools and the like. It was a warm day, and most of them had their shirts off. She wondered idly if any of them were into heavy S&M. Things with Mark had been tense.

Within another week, the work crews on Bourbon Island were beginning to accomplish things. Building supplies had been brought in, scaffolding erected, enormous sheets of plastic hung around the Imperial. Electric generators provided power and light, and they drowned out the sounds of the river. And three barges were brought in, and moorings built for them, for ferrying men and supplies from both shores of the river. There were only a dozen and a half men on the job full-time so far, but once more barges arrived to ferry heavy equipment, the work force would more than triple.

The foreman was Mike McKim. He was fifty years old, and he had thirty years' experience, and he had worked on all kinds of jobs, from Florida to Alaska. Even though he had grown up near Pittsburgh, this was his least favorite part of the country to work in. Too many of the construction guys around here resented having a foreman with darker skin than theirs.

Mike was absolutely certain that the Imperial Opera House was the ugliest thing he had ever seen. Why they weren't just knocking the thing down was a mystery to him. For that matter, why he'd agreed to come back to the Pittsburgh region to work on it was something he didn't quite understand about himself. But it was a well-paying mystery, so he kept his thoughts to himself.

One of the first jobs he had to get done was removing the old chandelier. The damned thing weighed well over a ton. With no crane on the island yet, it would be a real hassle to move.

Were they going to restore it or replace it? He consulted with Jo, who was in Pittsburgh working on her thesis—she was dividing her time between campus and the island—and she assured him that, no, the old one was not to be fixed up; there would be a gleaming new one to light the auditorium.

Mike and six of his men rocked it to one side till it was stable and away from the spot where it had been. The floor of the auditorium was littered with far too much broken glass for work there to be safe. Once he had the chandelier rocked to one side, he set two men to cleaning the floor. Then the heavier work—cutting the damned thing apart with acetylene torches and carting it away—could begin.

Neither Mike nor any of his men understood what they saw. Someone, or something, pushed the chandelier back to where it had been. It did not simply roll of its own volition. Something deliberately pushed it, that was clear—till it was back where it had fallen. The two men under it had their faces and bodies ground into the thousands of splinters of glass. Their screams were loud enough to be heard on both shores.

Glass slit their eyes. Glass slashed their throats. Long slivers like crystal pins pierced their wrists. One man's heart was punctured. Blood flowed so quickly, from so many points on their bodies, there could have been no hope of stanching the flow.

It took forever for Mike to persuade a nearby Ohio township to send ambulances. The men were dead before they arrived. Even with slower blood loss, the men would have died before anyone could get to them.

Mike called the construction company's owners, then Joanna. It was horrible, what had happened to his men. He dreaded all the questions and all the paperwork to come.

Joanna listened calmly as he explained what happened. "Did they have families?"

"I don't think so. They were both from Alabama. Both were what folks down there call 'bachelor men.'"

"I see. What about parents? Or siblings? People have to be notified."

"I know it sounds weird, Ms. Marshall, but most of the men who've come to work on this job don't seem to have anyone in the world. I mean, it's really so odd."

"Well anyway, Mike, I'll be out as soon as I can. I want to see. What are you doing with the chandelier now?"

"We've had to leave everything as it was. OSHA will have to investigate. We managed to secure it with cables, so it shouldn't shift again. My boss at Lanier Construction said he's calling OSHA. I imagine they'll get an inspector out here pretty quickly. They usually do. Holding up work for too long would cost too much money."

Another delay. She was starting to wonder if this project was such a good idea, after all. It had seemed so smart when it first occurred to her. Now . . .

Jo had a meeting with the advisor for her dissertation. There was a temptation to cancel; she wanted to get to the island as soon as she could. But she decided it wouldn't be a good idea; her advisor already disliked her.

Jo rushed to her office in the department.

They talked about how her thesis research was coming. "Jo, this isn't anywhere near complete enough for me to approve it. You'll have to push harder to get it done."

"I have other things on my mind."

"Such as?"

"Such as working in the theater."

Her advisor was Dr. Madeline Swartz, the only woman on

the tenured theater faculty. She and Jo had never liked one another. Though neither of them had ever said it, each of them thought the other one was a hard-nosed lesbian. Neither was right.

Jo had tried like hell to get a different advisor, but she had called in every debt anyone in the department owed her to get permission to abandon her ghost research and switch to something more conventional and therefore easier to do.

"This will never be ready in time for you to get your MFA, Joanna." Dr. Swartz seemed pleased by this.

"Then I won't get my degree till the fall."

"Not with thesis work this weak. I know the way they'll grill you when you're defending it."

"As I said, I have other things on my mind, right now, I'm afraid." Images of men lacerated by hundreds of shards of glass kept coming into her head, and she couldn't shake them. "Can you give me any guidance that might be productive?"

"I'm afraid it'll be really hard for you to come up with anything substantial enough."

"I see." She got up to go. The impulse to make a smartass crack—"thanks for all your help"—was almost impossible to resist.

"Joanna, this is your master's thesis. You can't take such a casual attitude."

"I can and I do. I have a theater to rebuild and a company to assemble. Are you telling me that a thesis is more important than living theater?"

"What I'm telling you is that it's a bad idea to let your thesis slide."

"That comes to the same thing."

Dr. Swartz was a short, plump woman, and she was pushing sixty. From what Joanna knew about her, which wasn't much, she had tried to found a company of her own once, back during the Cretaceous period. Which is to say that she was a tangible, visible, nagging reminder that Jo might fail, too.

"No, Joanna, it doesn't. Think. You've been here two years, working like hell to get your degree. Now you're throwing all that work away. I don't think this thesis will come anywhere near passing review. And, at that, it's better than that first silly thing you worked on."

Jo stiffened. "George Washington didn't have a master's degree."

"George Washington wasn't trying to work in contemporary theater. Except for the shlock they still do on Broadway, we're it. We academics have taken over the field. Regional theaters are where the action is, and they all have ties to academia. They won't touch your work unless you play the game. With no degree . . ." She smiled broadly at Joanna. "What do you think you'll be able to do?"

"I've never heard anyone say, 'Gosh, I really want to see this play—I hear the producer has a degree.' "

Dr. Swartz wrinkled her nose. "You mean you're a commercialite?"

She sat down heavily. "If Shakespeare wrote for money, why can't I produce for it? I could argue that the life went out of theater when people like—when academics got a stranglehold on it, doctor. And I wouldn't be the first."

"And you won't be the last. But you still need that degree."

"In case you haven't heard, the state arts councils in Pennsylvania, Ohio and West Virginia are all backing my company. With no degree."

Swartz let out a theatrically exaggerated sigh. "People like you will be the death of theater, Joanna."

"If you mean your kind of theater, reeking of universities and departments, I can only hope so. My mother dropped out of Bennington in her second year. I'd say she's done all right in the theater. Wouldn't you?"

Dr. Swartz narrowed her eyes and scowled. "Now, listen to me, Ms. Marshall. I'm your advisor. And I'm giving you the best practical advice I can. You had sense enough to drop your first thesis topic, thank heaven. Use your sense, and work on your thesis."

"I'll be sure to consider your advice for what it's worth, doctor."

"Joanna." For the first time she softened her tone. "You abandoned your damned ghosts. Now—"

"That's what you think. I just took them out of my paper.

I'll work on the thesis when I have the time. Thank you for your input."

She finally left.

Bickering with her advisor was not a good idea; she knew it perfectly well. And she knew that there were people waiting for her to fail, and that Dr. Swartz was one of them. Having to deal with her just after the horrible news from the island . . .

The morning had been sunny; now there were heavy clouds building. Jo didn't want to go out to the island alone. She tried to find Mark, but he was busy working with some actors. Mo, she couldn't find. Finally she bumped into John, told him what had happened and asked if he'd mind riding along with her.

"Sure, Jo."

John drove his own car, not one of the minibuses. Jo navigated and complained about Dr. Swartz's attitude.

"You shouldn't fight with your advisor, Jo. Smile at her, then ignore her advice, if you want to. That's what everybody does. Why make an enemy?"

"That's not the way we Marshalls get things done."

"It might be a good way to get things *un*done."

"I'll be out of West Penn soon enough. And away from Madeline Swartz. The more I think about it, the less I care."

They made good time. He nearly made a wrong turn, and they bickered about the correct route, but Jo finally persuaded him of the right way to go. It was nearly five o'clock when they approached the island.

John looked around disapprovingly. "I can never get used to the way the land here is so . . . so bare. It's not going to look good to customers. And I can just imagine how the critics will latch on to it. That smart-assed bastard who reviews for the gay paper will have a field day with it. 'The barren land is nothing compared to the barren show I saw last night.'"

"That's the least of our worries." She glanced at her watch. "Fifty minutes from the heart of Pittsburgh. Vince asked me to time the drive."

"It always feels more like two hours. I'm serious about this desert, Jo. It doesn't look good."

One more thing to worry about. She looked around and decided he was right. "I'll have to give it some thought. If that damn deputy was right and the earth here really is sown with salt, I'm not sure what we can do."

Most of the construction crew was on shore, getting into their cars. Jo glanced at her watch again. "Five o'clock."

"This is more traffic than the place has seen in years, Jo."

Mike McKim was among them. He seemed to be waiting for Jo quite anxiously. As soon as he saw them pull up, he crossed quickly to the car. "Jo. I'm afraid things aren't good."

"Hi, Mike. Why? What's wrong? How soon will OSHA be here?"

"They're not coming."

"What!"

"It's another damned jurisdictional dispute. Neither of their two 'regions' can find Bourbon Island on any of their maps. It's that same stuff—about which state the island's in."

"So they're not coming? Jesus."

"And we had to get a private ambulance for the two—for the men who had the accident."

"I thought we had the police/EMS thing straightened out, at least." She looked across the river to the Imperial. It was quite deserted. "Well, Marvin will be happy, anyway. This 'no man's land' thing seems to give him a kick."

Mike shifted uncomfortably. "Jo, I'm afraid I'm not explaining this well."

For the first time she realized just how agitated he was. She had to stop herself from barking at him. "All right, what's wrong?"

"With no government oversight, Lanier Construction is pulling out of the job. My boss says our lawyers insist. Anything could happen here, and we'd have no one to certify we've done our job right, no one to oversee our operation for safety—"

"So you could do anything you want. Is that so bad?"

"According to the lawyers and the insurance company, yes." He took her hand and shook it; she didn't resist, but she wanted to. "There's a letter on its way to Marvin Mittelberger, explaining our position."

"We have a contract, Mike."

Stage Fright

"Yeah, and it specifies that you meet all the appropriate government guidelines. You don't."

"You just said it yourself, Mike. There are no government guidelines here. So how can we not be meeting them?"

"I don't want to debate with you, Jo. I have to follow what my boss tells me. It's been good working with you." He took a step in the direction of his car.

"Wait, Mike. Can't you at least show me what happened before you go?"

He hesitated. "Sure. Why the hell not?"

He took her and John out to the island and into the theater. There was still splintered glass on the floor; it was mixed with blood. The chandelier was still up on its side, perched at an unnatural angle but stabilized by cables. Mike described the incident as fully as he could.

"Now I'd appreciate it if one of you could ferry me back to shore. I'm sorry things haven't worked out well here. My men are all out of work."

Jo walked him to the entrance. John stayed behind, gaping at the blood-soaked floor.

Just as they reached the launch, Jo had a thought. "I don't suppose you and your men would work here, er, unofficially?" She kept her voice low and confidential. "Would you, Mike?"

"With no government oversight?"

"So it seems."

"I don't think I could do that, no. Jo, two men died here today. Hasn't that sunk in?"

"That was a freak accident. You said so yourself. It would have happened whether OSHA was on the case or not." She cast off and started the motor.

"Well, I guess you have a point, but even so . . . no, I don't think I could. If more men die . . ." He looked around, as if there might be someone there who could overhear. "You don't know how the construction business works, Jo. I'd be blamed. It would ruin my reputation. I'd never find decent work again."

"Well, it's a damned shame, that's all I can say. You know we'll find someone to do the work here, Mike. I'd like it to be you."

"I'm sorry, Jo."

The last of his men were gone. He walked quickly to his car and got in. Jo called after him another time, but he either didn't hear her or chose to ignore her. A minute later he was gone, too.

In the distance, Jo saw Portia, watching, staring. It was so unsettling. The woman always seemed to be around when something bad happened. And with no police support, there was no way to keep her away.

She went quickly back into the launch and headed out to the island. John was waiting at the dock. She tossed him the line and he tied it off.

"Well." She slipped as she was getting out of the boat and nearly fell into the river. John caught her. When she steadied herself, she went on as if nothing had happened. "Well," she repeated. "That, it seems, is that."

"Will we be able to find another construction company?"

"My mother has connections." She strode off toward the theater. "Not all of them are legal."

"Oh."

Jo walked quickly through the lobby and back into the auditorium; John followed. She crossed to the chandelier, planted herself firmly, hands on hips, and glared at it. "There's no way that can have happened, John. It doesn't make sense. Things this large and heavy just don't move by themselves."

He stopped a few paces behind her and looked around. The place was eerily still. He couldn't even hear the constant splashing of the river. "Jo, I know this isn't exactly the right time to mention this, but this place creeps me out. Completely."

"How could it not? We keep having all these accidents."

"Do you really think that's what they are? I mean, this must have been one, sure, but what kind of accident could cause what happened to Annie?"

A low moan came from the organ. Joanna jumped at the sound of it. "We need to have that damn thing torn out."

"And who will do the work?"

She obviously didn't want to think about it. "Listen, I have to call Marvin. I'll meet you outside in fifteen minutes or so, okay? I just hope he's in, for once."

"Sure."

John went outside. The sun would be setting soon, and he decided to sit and watch it. Jo went with him as far as the lobby, then got out her phone and rang Marvin's office.

"Jo—I just heard."

"They called you?"

"Yes. We'll get someone else, okay?"

"Can't we force them to keep working, with the contract?"

"Not a chance. But don't worry about it. There are other companies."

"That doesn't solve the basic problem, Marvin. We are nowhere. Literally. No one who can help us will acknowledge we even exist."

"I'll see if maybe we can't work through one of the arts councils."

Idly, she climbed the stairs to the mezzanine. Then, more purposefully, she climbed to Fulton's old office or, as she was thinking of it more and more, her office.

No work had been done there yet. But everything in it was new, and it was completely furnished and richly appointed, as it was for her more and more often. Fulton was there. He was naked and smiling; she had the impression he'd been expecting her.

"Marvin, I have to go. We'll talk soon, okay?"

He had two young partners this time, a boy and a girl. They were, maybe, fifteen or sixteen, and they were both undressed. The boy was chained to the wall; the girl was on the bed, also tied down. The air was thick with opium.

Jo took it all in. But she was not in a mood for this scene, not today. She crossed to the bed and began to untie the young woman.

Fulton caught her arms and stopped her. "Do not." His voice was so forceful it was unsettling.

Jo froze for a moment. "What is wrong here, Samuel?"

"Mr. Fulton." Again, that forceful voice. The voice of a man used to power.

"Mr. Fulton, then. What is wrong with this place?"

Instead of answering, Fulton forced her against the wall, kissed her and fondled her breasts. From the corner of her eye she caught sight of the boy. There were welts on his sides; Fulton had been beating him. But watching them was arousing him. It was too strange, and too exciting. She kissed Fulton back, hard, but then pushed him away.

Slowly he walked across the room and got a whip. He used it on the boy, lashing him viciously, and the kid cried out in pain. Hearing it seemed to make Fulton more excited, and he lashed the boy even more furiously. Finally the pain had an erotic effect and the boy exploded with pleasure, then went limp.

Fulton held the whip out to Joanna and gestured to the girl on the bed. "Now you."

Slowly, not at all certain she wanted to be doing this, Jo took the whip. The girl cried as Jo lashed her. She was not as furious as Fulton had been with the boy, But the girl's blood flowed, and in time her pain turned to pleasure, too.

Fulton came up behind Joanna as she was doing it, and he put his arms around her again and fondled her. When she was finished with the girl, it was her turn. Fulton stripped her naked but did not tie her. She stood willingly as he whipped her, and in time the pain turned to intense, sweet pleasure. She became so absorbed in what she was doing, and in what he was doing, that she didn't notice that the air around them was filled with the haunted cries of tortured men.

When, finally, she came back downstairs, John was waiting impatiently. "What did he say?"

"He?" She recoiled from the question. "How did you know about—"

"Marvin. Isn't that who you were going to call?"

"Oh, yes, Marvin." She arranged her hair. "He said we'd get someone else to do the construction."

"That's all?"

She nodded.

"Jo, you were up there for nearly an hour."

She shrugged. "Let's go."

"If I didn't know better, I'd suspect you have a secret lover stashed away up in that loft."

"Don't be foolish."

"That's asking a lot, but I'll try." He grinned and followed her outside. "I guess."

There wasn't a lot of conversation on the ride back to Pittsburgh. At one point, John asked her, "Jo, I know—I know you and Mark have been having your troubles. But—"

"How could you possibly know that?"

"Everyone knows it. Except the kids, maybe. It shows." He said it slowly and pointedly.

"Well, what of it? Every couple has their rough patches."

"I guess so. But—"

"I don't want to talk about it, John."

That was that. A few minutes later, Jo fell asleep in the passenger seat; John got lost and had to ask at a service station for directions back to town. The attendant was young and cute. John made a note to try and remember the place. He was getting more and more bored with Tim. He did not notice the blood seeping through Joanna's clothes, here and there.

"You're getting carried away with this thing."

Mo and Tonya were having dinner at their favorite Italian restaurant. A quaint little place out of an old movie—there were actually checkered tablecloths and candles stuck in Chianti bottles. And they had that archetypal corner booth, for privacy, just like the young lovers in those movies.

"I don't think I am, Tonya." He scowled. "The eggplant parmesan isn't up to their usual standard tonight."

"You should have gotten the lasagna. It's terrific."

"Next time." He ate and hoped she'd forgotten what they were talking about.

But she pressed him. "You're working on these damn scripts more and more." Pointedly she added, "And not doing anything else."

"That's not true."

She lowered her voice and looked around. "When was the last time we made love?"

He couldn't remember. It had been weeks, at least. "I think there's not enough salt."

"Mo, will you for God's sake listen to me?"

"I am."

"Then stop avoiding the subject."

He sighed and put down his knife and fork. "You're probably right. I'm sorry. But, Tonya, this thing has gotten hold of me in a way I never thought it could."

"Putting on plays."

"Yes. No." He picked up his knife again, fiddled with it, then put it down again. "What I mean is, when Jo first talked to me about this thing, it didn't really occur to me the kind of potential it has."

"Can you hear yourself, Mo? Potential for what? You've heard all the theater people say most companies fail. It's all half of them can talk about."

"But—"

"They all keep saying how happy they are to have jobs, and they'll stick with this while it lasts, but they don't expect that to be very long. What can you say about people who pin their hopes on something they know is going to fail? Joanna seems to be the only one who thinks it will fly."

"But—"

"And who the hell wants to see plays about history, anyway? People don't even go to plays when they're entertaining." She made a sour face. "Except for *Phantom of the Opera*. I loved that."

"So, this is about you and what you like."

"No. I—"

"Listen, Tonya. I'm working in my field. I'm a working historian. Not on an academic level, sure, but what's wrong with your work being popular?"

"And what about all the other scripts? The Halloween ones? Zombies and vampires. Torture and dismemberment and slaughter. Go on, tell me that's history."

He put on a big grin. "You never know. Besides, they're bringing in some local horror novelist to work with me. John James Masters." He went back to his food. "You're only being like this because you're afraid of the river. You shouldn't want me to miss an opportunity like this."

"Opportunity? For what?"

"Do you know how many historians reach a wide public? You can count them on one hand. And they all write books and work for PBS. You know the kind of money I could make?"

"You think there are things wrong with America. PBS wouldn't touch you with a pole. Besides . . . I just don't like the place. It creeps me out every time I see it."

They were at a stalemate. Mo gave up trying to persuade her and concentrated on his dinner.

But later, when they were walking home, he took it up again. It was well after dark; the strange glow of sodium street lights colored everything orange yellow. The sky was overcast, there was a faint mist in the air, and, now and then, a few drops of rain fell. There wasn't much traffic.

"I haven't told anyone, yet, not even Jo. But I think I've turned up some stuff on the island itself."

"What is there to turn up?" She was sorry the topic had shifted back to this.

"Well, I'm not completely sure. There are references to a 'Whiskey Island.' I think that must be the same place. Anyway, there's no other record of a Whiskey Island."

"I could stand some whiskey myself, right now."

"There was a slave warehouse on the island. Warehouse and auction house. A big one, the biggest in the region. From the descriptions, it was downright huge."

"You knew that already."

"Yeah, but what I didn't know is that it was the site of the first recorded slave rebellion in America." He hesitated. "At least, I think so."

A city bus rumbled past. It was loaded with kids, high school age, maybe college, having what seemed to be a party. Tonya decided they must be on their way to or from some sporting event or other. They were blowing horns, singing off key, shouting. She wished she was with them. "What kind of slave rebellion?" She didn't really much care.

"Well, again, the sources are kind of sketchy."

"So you're not even sure?"

"I'm *pretty* sure."

"You want to go to a movie tonight?"

"Tonya, I'm trying to tell you about this."

"Okay. Sorry." She pretended to be interested.

"Well, there was a slave sorcerer or magician or some such."

"Oh, fine."

"Be quiet. This magician cast some kind of spell the slaves believed would make them invulnerable. And they really did believe it. So they started a revolt."

"I can guess where this is going." She said it with a sneer. "They weren't really invulnerable, right?"

"The white slave traders decided the easiest way to deal with the uprising was with fire. They launched boats onto the river with scores of lit torches. And their men threw the torches at the wooden warehouse. It caught fire, and in minutes it was engulfed in flames. All the slaves died."

"Like the angry villagers in an old horror movie, hunting the monster down with torches." For the first time, Tonya sounded like she was actually interested. "That sounds terrible. What a way to die."

"Yeah. There would have been dozens of them, I think. Maybe even more. I haven't found anything like exact numbers. One source says the sorcerer escaped, the only one to live."

"That's no surprise. Priests always manage to save their own asses."

"And the slave traders just built a new building and went right on with business as usual."

"Ah, the marvels of the free-market economy."

He hesitated. "I want to write this up as a play and have it performed there."

"Now, *that* is an idea." More and more—and against her will—she found herself getting caught up in Mo's enthusiasm.

"I'll have to talk to Jo and Mark about it, though. I don't know how we could do it all. The fire and things, I mean. And it would probably need a large cast."

"A lot of black actors. Work for them." She was smiling, now.

"It may not be feasible. But you see what I mean about this stuff, Tonya? You see why it's got hold of me?"

She did, and she said so.

"This all started because I wanted to learn as much as I could about the old minstrel shows and the culture that drove them. Now we've got something better. We can actually produce something that might be a corrective to them."

Suddenly Tonya's native skepticism resurfaced. "That's a lot of correction for one little play."

"You're right. But it's a start."

She kissed him lightly. "You've got me thinking about this in a whole new way, Mr. Settles."

"That's the idea. If I can do it to someone as stubborn as you, the rest of the company will be a cinch."

She slapped him playfully. "Now if you can only find a way to move that damn theater off that damn island."

For once it was Mark who had dreams about the Imperial, drunken ones.

The theater was newly restored, gleaming in brilliant sunlight. Everything was in the kind of sharp relief that seems to occur only in dreams.

He stood at the entrance, looking up at the façade. Sphinxes, griffins, unicorns, gorgons looked down at him in return. They were hungry.

Slowly, dazzled by the grotesque beauty of what, in his dream, he thought of as "his" theater, Mark walked inside. The fantastic creatures in the lobby watched him, exactly as the ones outside had done. Monsters in murals eyed him with ravenous fascination. Sculptures in black marble, motionless but aware, watched him and were glad he had come.

Some impulse led him to go down to the basement. It was dark everywhere, dark as night, but somehow he could see. He wandered from room to room, believing it was all his, knowing he could master it all any time he chose. Plays—his productions, living embodiments of his vision—would be preformed in this house. The world would see them, and through them the world would know him. It really was quite thrilling.

From the darkness ahead of him came a scream. A woman's scream. Idly, not wanting such things to be disturbing his reverie, he went to see what the problem might be.

And there on the floor he found a pair of arms, pale, slender woman's arms. They were alive, moving, writhing, crawling. Toward him. He turned to go but, in the way of dreams, he couldn't move. His feet were frozen in place. And the arms crept toward him and took hold of his ankles, tighter and tighter until it felt as if they might rip his feet off.

He woke.

And he screamed.

Or rather, he tried to scream. There was something over his mouth.

He tried to move. He was tied down.

In his sleep, he had been tied down to his bed, and a gag had been tied tightly around his mouth. He didn't think he had drunk so much this could have happened, but . . . He struggled, but the ropes were too tight to give him even a fraction of an inch to move in.

Suddenly frightened, he cried out, a muffled cry. There was no one else in the bedroom. But, he realized, there were dozens of candles burning. Black ones. The largest of them, six inches in diameter, was on the nightstand, not a foot from his head. Its flame danced. Then he realized there was something else, something like an incense burner in one corner; sweet smoke curled upward from it.

Joanna walked slowly into the room; like him, she was naked, and there was a faint smile on her face, just the trace of one.

Mark struggled, pointlessly.

Jo walked to the bedside. He saw that she was carrying a knife and a handful of large needles. She raised her free hand and slapped him, very hard. Then she leaned down and pressed her lips to his forehead. Gently she whispered, "It is time for this."

Slowly, carefully, she took one of the pins and stroked him with it, first his chest, then his right cheek. It tickled, and he squirmed. He tried to mutter, "Jo, please stop this," but the gag muffled the words quite effectively. He could have been saying most anything; he could have been asking for more. To his embarrassment and shock, he realized he was aroused.

Jo kissed his forehead again. "You are going to love this."

Slowly she lowered the gag and kissed him on the lips. "And so am I."

"Jo, please, you know I'm not into this."

She ignored this.

From the dresser she took a tall, thin candle. And she held it two feet over him. The hot wax dripped onto him, burning, stinging. He tried with all his strength to get free of the ropes that were holding him, but Jo had tied them much too efficiently, as if someone had taught her how to do it. When he tried to cry out, she replaced the gag.

Molten wax seared his nipples. His chest. Slowly she moved it lower. His abdomen. His genitals. His testicles.

The pain was worse than anything he had ever felt. He groaned loudly and fought against his bonds, but it was no use. Joanna lowered the candle, and the closer it got to his body, the hotter the wax was when it hit him. He tried to scream. Couldn't.

Jo put the candle back on the dresser. Mark watched, horrified, as she picked up one of the pins and sterilized it in the flame of the large candle on the nightstand. Then she pushed it, quite forcefully, through his right nipple. He felt it puncture the skin; he felt it move through his flesh. And he felt blood trickle down his side.

A second pin; his left nipple. A third; his scrotum. The pain was horrific, like nothing he'd ever felt or imagined.

Joanna took up her knife. She ran its tip down his chest, from his right nipple to his groin. Not too hard, not too deep, just enough to break the skin and make more blood flow.

And the pain, finally, had an erotic effect. Mark climaxed. It seemed the most intense thing he'd ever felt, even more than the pain that had come before it.

Slowly his body went limp. Joanna lowered his gag and kissed him, hard and deep.

"You loved it, Mark. I knew you would."

Slowly, carefully she removed the pins from his body. And she kissed the hardened wax that covered parts of his anatomy.

From the pain and the fear and the intensity of his response to them, he was weak. But he managed to say, just before he fell into a deep, dreamless sleep, "I did."

* * *

"You little shit."

John was drunk, more drunk than he'd been since high school. And he was angry, not for any special reason except that he was drunk. He burst into the bedroom where Tim was reading a superhero comic book.

"You goddamned little shit."

Tim looked up at him, alarmed. "What did I do?"

"How many times have I told you to keep my original cast albums in alphabetical order?"

"I did."

"Why is *70 Girls 70* after *Sweeney Todd*?"

"Huh?"

"You heard what I said."

"I've never even heard of—"

John threw himself onto Tim and began punching him in the face. "Self-absorbed little fucker."

Tim fought to get away, but John was taller, heavier and stronger. Frantically Tim grabbed for the telephone. John knocked it out of his hands. Trying to get away from him, Tim stumbled and fell to the floor. John kicked him in the head, then stomped angrily from the room.

Weakly, Tim got to the phone and dialed 911. "My lover just attacked me. I think I'm hurt bad."

The operator asked him to repeat it. When he did, the woman asked, "Did you say your lover?"

"Please. I think he broke something."

"Is this homosexual rape we're talking about?"

"Not rape, no. Please. He kicked me in the head. I don't feel . . ." Then he fell into unconsciousness.

It was more than twenty minutes before the EMS team arrived. By that time, John had gone out. At the hospital, Tim was diagnosed with a concussion, and his right orbital bone was shattered.

A police detective came and asked him what had happened. Tim said he had fallen in the shower.

"You told the 911 operator you were attacked."

"No, I fell."

"You said your 'lover' "—he said the word with a faint sneer—"assaulted you."

"No."

"Tell me the truth."

"I am."

The detective tried repeatedly to get the truth out of him, but Tim held fast to his story. He had been raised to keep family business inside the family. It was private. Secret. No one else's business.

Vince Gallardo and Mo Settles met for lunch at the Z. They were, by this time, both drawing salaries from the corporation. The music in the place was especially loud, and Vince suggested they head to another place, a block away. "It's more for grown-ups."

"You don't have to ask twice."

It was a bright day, unusually warm for late spring. Guys were running in just shorts; girls were sunbathing on the lawn in front of Academic Tower. Vince, oddly, was in a shirt and tie. When Mo commented on it, he shrugged and said, "This is work. Professionalism means a lot to me."

Mo seemed to find it funny. "I'm glad it does to someone. These theater types we're working with . . ."

"Hm?"

"Well, let's just say they're a long way from Edward Gibbon and Arnold Toynbee."

"I'm a theater type myself, you know."

"Oh."

They reached the restaurant, which, it turned out, wasn't much more than a neighborhood bar. But Vince assured Mo they made the best burgers in Oakland. "And they actually cook them right when you order them. Can you imagine?"

"What won't they think of next?"

When they were seated, had ordered and got the small talk out of the way, Vince got down to business. "I'm compiling PR bios of all the principal people in the company. I need one for you."

"Me? I'm just a historian."

"You're our resident writer."

"Oh."

"And your credentials will help sell—I mean, will lend a note of prestige to the operation."

So Mo told him about his life, at least the parts of it he wouldn't mind having in a newspaper. He warned Vince there was nothing all that interesting, and there wasn't. Lower middle-class background; good, solid but not brilliant academic record; a few adolescent scrapes with the law, nothing juicy enough to be worth mentioning.

"What about your family?"

"They're Catholic. They keep telling me I shouldn't work in the theater."

"Everybody's parents tell them that." Their burgers came, and Vince bit into his with obvious pleasure. "Oh—and I need a good PR photo of you. Do you have any we could use?"

"Nope. 'Fraid not."

"That's okay. We'll be hiring a photographer. I'll make sure you're on the list for him."

When they had this business out of the way, the talk shifted to all the accidents on the island. Mo wanted to know how Vince thought he could spin them.

"Well, we're not really on anyone's radar yet. And there's the fact that we're in the middle of nowhere. So far there have only been a few minor items."

"But you're planning a big PR blitz when we open, right?"

Vince nodded. "And even when construction's near complete. 'Landmark building renovated by thrilling new theater company.' It's the kind of story they'll love."

"Then won't they want to know about all these awful things that have been happening?"

"Old news." He shrugged. "Nobody cares about what happened yesterday. You're a historian. You ought to know that."

From the back of the bar there came a sudden commotion. A patron, loud, belligerent and apparently drunk, was threatening the waitress. They both craned their necks to see.

It was John Bartlett. He was apparently furious about something, shouting incoherently and throwing everything he could get his hands on. Vince got up and rushed back to him. "John, for God's sake, what's wrong?"

The bartender was coming at them with a baseball bat. Vince waved him back and gestured that he could get this guy calmed down.

It took John a moment to recognize him. "Fuckers."

"Who? John, quiet down. What's the problem?"

"Not enough fries."

"Is that all? Come on, then. I'll take you down to the Z and buy you a large basket."

John looked at him as if he was trying to make sense of this, then looked around the bar dubiously. "They didn't give me enough fries."

"Come on. It'll be all right."

Mo watched all this, more than slightly alarmed. Vince caught his eye and waved him off, as if to say, "Don't worry, I can control him." So Mo left a few bucks on the table and left quickly and quietly.

Just behind him, Vince managed to steer John outside. Instead of the Z, he guided John in the direction of his own apartment. By the time they got there, John had forgotten all about his french fries. Vince managed to get him undressed and into bed.

But John wouldn't sleep. "Don't let him in here."

"Who?"

"That little shit who's been living with me. He called the police on me."

"Just quiet down, John. Close your eyes, relax and try to get some sleep."

"Little fucker."

Vince waited a few minutes for John to nod off, then left, making as little noise as he could. He hoped Tim wouldn't get home till John had slept it off. Something told him he should wait and warn him, but he had a date.

Two nights later. Late, after two A.M. It was cool, and there was just enough of a mist in the air to blur everything. Overhead there was a bright moon with a halo around it; the stars, obscured by the mist, weren't more than bright little smudges in the sky. Jo and Mark walked hand in hand across the lawn in front of Academic Tower. Traffic was sporadic; occasional cars passed, not many, and a city bus rumbled by.

Their relationship had—as Jo always insisted, been made more rich and more stable by the brutal sex. Mark was beginning to like it more and more. Even the blood. His blood. Jo licked it up, and watching her excited him even more. He was thinking more and more about permanent piercings, everywhere.

Jo had done her homework; she knew what she could do safely, what to avoid, and she always had disinfectant and first aid near at hand. As for Mark, having this new secret thrilled him a bit. Aches, pains, bruises that he and Jo knew about but no one else did—it was a secret world she was taking him to, and the secret was delicious. The more she hurt him the more he loved her, and the more sure he was that she loved him.

They had been at a party. Most of the crowd were theater people, though there were a few from other departments. Word was getting around more and more about the Bourbon Island company, and people were dropping unsubtle hints that they could use jobs. Even Jo's professors were being deferential. And she was enjoying the hell out of it all, keeping them hanging, giving them hope then blowing them off.... It was the loveliest game, and she had learned it at an early age, from her mother.

Mark watched the moon. "We haven't held hands like this since we first met."

"I know it. We're kids again."

"Twisted kids." He giggled. "I'd have thought we were too young for our second childhood."

"We're all children in the theater, Mark. We play at being grown-ups, at being sophisticated, even. But put two actors in a room together and watch the childish games they play with each other."

"Worse yet, two directors."

"Or producers." Her nose was itchy. "I think a mosquito

just bit me. You should see the cat fights mother gets into with other producers."

"Does she win?"

"Almost always."

"Good. Then so will you."

"Are you saying I'm like Mother?"

"I don't know. I've never met her. Should we sit on the lawn and neck?"

"You really are in your second childhood, aren't you?"

He nodded enthusiastically.

"This isn't *American Graffiti*. Besides, there's too much dew."

At the far end of the lawn was a solitary man, kicking a soccer ball around and laughing loudly. Mark wanted to change directions so they wouldn't have to get too close to him. He didn't want anyone to interrupt their intimacy. But that was the shortest route home. Jo led the way, pulling him after her.

As they got closer, they realized the soccer boy was quite naked. And there was something wrong; the ball was too heavy, too lopsided, not responding the way a soccer ball should.

A few steps closer, and they recognized him. It was John Bartlett. His body was smeared with something dark. Then they realized it was not a ball he was kicking. It was Tim's head.

"John! For the love of God, what have you done?"

They both rushed toward him, not stopping to think he might be dangerous.

John saw them and froze. "You." He looked down at the severed head on the ground in front of him.

"John, for Christ's sake!"

Suddenly deflated, he sat heavily down. "I'll catch a cold like this, don't you think?"

Tim's eyes were open. His mouth gaped widely. John took his head and cradled it in his arms. "I loved him. I did. But he was making me crazy."

Mark got a hand under his shoulder and pulled him to his feet. "John, what in God's name have you done?"

"Nothing in God's name."

Jo, without thinking, bent down to pick up Tim's head.

Then she realized what she was doing and stopped herself. She looked from the head to John and back again. "I thought you and Tim were lovers."

"This is what love turns into, sometimes."

Suddenly, as if he was waking from a nightmare, John looked down at the head again and began to cry, loudly, horribly. He wailed. He howled. Mark put an arm around him to try to comfort him, but it didn't do any good; John pushed him violently away.

Someone came walking past, twenty feet away, on the sidewalk, not the lawn. Joanna called out, "Call 911. Please. Something terrible has happened here."

The passerby stopped, craned his neck to see, asked them, "What happened?"

"Please just get to one of the emergency stations and call the campus police." She pointed to a post with a blue light on the top, thirty feet down the sidewalk from him. "There. Just hit the button and tell them to get here as soon as possible."

The man hesitated, then moved quickly to the post. Both Jo and Mark could hear him exchange words with the operator on duty; they couldn't be sure what was being said. Mark shouted, "Thank you."

From the post, the man called back, "Do you need any help?"

"You don't want to see this."

Naturally the man walked toward them. "What the—?"

When he was close enough to realize what had happened, he stopped, obviously terrified. He looked from Joanna to Mark to John. "What have you people done? Who are you?"

"Do yourself a favor and go home before the police get here."

As if on cue, a campus police van pulled up; its lights were flashing, but there was no siren. It approached quickly, then braked abruptly. A pair of officers got out, leaving the lights spinning, and crossed the lawn to them.

"Jesus fucking Christ."

Joanna decided, as usual, that she had to be the one in charge. "No, officer, John Allan Bartlett."

"How did this happen? Who are you?"

The cops were both young. They were probably jocks; the

Stage Fright

university gave jobs to its poorer athletes. Mark, with his director's eye, saw that they were both working at a façade, cool police officers not shaken by anything they saw. They weren't being very convincing.

Joanna introduced herself and Mark to them. The passerby said his name was Christian Caparato. He didn't know anything, he said; he was just walking by, when . . . After a minute or two of questioning, and after getting his contact info, the cops let him go.

While all this was happening, John sat down on the ground again. Slowly, tenderly, he picked up Tim's head. And he kissed it, a long, deep, passionate kiss. Then, even more tenderly, he began to lick the drying blood from the jagged bottom of the throat.

An ambulance pulled up, lights spinning. Shortly after that, city police arrived. They and the EMS crew had to fight John to get Tim's head away from him.

It was more than an hour before the police were satisfied they had gotten all the information they could for the time being and let Mark and Joanna leave.

The mist had thickened steadily; by the time they were able to continue their walk home, it was a dense fog. Headlights of occasional cars and buses were bright spots in it; the moon and stars were gone. Neither of them said much; they were much too shaken by what John had done. Joanna found herself thinking about the night she and Tim had gone to the island, stoned. He had been a sweet boy, mostly; she had liked him and was looking forward to working with him. Mark and John had been close; Mark was having similar thoughts about him.

Briefly, quite fleetingly, the fog parted and the moon showed, bright and white above them. It was so unexpected, they both looked up. Neither of them said a word, but each of them was quite certain that there, in the moon's face, was the face of Portia, looking down at them and laughing.

Neither of them said a thing about it. It was illusion, or imagination. It had to be.

SIX

Marvin Mittelberger was short, dumpy and unattractive. His suit didn't fit even remotely well, and he was wearing eyeglasses ten years out of style. Joanna had loved him since she was a little girl and he was "Uncle Marvin." And what she loved about him was that he was as much actor as lawyer.

He was one of the richest, most wildly successful corporate attorneys in Manhattan, and he'd made even more on investments, but he looked, dressed and acted like a shyster lawyer out of a Billy Wilder movie. And got away with it. No one who didn't know him took him seriously, which was the way he wanted it. The ones who did know him . . . knew better than to underestimate him.

He had worked quite actively with Vince Gallardo at keeping the Bourbon Island company's connection to the Myers murder out of the public eye. Thanks to their combined efforts, all the very sensational coverage had included only one brief mention of the development on the island, and not even that had mentioned theater or the arts. Marvin made certain that the state bureaucracies that were financing the enterprise knew about this, too; and they were so grateful, and so impressed, they increased the grant money. Such an efficient

Stage Fright

operation merited that, and Marvin made absolutely sure they knew it.

Marvin had made several morbid jokes about "quitting while you're a head." He and Joanna decided it was time for him to come to Pittsburgh to meet her key people and to see the operation for himself. He would almost certainly have a few suggestions for improving and streamlining, which would save money and impress the agencies even more.

Vince met him at the Pittsburgh airport. He was expecting someone tall, distinguished and dressed to the nines. When Marvin walked past him, he had no idea this might be his man. Ten minutes later, they were the only two people left at the gate, except for a few of the flight crew. Vince approached him hesitantly. "Uh, you're not Marvin Mittelberger, are you?"

Marvin looked up at him and smiled a shy smile—a very carefully practiced one. "You're wrong. I am."

This threw Vince. "You are!"

"Do you want to see my ID?"

"No, no!" It took him a moment to recover himself. If he had to cast the role of this Marvin Mittelberger in a movie, the part would have gone to Moe the Stooge, hands down. "Welcome to Pittsburgh."

"I've been here before. It's not much of a town, is it?" He sniffled and wiped his nose on his sleeve.

Vince pretended not to notice. "I guess it must seem quiet to a man like you. After Manhattan, I mean."

Marvin's game of one-upmanship continued. "What do you mean, a man like me?"

But Vince was experienced enough at this kind of thing to catch on to what Marvin was doing. He decided there was no real reason for him to play. "Come on. I'm parked in the short-term lot. You only brought one bag."

"I'm not planning to be here long."

"Joanna might have something to say about that. She keeps insisting we need a lawyer full-time."

"Let her find someone local, then."

"There's no one local with your clout and your connections, Marvin."

"Carry my bag, will you? I have a bad back."

"So do I, I'm afraid."

Mittelberger realized Vince was on to him and dropped the game playing. He followed Vince through the terminal to the parking lot. There was a good bit of small talk, the weather, Marvin's flight, nothing very substantial or interesting. But Marvin knew Vince was one of the key people here. Schmoozing him couldn't hurt.

He had in fact found a construction company that was not too scrupulous about government rules and oversight. It was called Harp Construction, and in the six weeks since they'd been hired, they had made remarkable progress with the restoration. There had been several freak accidents, two of them resulting in deaths. One man was electrocuted; another was buried in the concrete foundation that was being laid for the main auditorium, prior to putting on the new roof. But the foreman, Hank Broughton, took everything calmly and insisted there was nothing to worry about. "We're used to that kind of thing."

When Joanna raised questions about investigations and insurance claims, Hank nodded calmly and told her, "Just leave everything to us." It was fairly obvious Harp was mob connected; no one had the bad sense to say so.

By midsummer, Annie Moore's family had raised an incredible amount of grief for the corporation. They suggested she was involved in some kind of rough-sex cult with someone else from the Bourbon Island company, demanded a police investigation and got it—briefly. But they ran into the same snag the company itself knew so well, the jurisdictional bickering that kept anyone from paying very close attention to what was happening on the island. Finally, Marvin explained to them in quite vigorous terms that continuing with their attempts to sue would only lead to unhappiness. They got the message and settled for a nominal amount.

There was still no sign of Jack Bilicic, and no indication what might have happened to him. To the extent the police had searched—not very far—they concluded that he had simply run off, for whatever reason of his own. It didn't make sense, not to anyone who knew what had happened, but it kept the heat off the company. He had had no family except a stepsister in Oregon, and they weren't close. She made a perfunctory inquiry through a lawyer, but Marvin had told them emphatically that unless they could prove where Jack was or what had happened to him, they had no grounds for any kind of claim.

As for John Bartlett, he was in a state hospital for the criminally insane—persuaded to cop a plea and go there quietly, by Marvin of course. John insisted he had loved Tim and had no idea what possessed him to do the terrible thing he did; and he explained that Tim had still been alive when he started to saw through his throat. He was given to long, loud, rather embarrassing crying jags and even spells of severe clinical depression. Mark visited him a few times, then stopped. They had been friends, and so he felt guilty about it. But he couldn't stand the smell and the general atmosphere in the madhouse. He told Jo it was horrific, like something out of the eighteenth century.

She was relieved; it gave her an excuse not to go. But like a good producer, tending her company, she pretended to be concerned. "You're exaggerating, Mark."

He was hurt. "Why would I do that?"

"We're theater people. We all do it. We thrive on drama."

"Not like this. You should go and visit him sometime."

She shook her head. "A theater company is madhouse enough for me."

Mark was now pierced. In eight places, none of which showed. Nipples, testicles, penis, navel, tongue . . . Joanna had watched each piercing, and each one was more of a turn-on for her. And Mark knew it. But the more he permitted himself to be perforated for her, the more she wanted him to keep doing it. Their sex and their relationship had improved for a while; now tension was creeping back. He felt pretty strongly that he was pierced enough.

As for Mo, his relationship with Tonya had grown similarly tense; and he wasn't sure why. But more and more, everyone's work was shifting to the island, and she liked it less and less. They fought at times; mostly, though, she just became increasingly distant from him and the company. She came to the island when it was necessary, but she usually worked at home. He was well into drafting scripts for the "after school" plays that were to be the company's bread and butter, and he found he liked writing more and more as he got into it.

Joanna worked with him quite actively, teaching him things like how to build tension, how to structure a scene for maximum impact, and so on. And she made certain he knew to prepare an outline of his play first, so he'd know exactly where his work was going—and so she could approve or reject it without him wasting too much effort. He learned the lessons so quickly, and took to the work so enthusiastically, she kept telling him he was a natural for the theater. Seeing what was happening to everyone's personal life, he wasn't sure he liked that. But there was the work, and he loved it.

He did less well at coming up with ideas and actual scenarios for the "fright" pieces, the plays that were to open the Imperial in October. But by late July that local horror novelist, John James Masters, was due to come on board to help.

Mark was amused. "There's a professional horror novelist in Pittsburgh!"

"Why not? I saw a chicken play the piano once." Jo was waiting for the guy to show up. She stood at the dock on the island, watching for his car. All she saw was Portia, standing on the shore and glaring as usual, in a way she must have meant as menacing. Her constant presence was unnerving, and neither Jo nor anyone else had gotten used to it or found a way to discourage her.

Mark pressed the subject. "What is there in Pittsburgh that you could find horror in?"

"Just look around sometime."

The three of them—Jo, Mark and Mo—had gotten their graduate degrees at the end of May. Jo had used the lure of jobs to "persuade" the faculty to accept her thesis. Now they were all living more or less full-time at the island, in that temporary housing she had planned, back when. This had its advantages, of course. But it also forced them into a kind of proximity Mo was finding more and more uncomfortable.

* * *

Then John James Masters appeared. He was short and had a tight body like a gymnast, which he was not. His hair was blond, his eyes green, his looks quite striking. Mark and Mo despised him on sight.

Joanna took the launch ashore to get him. Mo and Mark watched as they shook hands, got into the boat and cast off. A moment later Jo was introducing them. "This is John James Masters. Mark Barry, Mo Settles. You'll be working closely with Mo."

Masters smiled and looked around. Writer that he was, he had an instinctive sense that Joanna was the one with the money; the others could be ignored, at least for now. "So this is Bourbon Island. I've never heard of it. Nobody has."

Mark shook his hand halfheartedly. "Well, we're expecting your work to change that." He put on a tight smile. "Okay?"

Jo pointed to one of a row of clapboard bungalows. "That's your place, there on the end."

He did an exaggerated double take. "You expect me to live here?"

"I thought you understood that. We do."

"Even so. I have a wife and kid back in town. I'm not sure I want to—no, I don't think I could—"

"We'll discuss it later."

She left Mark to show him around the island.

Later that afternoon, Hank Broughton, the construction foreman, took Jo aside. "I think there may be a problem."

She sighed. "Another one?"

"Maybe the same one. You've heard these weird sounds that echo through the theater every now and then?" He was wearing a dress shirt and necktie. And he absolutely refused to call her by her first name. Joanna had tried to get him to go casual, like her theater people, but he insisted. Even so, she liked him.

"Yeah. It's got to do with the river, right?"

"I'm not sure. This is coal mining country, you know."

"Good. If the shows don't take off, maybe we can dig in the basement and realize something on what we find there."

"I'm serious, Ms. Marshall. There are old, abandoned

underground mines all through this region. Technically, they wouldn't have dug under the river, but you never know."

"That would have been really dangerous, right?"

"It would, yes. But, like I said . . . you know American corporations."

"Fortunately, no."

"Aren't you a liberal? I thought all you arts people—"

"I'm about as political as a tadpole, Hank. Anyway, what do I need to know about this?"

"Well, we can bring in one of our engineers and do some soundings. We might even need some bores."

"I can introduce him to the faculty at West Penn."

The joke was lost on him. "If the island's unstable because of something like that, it could explain a lot. That might be what made the chandelier fall."

"I thought it was a weak roof."

"That's what everyone's been guessing, but since the roof's gone, there's no real way to know."

This was exactly the kind of news she didn't want. "Well, do what you need to do, and keep me posted, will you?"

"Sure thing, Ms. Marshall."

She glanced at her watch. *Marvin should be here by now.*

On the drive to the island, Marvin and Vince made idle chitchat. But each was astute enough to know that the other was after information.

"So, how's the construction going?" Marvin pretended it was a casual question.

Vince shrugged. "It's coming along. They've got most of the new roof on, and the restoration of the lobby is almost complete. There are a couple of arts firms around, one restoring all the sculptures, the other one working on the murals in the lobby, mezzanine and in the rest rooms."

"Man, that's high living."

"Work hasn't started on the basement yet; everyone thinks it should be done last."

"They're afraid?"

Vince nodded.

"Where are we going? This isn't the way to downtown Pittsburgh."

"We are heading," Vince told him with a grin, "to Bourbon Island."

"I'd rather check into my hotel first."

"What hotel? You're staying on the island with Joanna."

"What!"

"There's some temporary housing set up on the south end of the island. The key people are all staying there."

"You're shitting me."

"No, honest. Jo says she wants you there, so you'll be available when she needs you."

"Jesus Christ."

"No, Joanna Marshall."

"Are *you* living there?"

"No, thank heaven. I can do my PR work a lot better from Pittsburgh."

Marvin harrumphed. There wasn't much more talk on the drive. When they pulled up and parked in what used to be Bourbon, Pennsylvania, Marvin took it all in, fascinated. "So this is what a ghost town looks like."

"And it's one of a matched set. Right over there is Bourbon, Ohio, and across the river is Bourbon, West Virginia."

Marvin shaded his eyes and looked. "I thought West Virginia was one huge ghost town anyway."

"They've come up with more arts money than either of the other states."

He remembered. "That's right. But then, what else do they have to spend money on? It's West Virginia."

They waited for someone to notice them, but everyone seemed to be either inside the Imperial or in one of the smaller, temporary buildings. Vince got out his cell phone and was just about to call Joanna when a movement caught their eyes. In some bushes about twenty yards away, some people were rolling around.

It was Helen and two of her customers. They were both boys. When they realized they weren't alone, they got quickly into their clothes and ran off. Helen was left there alone, glaring at Marvin and Vince. "Why don't you go back where you belong?" she shouted. "You're ruining my life."

Vince muttered that, from what he had seen of her, ruining her life wouldn't take much. Marvin was obviously puzzled, and Vince explained, "She's a local whore. She's crazy, or retarded or something."

"Places out here come with their own whores?"

Helen shouted a few choice words of abuse and walked off. Marvin watched her. "I wonder if she used to be pretty."

"Who knows? Does it matter to you?"

"Women matter, yes. But *her* . . . ! She has to have seen better days."

"What were you saying about West Virginia a minute ago?"

"Point taken."

Vince called Joanna. She was in the middle of a meeting with Mo, Mark and John James Masters, coming up with plots for the horror plays. She found one of the construction workers and asked him to go ashore to get them.

Joanna made a big show of greeting Marvin, who she described to everyone as "our savior." Then she left Vince to show him around the island. "You'll love the theater, Marvin, it's a remade ruin, like Mother."

Her meeting wasn't going well. John James Masters didn't seem to have anything like an original idea. He wanted to do *Night of the Living Dead*-style zombies. That was the extent of his invention.

"It's a natural," he chirped. "The original movie was made around here. So were most of the sequels. Everybody knows it. It's a natural."

Mark hated the idea and didn't try to hide it. "If it's such a natural, why hasn't someone else done it already?"

"No one else has thought of it, I guess."

"Then it's not much of a natural."

Joanna asked if they'd need to pay royalties to the people behind the movies.

"Gee, I hadn't thought of that."

Mark scowled at him. Actors were bad enough; horror novelists . . . !

A moment later, Marvin joined them. Joanna had asked him to draft a contract for John James Masters. Masters read the document, obviously puzzled by some of the language in it. "Why is this so different from a publishing contract?"

"Because," Marvin said patiently, "it's not a publishing contract."

"Oh." He went back to reading it, and he seemed more and more confused. "This says my royalty will be two percent. I get six."

"Keep reading. It's two percent off the gross."

"Off the top? Wow, I've never heard of that."

Suddenly the office they were in began to shake. Mark cried, "Let's get out!" and they ran outside. But it was the whole island that was trembling. It wasn't a violent quake; it wasn't even bad enough to knock things off walls and shelves. But the vibration was unnerving. Joanna made a mental note for herself, to make the engineer and his soundings a priority.

Then she realized that across the river, standing side by side on the Ohio shore, Portia and Helen were watching them and laughing.

"Jo, I've found something." Mo was settling into life on the island, away from the city—and life without Tonya, most of the time; she still refused to live there.

Jo looked up from her desk. "Good. That's the point of research, isn't it?"

"Something weird. I don't know what to make of it."

"Then it'll fit in just fine around here. What have you got?"

The island trembled again. These minor quakes were becoming so routine no one paid them much attention. Marvin was originally from San Francisco; he said they were nothing.

Nonetheless, Joanna and Mo stepped out of the hut. The day was brilliantly sunshiny; the river was flowing slowly, leisurely, as if it had no place special to go. It was a perfect July day.

On the Ohio shore, some heavy equipment was just pulling up. Mo watched it, a bit fascinated. "Construction stuff. How are they going to get it over here? It's way too big for the barges."

"It looks like road-grading stuff."

From the shore, a man who seemed to be in charge waved at them. "I'm looking for Joanna Marshall or Marvin Mittelberger," he shouted.

"I'm Joanna Marshall. I'll be right there."

Curious, Mo crossed with her to the shore. There, making an enormous racket, were a road grader, a backhoe, an asphalt spreader and another piece of heavy machinery he couldn't identify. Just as they were landing, he wondered aloud if they were what was making everything quake.

"I wouldn't think so, Mo. They just got here, and the island has been quaking a lot."

The foreman came down to the dock to meet them and introduced himself as Thomas Douglas, of the Ohio Department of Highways and Transportation. "We're here to start work on your bridge."

"Our—" It took a moment for it to register. When it sank in, Joanna's face lit up, and she shook his hand enthusiastically. "Pleased to meet you, Mr. Douglas."

"Tom, please."

"Call me Jo, then."

She introduced Mo, who then went off to get a close-up look at the machinery.

"Of course, we're just going to do some preliminary stuff today. The engineers that were here last month said the old piers are still usable, so we can do this pretty quickly and cheaply."

"Good."

"But we're going to reinspect them anyway, just to be sure."

"That makes good sense. Do you know how old they are?"

He smiled. "Damnedest thing—all the original plans and authorizations seem to have disappeared."

"If you knew how familiar that sounds. . . . Do you know anything about this place? Its history, I mean?"

He shook his head. "Nobody seems to." He shaded his eyes and looked out at the four piers stretching from the Ohio shore to the island. "I don't think they built in anything like that style after World War I, though."

She frowned. "We *are* planning to do classic plays here. Maybe an old-style bridge will help set the mood."

"Anyway, please don't let us interrupt your routine." He shaded his eyes again and looked across the river to the island. "So that's the Imperial Opera House, huh?"

"The temple of our art. What's on your agenda first, then?"

"Like I said, today we're going to double-check the piers, just to make sure. I think that third one may be trouble." He pointed. The piers were made from some heavy stone; the river stained them just above the water line. The third from the shore looked as if it might be starting to crumble, just ever so slightly. "Funny the engineers didn't notice that."

"Well, Tom, if I remember the stuff we have in our archive, the bridges must have been built when the Imperial was. If the theater's still in solid shape, they might be, too."

"You're no engineer, Ms. Marshall."

"Joanna—Jo."

"They said we'd be able to use one of your barges."

"Help yourselves."

Mo rejoined them. "This is so cool. Ever since I was a kid, I've loved heavy equipment."

"You sound like an actress I know." Jo laughed, turned back to Douglas and handed him one of her cards. "We'll be out on the island. If you need me for anything, that's my number."

"Bourbon Island Arts & Development Corporation." He whistled. "Sounds impressive for a theater group."

"Let's hope everyone else thinks so, too."

They shook hands all around, Douglas headed back up to rejoin his crew, and Mo and Joanna got back into the launch. She had trouble starting it for a moment, but the motor finally kicked in.

As she cast off, she asked Mo, "Now what was it you were going to tell me about?"

"Well, like I said, Jo, it's weird. I mean, it has to be the flukiest coincidence you can imagine."

"Try me."

He took a deep breath. They reached the island, and he used that as an excuse to stop talking and tie off the launch.

"You're dodging the question. Shoot."

"Well." He inhaled deeply a second time. "I came across another account of that old slave revolt that happened here. The slave magician, the so-called magic spell that was supposed to make the slaves invulnerable, the massacre that resulted."

"Yes?"

"In this account—I have it in my office, you can read it if you like—in this account, the magician was a woman."

"What of that?" She climbed quickly up to her office.

"There's a fairly vivid description of her. In early eighteenth century English, but unmistakable."

Jo narrowed her eyes. "You're being cryptic."

"She was a Negro woman. Negro born, but with unnaturally pale white skin and shockingly bright red hair."

For the first time, this caught Jo's attention. Suspiciously, she told him to go on.

"Well . . ." He pretended to look at the heavy road equipment on shore.

"Mo, tell me what you found."

"Her name was Portia."

She opened her office door. "Come in here and sit down and tell me that again.

He did. "Yes. Her name was Portia. Just like our little nemesis on shore."

"But—but—that can only be a coincidence."

"I told you you'd say that."

"Don't be smug. I mean—I mean—it can't be. Not unless she's a real magician. And we both know perfectly well there's no such thing."

"Of course we do."

She stared at him for a moment, trying to figure out how serious he was being, or how he could even *be* serious about something like this. Then they both broke out laughing. Playfully, Joanna took his hand. It was meant only as a friendly gesture. But they stood holding hands for longer than seemed quite appropriate. Finally, Mo pulled self-consciously away from her. "I ought to get back to work. Masters is waiting for me."

"Does he know about this Portia thing?"

Mo shrugged. "He seems to be off in his own little world all the time."

"And he doesn't even work in theater."

That night Mark was restless, tossing and turning. Partly because he wanted it, partly because he could, he had asked for and gotten his own little temporary bungalow on this island. No pins, no candles, no Joanna. They still had sex, some nights in his place, some nights in hers, but having his own place gave him a bit more independence and control.

The cots they used for beds weren't very comfortable, which made sleep even harder. The alarm clock on the nightstand announced 2:00 A.M. in bright red numerals; even they seemed to be keeping him awake.

He got out of bed and pulled on a pair of shorts. A walk would tire him out; he only hoped the night air wouldn't wake him up even more. He slipped into a T-shirt, put on a pair of sneakers and stepped outside.

There was a moon. It lit the island brightly. The façade of the Imperial might almost have been floodlit. The creatures on it seemed to be moving, crawling about. It was an optical illusion he had seen before; and other people had commented on it. At night, the Imperial came alive, or seemed to. It was something of a standing joke, at least among the ones who actually lived on the island. The theater will get you if you don't watch out. Annie Moore's death was far enough in the past for it to be funny.

On the Pennsylvania shore there was a fire. He peered at it, trying to decide if it was a campfire of some kind, or whether an actual wildfire had started there, despite the sparseness of the vegetation. There was no way to be sure, but it didn't seem to be spreading. There were only two people he could think of who could have lit it.

"You can't sleep either."

Mark turned, startled. It was Mo, dressed like him in shorts, T-shirt, sneakers. "You scared the hell out of me."

"Sorry."

"It's okay. I'm just never really comfortable here at night."

"No one seems to be, except Joanna. How will audiences feel?"

Mark ignored the question. "That sphinx over the entrance to the theater—I could swear it used to be more to the left."

Mo looked. "I know what you mean. The architect who built the place—Beatty—did some really interesting tricks with perspective or something. Sometimes the dragon's tail looks coiled to me, sometimes not."

"I wish I could convince myself it was just perspective."

Mo hesitated. He and Mark had never been close; they'd never even opened up to one another very much. But impulsively he said, "I miss Tonya."

"She'll come around."

He shook his head. "I don't think so."

"It looks like we'll have a bridge soon enough."

"From the wrong state. Besides, it's not just the water thing with her. She just doesn't like this place. She's never actually said it, but I think she's afraid of something here."

Mark shrugged. "I don't know anything about women."

"Who does? I think . . . hell, I don't know what I think."

"Oh." They fell silent. Mark watched the river, the way the moonlight played on the surface. It was his turn to say something impulsive. "You know, ever since we first came here, I've had this temptation to sit and fish and dangle my bare feet in the water." He felt self-conscious saying it, but he added, "Like Tom Sawyer."

"Maybe we can build a raft and float downriver."

"Joanna likes you."

"Does she?"

"I mean, really likes you. She doesn't like many people. I think that's what makes her a natural producer."

Mo wasn't certain whether this was a joke. "She's not like anyone I've ever known."

"We theater types are a breed unto ourselves."

"You can say that again."

"Someday soon you and I have to get together and go over the scripts you've got drafted. I'll have to start thinking about how to stage them."

"Sure, Mark."

On shore, the fire burned suddenly brighter. It licked up high into the air, like a student bonfire. Mo hadn't noticed it before. "Who's over there?"

"It can only be Portia or that dumb, crazy whore."

"Did Jo tell you about the Portia thing?"

"What Portia thing?"

"She didn't." He put on a wide smile. "It's the weirdest thing."

He told Mark about what he'd found, the magician named Portia, the slave revolt, the supposedly magical spell that failed. And the massacre that followed.

It all came as news to Mark. "She's never said a thing about any of it. I wonder why."

"She's got a lot on her mind."

A slight breeze came up. The fire danced in it, more than seemed quite right in such a gentle wind.

"Come on, Mo, let's see who's over there."

Mo laughed. "Whatever you say, boss."

The river was flowing slowly and gently. They got into the launch and pushed off. Rather than start the engine, which would have wakened people on the island and alerted whoever was on shore, Mark rowed. It took him a moment or two to get the hang of the oars; then he made pretty good time.

As they approached the Pennsylvania shore, they heard voices. Women's voices—more than one. The fire was still there; the actual flames were hidden by the shoreline that rose above them, but they could still see the glow.

Quickly, Mark tied off and followed Mo up the path. They should have some steps built, to make the climb easier; he made a mental note of it. At the top, the barren plain that had once been Bourbon, Pennsylvania, stretched out in front of him. Bright moonlight made it seem more vast and empty than it ever had. Barren, all that land, barren. They had sown it with salt. Why?

At the center of the plain, the fire burned. A large campfire, six feet high. Two figures sat beside it. Portia the madwoman and Helen the prostitute. They stared into the flames as if they were hypnotized. Mark looked to Mo and nodded, as if to say, "Come on, let's see what this is about."

The women didn't notice them till they were ten feet away. Then, with quite startling speed, they got to their feet. Simultaneously they said, "What do you want?"

Mo smiled. "We saw the fire. We wondered who was here. That's all."

Portia took a step toward him. She seemed to be trying to convey menace, but she was so small, the effort came off absurd. "What do you want?"

He made his smile even wider and hoped it didn't look too insincere. "Like I said."

Helen took a few steps back and away from them and the fire. "Go away. Get off our island."

Mark didn't move. But he felt like he had to respond to this. "It's *our* island, now. The states all say so."

"They never cared till you came. Get off our island."

Mark looked at Portia. "Do you want in on this, too? You think it's *your* island, right?"

"I've been here longer than you." Unlike Helen, Portia seemed not at all intimidated by the men. "I know this place in small, precious ways you never will." She snapped her fingers, in a very pointed way, and the fire rose up. For a brief moment it soared up to more than twelve feet tall; then it subsided.

"You think you can frighten us off with parlor tricks? Any good stage director could come up with a better fire effect than that."

Helen picked up a rock and threw it at him. It hit him in the forehead, surprisingly hard, and knocked him off balance. The skin was broken. Blood flowed. The fire rose again and danced wildly, even though there was no wind.

Mo rushed to Mark's side and put an arm around his waist. "Are you okay?"

"Jesus, I don't know." He sank to the ground, with Mo still trying to steady him, and reached up to touch the cut on his head. "Crazy bitch."

Helen laughed and ran off into the surrounding darkness. But Portia stood her ground, grinning at Mark as if stoning was the most natural thing in the world.

Stage Fright

The pain in his head was not subsiding; it was getting worse by the moment. He pressed it hard with the palm of his hand.

"Come on, Mark. Let's get back out to the island. There's first aid stuff there."

Mark nodded; with Mo's help, he got back to his feet. Mo told him, "Maybe I should get you to a hospital. There might be a concussion."

"No, just get me back out there."

Portia took a step toward them and held out a hand, as if she wanted to help. Mark instinctively pulled back from her. And she looked offended.

"Foolish white man. You don't belong here. Foolish black man. There is nothing here but death and the dead. You should know. You should understand. Go away while you can."

"What are you then? Death, or the dead?"

She laughed. "Me? I am Portia. I belong here."

"Right."

Mark staggered, and Mo worked to steady him. It seemed to take forever, but finally they got back down the bank to the landing, then into the launch. Mark planted himself squarely at the center, leaving Mo no place to sit where he could row. "You have to move. I have to work the oars from there."

"I'll row."

"Don't be foolish, Mark."

Mo glanced up, expecting Portia would be there watching them. There was no sign of her. The glow from the fire seemed not so bright. He reached into his back pocket and pulled out a flask. "Here. Drink something."

Mark looked at it as if it was an alien object. "What is it?"

"Bourbon. What else?" He unscrewed the cap and handed it to Mark, who took a long swallow. Mo expected him to pass it back, but he held on to it and took another drink. Mo helped him to his feet again and moved him to the rear of the boat.

Then Mo pushed off and took up the oars. They gave him trouble "This is harder than I thought." Sheepishly, he grinned. "I've never done this before."

"You'll get the hang of it." Mark took a third long drink,

then put the flask on the floor of the launch. "Women. Women are all crazy bitches."

"And some of them have good throwing arms. Are you including Joanna in that?"

Instead of answering Mark snorted.

"Are you sure you don't want me to get you to an emergency room?"

He shook his head. "I'll be okay. I don't even know what Jo thinks of me, really."

"She's your fiancée. She must love you."

Slowly, drunkenly, Mark looked directly into his eyes. "Yeah?"

On the eastern horizon there was a series of lightning flashes. They were too far away for thunder, and the sky was still cloud free, but Mo watched them, concerned. "We've been lucky with the weather, so far. I can't imagine what it will be like here in a storm."

"Wet." He touched his cut again.

"Stop doing that. We need to get some disinfectant and a bandage on it."

"I love Jo, but I really don't know what she thinks of me, down deep. There are times when I have the feeling she's always laughing at me. Why are women like that?"

"I'm not sure they all are."

"You ought to make Tonya live here."

"Right. And if she doesn't pick enough cotton, I could whip her."

"I didn't mean it like that."

Mo wasn't offended; he assumed the head wound was affecting Mark's judgment. He concentrated on his rowing. Getting from shore to the island was taking longer than it should. He realized the river was beginning to run faster than he'd seen before. Those storms off to the east . . .

But Mark was in a rut. "My mother never liked me, either."

"Where is she, Mark?"

"Dead. Died when I was eight."

"I'm not sure I'd rely on an eight-year-old's perceptions. Not to the point of carrying them with me all my life."

Stage Fright

"I was a good boy. Well-behaved. Nice. Women are all crazy bitches."

"Yes, sir."

Finally, Mo managed to maneuver the boat to the dock. It had been much more of a struggle than he'd expected. He jumped onto the landing and tied off, then got back in the launch to help Mark, who was still quite unsteady. When he had him safely on the dock, he got back in again and picked up his flask. He looked around as if he was a child about to do something naughty, then took a long drink himself, draining the last of the liquor.

"Can you make it up the path, Mark?"

"I'm okay." He staggered.

There was more lightning, closer this time. The sky was clouding up more and more. Mo cursed the weather. If Mark got much worse—and it looked like he might—they'd have to get him to shore through a rainstorm.

He got Mark up the path. To their mutual surprise, they found Marvin Mittelberger there, alternately watching the sky and the Imperial. Marvin saw them coming up, with Mo supporting Mark. But instead of asking what was wrong, he said, "The place is alive."

Mark laughed. "With the sound of music."

"I mean it." Finally he realized something was wrong and gave Mo a hand with Mark. "What happened?"

Mo described the scene on the Pennsylvania shore. "Who'd have thought that half-witted whore could throw like that?"

"Maybe"—Marvin helped him ease Mark to the ground—"she can't. Maybe she was aiming at you."

"That's not what I need to hear, Marvin."

"I've been watching the theater. It has to be some kind of optical illusion, but it looks like the things on it, all the statues and reliefs and what not, it looks like they're moving."

"We've all seen it. It's a trick of the eye. William Beatty, the architect who built the place, was a master of that kind of thing. I don't know if there's an actual name for it, but it's the architectural equivalent of those optical illusions you find in children's books."

Marvin looked at the Imperial. "You sure? I mean, you have to be right, but . . . It's mighty convincing."

"Beatty was a master. Between Jo and me, we've found a good bit about him. He was really famous, in his day."

"Which was . . . ?"

"Up till the end of World War I, roughly. He was as well known as Frank Lloyd Wright or Stanford White. But nobody remembers him today, I think because he designed and built theaters instead of doing 'serious' work."

Mark fell backward; his head hit the ground.

"Shit, he's passed out. Give me a hand, Marvin. We've got to get him to—"

Suddenly, seemingly from nowhere, there came an enormously bright flash of lightning. They both looked to the sky; it had clouded over completely, with astonishing rapidity. A moment later there came a clap of thunder so loud the ground shook.

"Did you see the Imperial?"

Mo looked at Marvin, puzzled.

"In that lightning. All the monsters looked up at the sky, like frightened animals."

"You're seeing things, Marvin."

"No. They did."

Mark rolled on the ground and moaned loudly.

"Come on, Marvin. Let's get him down to the launch. We have to get him to a hospital."

"We should tell Jo."

"No, we have to move. There's a storm coming."

"She won't like it."

"I don't care."

"She's the producer."

"Marvin, will you come on?"

"Her mother would turn into a fury."

"Women," Mo found himself saying, "are all crazy bitches."

"The Marshall women, anyway."

Reluctantly, looking over his shoulder like a naughty schoolboy afraid he might get caught, Marvin helped Mo pick up the patient and carry him back to the path that descended to the dock. For a moment Mark regained consciousness and fought them, then he passed out again.

There was another lightning stroke, brighter and closer than the last one. They braced themselves for the thunder. When it came, it was louder than anything either of them had ever heard. They put Mark down and covered their ears with their hands, not that it did any good. A few scattered hailstones hit the ground.

Joanna and Masters came running out of their huts, both obviously terrified. Masters shouted, "Is it an earthquake?"

Marvin shouted back, "Have you ever heard of an earthquake with hail?"

A sudden storm of hail, with stones half an inch in diameter, pelted them. They lay so thick on the ground it was covered in a matter of moments. Then came the rain, heavy sheets of it. Mo looked to the river, and it was running high and swift; there was no way they could get Mark across.

A violent gust of wind tore the roof off one of the huts. The four of them, Mo, Joanna, Marvin and John James Masters huddled together, as if that might protect them. Over the wind's roar, Mo shouted, "We have to get somewhere safe. This is tornado country."

Marvin did a double take. "This is Pennsylvania, not Kansas."

"Even so." He pointed at the theater. "Let's get inside. It's the most solid thing here."

Joanna hesitated. Looking at Mark, she asked, "Mo, what happened to him?"

"I'll tell you when we're inside. Everybody, help me get him up there."

They carried him. Masters kept looking anxiously at the Pennsylvania shore. "We ought to get out of here."

"How? Look at the river." Marvin didn't try to hide his contempt. He and Masters had disliked each other from the start. Marvin kept saying he "wasn't theater."

The Ohio was running higher and faster than any of them had ever seen it, so high and fast it was rather frightening. They all had, in the back of their minds, a terror that it would flood the island and carry them away. None of them put it into words.

Finally, they got Mark inside the Imperial lobby. Mo pulled the doors firmly shut, and the noise of the storm subsided somewhat. The work crews had cleaned out most of the clutter and litter from the place. It was now filled with equipment—large metal tool boxes, huge coils of cable, ladders and scaffolds waiting to be erected. They propped Mark carefully against a wall. Marvin asked if they should lay him down. "Wouldn't that be better for him?"

None of them knew. Just to be safe, they eased him into a face up position on the floor. He was quite unconscious, but somehow he fidgeted and moved himself up again, back against the wall.

Masters looked around. "I knew I should never have let you talk me into living here. I can do everything I need to from home and e-mail it to you."

"This is the theater, John." Joanna's tone made it clear this was not a discussion she wanted to be having, just now. "We expect our playwrights to be hands-on professionals."

"I never agreed to this."

Everyone ignored him. He started to say more, then he realized there wasn't much point.

The wind was picking up even more; they could hear it.

But they could hear worse things than that. The inside of the theater was filled with sounds. Cries, moans, sobs, screams, they were coming from everywhere in the building, it seemed. Among them there was one particularly agonized shout, the voice of a young woman. Mo took Joanna aside and whispered, "That's Annie Moore. I know her voice."

"Don't be foolish, Mo."

"I mean it. It's her."

"But . . . she's dead." Her own experiences with Samuel Fulton got pushed conveniently out of Joanna's mind; they didn't fit what she wanted to believe was happening. She listened, trying to recognize what they were hearing, but she realized she wouldn't know Annie's voice if she heard it. She had never paid much attention to the girl; she was only an actor, after all. "She's gone and buried, Mo. She can't very well be haunting the place when she's somewhere else."

"Why not? Do you think body and soul are so closely bound together?"

"This is absurd, Mo. We should be taking care of Mark."

He looked around. The ghostly cries were growing louder and more concrete, less ghostly. "Let's see how he is."

The cut on his head was still bleeding. He was sitting, propped against the wall, groggily fighting Marvin, who was trying to examine the gash. Mark pushed him away. "Leave me alone, Annie."

"I'm not Annie, Mark. I'm Marvin."

"Leave me alone."

Joanna got down on a knee and tried to help Mittelberger, but Mark pushed her away, too, quite violently. "Leave me the fuck alone, I said!"

They didn't have much choice. Short of pinning him to the floor, there was no way anyone was going to check his wound at all closely.

Meantime, Masters was walking around the lobby, trying to make out what details he could. At the foot of the steps he inspected a black marble statue of a woman with snakes for hair. "This," he announced loudly and happily, "is a gorgon."

Joanna looked at him. "No kidding."

Outside, there was a series of violent, blindingly bright lightning flashes. It must be striking the ground somewhere nearby. The island and the Imperial shook.

Mo caught Joanna by the arm. "Have we been hit?"

"I hope not. We can't afford any more delays getting this place up and functioning."

They walked to the front doors and opened one of them a crack. The rain was pouring down, roaring as it hit the ground. She had never seen anything like it.

"This is like the end of the world."

She pulled the door shut again. "Or the beginning. Just look at the world."

A violent burst of wind blew all the doors open. Gusts blew into the lobby; debris flew about. Then the worst lightning yet struck. This time there could be no doubt it had hit the island. Joanna, Mo, Marvin and Masters struggled to pull the doors shut again. The sound of the storm outside was almost deafening.

Joanna shouted. "We have to go out and check."

"Check what!" Masters was horrified at the idea.

"We have to make sure the theater hasn't been hit."

"We can see that after the storm passes."

Mo tried to reason with him. "It could come down around us. Besides, you're a horror writer. This is your element."

"We'll be able to check better after this passes."

Joanna put her foot down. "No—now. We need to see."

She took charge, and the others acquiesced. Reluctantly and rather fearfully they went outside, all but Masters, who stayed to tend Mark. Marvin was more annoyed than afraid, and he looked it. Mo followed Joanna quietly.

The river was raging, but the storm, finally, seemed to be subsiding. Rain was still heavy, but the wind was dying down and there didn't seem to be any more lightning. Joanna took Mo's hand and told him, "Everything looks okay here. Let's go around the back, to be sure."

"Okay."

The rain slowed even more; it wasn't much more than a light shower, now. But the air was charged with electricity; they could feel it. When they reached the rear of the building, the rain stopped completely.

When Mo realized the storm had passed, he relaxed and smiled. "Well, we survived."

"But look at the river, Mo. I've never seen it so high or so rapid. We'll never get Mark out of here."

Just at that moment, one last, painfully bright bolt of lightning struck. It hit the third bridge pier from the Ohio shore. There was the sound of an explosion; the pier smoked for a few moments. But it held solid. Joanna was tempted to say something about how firmly everything was built, but somehow it didn't feel right.

Inside the theater, Mark pressed himself against the wall; that final bolt of lightning terrified him. His head ached, and he couldn't remember why. Masters drifted to the doors, stepped outside and lit a cigarette.

From out of the darkness inside came a figure, a woman.

Stage Fright

She was blond, blue-eyed, delicate, pretty. She had no arms. They had been torn off, and blood poured from the stumps. It was Annie Moore; Mark had sensed her presence earlier; so had Mo.

Seemingly in a trance, quite oblivious to the volumes of blood pouring from her shoulders, she circled the lobby. After what seemed a terribly long time, she noticed Mark, who had been watching her, numb, groggy and still unnerved from the storm.

She walked to him and stood at his feet. "Mark Barry." Her voice was like a whisper, yet it echoed clearly through the building.

"Annie." He pressed himself against the wall; if it had been possible, he would have pushed himself into it and vanished. "Annie, I'm sorry."

"You hated me."

"No." Her blood was pouring onto him, soaking him. An impossible amount of it had spilled already, and more and more was flowing.

"I loved you. I wanted you. And you hated me."

"No, Annie, I—I never knew."

"Why? What did I do to earn your contempt?"

"Nothing. I never knew, I—"

"Mark."

She spoke only that one word. Then she approached him, nearer and nearer. And she bent down and kissed him. Her blood never stopped pouring, it seemed; terrible volumes of it covered him. And they kissed, a long, deep and passionate kiss. And all the stone monsters around the lobby, and all the figures in the murals, turned their heads to watch.

Mark closed his eyes. This was the best kiss he'd ever tasted. So sweet, so warm, not at all like the way Jo kissed him. The warm blood covering his body made it seem even sweeter, somehow.

Annie's clothes fell away, and he began to use his mouth on her body. And the statues around the lobby watched them still more intently. The figures in the murals craned to see the lovemaking that was beginning in their place. And one by one, stone figures and painted ones, they smiled.

Mark opened his eyes again. It was not Annie he had been kissing at all. It was his mother, young and pretty as she had been before she died.

Mark recoiled. Annie was one thing. This . . .

But his mother, naked and hot, took violent hold of him and pressed her body into his face. Mark struggled, he tried to scream, but she was much too strong for him. He could smell her, taste her, and he could not stop crying.

It was not his mother. The body forced against him was a man's. A dark-skinned man. Tall, muscular, handsome in a ruined way. A black man Mark had never seen before. Like Annie and Mark's mother, he was naked. And his body was covered with welts, fresh, newly opened, it seemed, from which blood flowed as abundantly as it had from Annie's arms.

The ghost forced himself on Mark. Beat him. Tore his clothes off and raped him. Mark cried out, but everyone else was outside.

And yet . . . through the pain and tears he thought he could see someone else. Another man, a white one, standing twenty feet away, watching. He was dressed in some kind of old-fashioned clothing. Mark tried to ask him for help, but when he opened his mouth, his assailant hit him brutally.

The white man's ghost was stroking himself, stimulating himself. The sight of the rape was exciting him.

There was no way Mark could know him. But Joanna would have. It was Samuel Fulton.

When, finally, after inspecting the Imperial as thoroughly as the night would permit, Joanna and the others found Masters on the front steps. They came back inside and found Mark on the floor where they had left him, naked, trembling violently. He was having a seizure. His limbs flailed; his breathing was intensely difficult; froth appeared at his mouth.

Marvin quickly pulled the wallet from his back pocket and pushed it into Mark's mouth. With uncharacteristic modesty he said, "I used to be a Boy Scout."

After a few moments Mark's body relaxed. The seizure became less and less violent, then ended. Marvin moved close to him and examined the wound on his forehead. "This is worse

Stage Fright

than it looks, I think. He may have suffered some serious damage."

Mo got down on a knee beside him. "You saw how the river is. We'll never get him to a hospital."

"As soon as the water subsides, then."

Joanna found herself watching Mark, fascinated. She wished she'd been there to see his seizure. At the far end of the lobby she saw Fulton, watching them all and smiling.

Suddenly she exploded. "Shit!"

"What's wrong?" Marvin was turning into a caregiver, more to his own surprise than to anyone else's. He got a large handkerchief out of his pocket and wrapped it around Mark's head.

"I was supposed to audition some actors tomorrow. I'll have to call them all and tell them to hold off a few days."

Masters seemed appalled at this. "We should all just get out of here."

"Unless you have a helicopter on you, I don't see how we could."

"There's something wrong here. This place is . . . I don't know, not right, somehow."

"You've been taking your own novels seriously, haven't you?"

Mo quickly got between them. "Why don't you make a list of all the actors who are coming? We can each call a few."

"He's asleep, I think." Marvin got to his feet.

Mo looked up at him. "You're sure he hasn't just passed out again?"

Marvin shrugged. "What difference does it make? If he's out, at least we know he's not in any pain. There's nothing we can do for him."

Masters shouted, rather violently, "Are you all blind or something? This place is—is—"

"Is what?" Jo was losing patience with him.

"I don't know, it's haunted or something. Cursed."

"You're crazy." She had to force herself not to watch Fulton. Masters was perfectly correct, but only she knew it, and she would not close again the doors Fulton had opened for her. "We have work to do. Let's get back down to our huts. Marvin, can you and Mo manage Mark?"

"Sure."

"Put him in my bed. I'll sleep on the couch."

The two of them picked Mark up, quite gingerly, and carried him to the door. Masters, seemingly appalled that no one would listen to him—or, as he thought, listen to reason—held it open for them.

Joanna stayed behind. She watched the others go, told them she'd follow in a moment, then tuned to face Fulton. He was gone. Annoyed, she climbed the steps to his office. He was there, quite naked, with a boy, who was also undressed.

"Let him go."

Fulton said nothing, but he smiled at her, a rather vicious smile.

"I said let him go."

"This is the prettiest boy I've had."

"I want to know the truth about you and about your theaters. About *this* theater."

Fulton laughed at her and turned on the boy. The two of them began to make love. The boy wasn't more than ten years old. For the first time, she found him and his sexual games disgusting rather than fascinating. She turned to go.

"If you can't guess," Fulton called after her, "you're a considerable fool."

She paused, looked back at him, then continued down to the lobby. From behind her, she heard Fulton laughing at her. And the boy was laughing, too. And the lobby was filled with a hundred other voices, all of them torn with laughter. Some of them were coming from the basement, some from the auditorium, some, seemingly, from nowhere at all.

She pulled open the door to the auditorium, and it was filled with people and light. A woman who looked like Portia played the theater organ. Men and women in chic evening dress, twenties-style, talked and socialized. The great chandelier above them began to sway and shudder. It was going to fall; Joanna knew it. She couldn't watch. She closed the door and left as quickly as she could.

Outside, it seemed to her still again that the theater was alive, or at least the beasts that adorned it were. None of them moved when she had her eye on them, but just outside the range of her vision, they crawled and writhed and danced. When she looked at any one of them in particular, it would be quite still. When she looked away, then back, it would have changed its pose or its place.

There was some bourbon in her hut. She needed it. Christ, did she need it.

The theater was alive.

In the morning, the river was running swiftly and the sky was still dark and overcast. The launch was gone, carried off by the current. Mo blamed himself; he should have tied it more securely. But Jo told him the water was flowing so quickly, it would have torn loose no matter what.

They had not managed to get hold of all the actors who were due for auditions. It was only a matter of time before they showed up. Awkward situation. But Jo wasn't concerned. "They're actors. They're desperate by definition. They'll cope."

Her cell phone rang at six thirty A.M., and it was Tom Douglas. "Morning, Jo."

"Tom. Hi."

"The river's running high everyplace. We're figuring we won't get any work done today, so we're not coming."

"Oh."

"Don't worry, we'll get back on schedule."

"It's not that, Tom. Someone's injured here. Mark. We were hoping you'd have a power boat that could get him to shore and then to a hospital."

"Not in this current, I wish I could do something."

"Can you arrange for a helicopter to get him?"

"I'll see what I can do."

"Thanks."

That was that. It had never occurred to her to think about it before, but she decided, yes, she really did love Mark. He was a good director, and the project would be hurt if he was lost to it.

Mark hadn't wakened. He had slept fitfully all night, never actually waking up but crying out every few minutes. Sometimes it seemed to be in pain or in fear; other times it was in sexual pleasure. Jo had heard him often enough to know. She never switched the lights on in the middle of the night to see, though; she didn't want to. Come morning, he was covered in sweat, and now and then he seemed to tremble as if he was freezing.

Marvin undertook to call the authorities and swear out a complaint against Helen and Portia. The Pennsylvania state police didn't seem anxious to look into the matter, but he finally persuaded them to try and do something. Everyone had known for a long time that the two of them were not right in the head; now, it was quite clear they were dangerous. But there was the question of where they were. No one knew. It occurred to Marvin, quite uneasily, that no one really could.

Just before nine o'clock the first of the actors arrived. There were two of them, a young man and a slightly older woman; they came in the same car. Joanna found herself wondering if they were lovers or just friends. They parked their car in a spot that seemed uncomfortably close to the bank. Then they got out and stared at the island, as if watching it long enough would show them how to reach it.

Joanna shouted to them. "We tried to reach you by phone. Auditions won't be possible for a few days."

"The phone lines were down. I'm Jerry Early and this is Megan Cantwell." He was blond and virile; she was slight and wispy.

"I'm sorry for the mix-up. The storm really had it in for us."

"Should we come back?"

"Yes. Definitely. We'll call you when we're ready for you."

"Great."

When they tried to leave, their car was stuck in the mud. It took them nearly fifteen minutes of trying to get it loose. He got out and pushed, and he nearly fell into the Ohio. The current would have swept him away in a matter of moments.

Mo stood with Joanna and watched them go. "We'll never see them again."

"Want to bet?"

"They'd be crazy to come back here."

"They're actors."

"We're crazy to be here at all."

Stage Fright

She frowned at him but let it drop.

A few minutes later another actor showed up. His name, he shouted, was Josh Feore. He was tall and handsome, a perfect leading man type. There was the same conversation, called out from island to shore. He registered disappointment, shrugged, promised to come back when Jo called, and left.

Jo regarded Mo smugly. "You see? Actors. Most of them would sell their mother to the Patagonians for a part."

"I think the river's starting to go down. I couldn't see that rock before." He pointed.

Jo looked at him. "Wishful thinking. It'll be days."

"Jo, I want to get off this island. I want to see Tonya."

"This will pass, Mo."

Just then, Marvin joined them. "Joanna, I think you better come down to the huts."

"What's wrong?"

"Come on, will you?"

"Marvin, I—"

"Just for once, Joanna, do as you're told. Come on."

They got to her hut quickly. Masters was standing just inside the doorway, looking pained. Mark was on the couch, not moving.

"It happened a few minutes ago." Marvin's voice was just barely above a whisper.

"What—?"

"He muttered something. It sounded like, 'Jo, please don't.' Then he stopped breathing."

"He's—?" Her eyes widened, and she went slightly pale.

Marvin and Masters both nodded.

"No. He can't be." She looked alarmed and crossed the room to the couch. Agitatedly, almost angrily it seemed, she shook him. "Mark! Mark!"

Marvin moved beside her and pulled her away from him. "It's no use, Jo. He's gone."

"No!"

She shook his body again, almost violently. "Mark, for Christ's sake, open your eyes."

"Joanna, stop it."

She ignored him. When Mark didn't respond, she became

even more upset. She began slapping his face and pounding his chest. "Mark! Mark! Mark, wake up!"

Finally Masters and Marvin caught her by her arms and pulled her outside again. Masters told her to calm down. She looked at him with something like contempt.

"How can I calm down? Mark was my fiancé. My *director*, for Christ's sake. Do you know what this does to this project? We've been talking for months about what I want for our shows. I'll never find another director I'm in sync with the way I was with Mark."

Masters tried to make his voice soft and kind. "Everyone loses people they love, Joanna. It's part of life."

She looked at him as if he was insane. "Where am I going to get another director?"

Mo had stayed outside, near the riverbank. The commotion caught his attention, and he joined them. "What's wrong?"

"Mark's dead." Marvin said it in a low voice, almost a whisper.

"Oh, God, no. But . . . but I saw what happened to him. That rock didn't hit him hard enough to—"

"Nevertheless, Mo."

Suddenly Joanna was in charge of herself again. "I'll have to direct, myself."

It caught the three men off guard. Mo was the first to respond to it. "Sure, Jo."

"I directed for my classes. Everyone has to take a directing class. I took two. I can do it."

"Of course, Jo. Now we have to think about—"

"There's nothing to being a director. Just good, common sense."

"Jo, we have to decide what to do with Mark. We can't just . . . leave him in your hut."

"These aren't exactly complicated plays. I know I can handle them. We can always bring in someone else to help later, if we have to."

"Jo."

Just then another carload of actors pulled up on the Pennsylvania shore. Joanna saw them and brightened almost at once. "More cast!"

Stage Fright 215

She waved to them and shouted her apologies. "I promise you'll get priority when we're able to do auditions."

But the actors had noticed something. "Who's that?" one of them shouted, pointing out to the middle of the river.

Everyone looked. Sitting on the third pier from the Ohio shore—the one that had been struck by that lightning bolt, were the two women, Helen and Portia. They sat serenely, holding hands and watching the island. When they realized everyone had seen them, they smiled and waved. Sunlight lit them brilliantly.

It was impossible they were there. The river was running high and swift. There was no way they could have maneuvered a boat to the pier, and for that matter there was no sign of a boat. They certainly couldn't have swum there.

Of everyone there, Mo was the most unsettled by it. He moved apart from everyone else, got out his cell phone and called Tonya. "Honey, you were right about this place."

"I told you so, Mo."

He gave her a brief account of what had happened. "I wish to God I had another job offer. Anything."

"You wouldn't be the first MA to turn burgers for a few months. If I don't find something soon, that's what I'll be doing."

Hearing it made him stop and think. "No, I can't do that." He explained to her that they'd be trapped on the island for a few days and promised to get home as quickly as he could. "I'll have to follow up on all those applications and resumes I sent out."

"I told you to do that two months ago."

"Don't. I know you told me so. You don't have to rub it in, okay?"

Meantime, Joanna had made a note of the actors' names. They left, feeling as if they'd been all but guaranteed jobs.

Marvin made calls. First, the police, then the three state health departments, trying to get someone to do something about Mark's body. The response in every case was, in effect, "Bourbon Island? Never heard of it." Finally he located a funeral home and arranged for a helicopter to come and get the body. It would cost a fortune, but the corporation would pay for it. He didn't bother to clear it with Joanna. He also didn't tell her the helicopter would have room for only one passenger, and that he planned to be that one.

When the actors were gone, Joanna offered to make breakfast. It surprised everyone. Mo had been doing most of the cooking, with Masters helping now and then. She cooked in Mo's cabin; Mark's body was in hers. When they finished eating, they came outside again to check on the river's level. And the third Ohio pier was empty; somehow, Portia and Helen had gone.

It wasn't possible they had been there at all, but everyone had seen them. It wasn't possible they had found a way back to shore, but they weren't there.

But the pier itself was damaged. The lightning had weakened it, and as they watched, a few bits of stone and concrete splashed heavily into the river. It was crumbling, slowly but surely. More work, more expense.

Jo's phone rang. It was Vince Gallardo, checking on conditions at the island, making certain everything was all right. Jo brought him up to date. He asked her to keep Mark's death as quiet as possible. "No sense stirring up bad publicity."

"No." She kept her voice neutral. "No sense doing that. Vince, there's something wrong here."

"Nonsense, you're just upset about losing Mark. He was a good man, Jo."

As she talked with him, her eyes drifted to the damaged pier. More stones fell. And when they fell, something was exposed. A human arm.

More stones fell, and more. Finally a male body was exposed there. It was quite naked. And the fact it was there was even more impossible than that fact that Portia and Helen had been. If Tom Douglas had been right, the piers hadn't been touched since they were built. How could there be what appeared to be a fresh human body in one of them, whole and undecayed?

Two hours later the helicopter appeared. It circled the island four times, as if the pilot couldn't convince himself that was where he was to land. Finally, he set down, midway between the theater and the huts. For whatever reason, he kept the blades spinning.

He was a central casting pilot, virile, hearty, dressed in safari clothes and wearing dark aviator sunglasses. He greeted everyone, asked where they had the body he was to pick up, got a stretcher out of his craft and unfolded it. Mo helped him carry Mark's body and get it secured.

Marvin suddenly emerged from his own hut, carrying his luggage. He introduced himself to the pilot, stowed his things inside the chopper and began to climb in.

"Marvin! What do you think you're doing?"

"Why, Joanna, don't tell me I've managed to surprise you?"

"You can't leave."

"Watch carefully."

"This is no time for wit, Marvin. I need you here."

He climbed aboard the helicopter. "I can do more for you from my office than I could ever accomplish here. I'm leaving, Jo."

"Don't. You're my rock."

"I am no one's rock, Joanna. And I'm heading back to Manhattan, where the only rocks are in Central Park."

"My mother—"

"There's no use invoking her name. She wants me back up there." He put on a wide scowl. "She says I'm wasted in a place like this. And she has a point."

For the first time, Joanna's self-confidence seemed to be wavering. She lowered her voice as much as she could, to sound a personal note yet still be heard above the whirling blades. "Please, Marvin. You're important to this project. You're important to theater, and it's places like this where the theater lives nowadays. Broadway is nothing but a theme park for tourists, and you know it."

"It's a very lucrative theme park, Jo, at least for smart lawyers."

The pilot climbed aboard, checked the bindings on the stretcher and took his place at the controls. Marvin promised he'd be in touch every day, and the chopper lifted ungracefully into the air above Pennsylvania, Ohio or West Virginia, as the case may be.

Once the sound of it receded. There was another loud noise. More of that pier crumbled into the river. And the body that had been inside it dropped into the water with a loud splash. Everyone watched as it floated in a small circle, as if it was caught in a whirlpool. Slowly at first, then more and more rapidly, it drifted toward the island. Before long it washed up on the eastern shore.

The three of them walked quickly down to see it. Masters had no idea who it might be. But Mo and Joanna recognized it at once. It was the corpse of Jack Bilicic. The *fresh* corpse.

There was more of the usual jurisdictional wrangling. Finally, because a report of Jack's disappearance had been taken by the Pennsylvania state police, they conceded they ought to follow up. From New York, Marvin pulled what strings he could to try to get the investigation, such as it was, closed and the publicity kept to a minimum. Vince did his part in Pittsburgh. Joanna wanted to be the one to notify Mark and Jack's families of their deaths, but Marvin made her agree it would be better if he did it.

Another launch was bought and delivered; they weren't pris-oners on the island anymore. Joanna's actors came back, and in fairly short order she had her resident company. Several of them had heard rumors about strange goings-on at Bourbon Island, but she managed to reassure them. "You know how superstitious theater people can be. They'll even tell you the ghosts of Shakespeare's actors haunt the site where the Globe Theater stood." They weren't quite convinced she was dealing with them honestly, but like all actors everywhere, they needed work.

It was neediness that kept John James Masters on the job; he kept complaining that his agent wasn't working hard enough to sell his new book. And Mo's job search had gone nowhere. Specialists in African American theater history weren't exactly in demand, it seemed. So he stayed; more and more it was out of necessity and even desperation, not conviction.

Even more unhappily, Tonya returned to the corporation. Her job search had likewise gone nowhere. She was in a more practical, in-demand field than Mo, and her transcript and references were sterling; neither of them understood why she hadn't been hired anywhere.

Restoration work on the theater continued at a rapid clip. The state highway departments put up their bridges. There were originally to have been three, but Pennsylvania and West Virginia decided to build one jointly. It was larger and wider than the one from Ohio, and it had a sleek modern design; it looked jarringly out of line with everything else on the island.

Harp Construction also put up a suite of permanent bungalows to serve as residences for the staff and actors. Masters said they looked like pieces for a puzzle of a motel, which they more or less did. But Harp had managed to find brick that matched the materials in the Imperial, so at least the bungalows weren't too startling to the eye.

Joanna found an unemployed director, which wasn't hard; he came to the island in late August. His name was Peter Fulton. Joanna quizzed him at length about possible connections to Samuel Fulton, but it appeared all the two men had in common was their surname. She was relieved; Vince was disappointed, saying it would have made a neat story. It was understood that Peter was to receive full directorial credit, even though a lot of the actual work was to be done by Joanna.

Mo and Masters had scripts ready by the time Fulton joined them. There were a half dozen of Joanna's historical/educational presentations, plus an elaborate horror piece designed to inaugurate the new theater for its opening in October. Vince was delighted with it. He could tie it to the legends of actual hauntings at the Imperial. Of course, he'd have to avoid any mention of the recent deaths there, but that was duck soup for a good publicist like him. After October, Jo planned a season of "contemporary classics"—Albee, Tennessee Williams, Eugene O'Neill.

There were accidents during construction. Electrocutions, an accidental decapitation, other less lethal occurrences. Joanna wondered if they were due to the fact that she was using a not-quite-kosher construction firm. Were they cutting dangerous corners? But everything went well, for the most part.

Peter Fulton hit on the idea of getting a new organ for the theater; when there were no plays on, they could screen classic silent movies there, with live organ accompaniment. It was ordered, manufactured on a rush order, and installed quickly.

The crews all worked double shifts. It was expensive but there was more than enough grant money. By August 30, the chandelier was hauled into place; Joanna and her cast and staff watched. The new auditorium was illuminated brilliantly, and when the chandelier itself was lit, the effect was perfectly magnificent. They had champagne under it. "Here's to the Imperial Theater," Joanna toasted, "and to long, happy professional lives for all of us."

SEVEN
Bourbon, 1769

Among the ideas Mo worked on was one that meant a great deal to him. He had synthesized all his research into the history of Bourbon Island and drafted a scenario. But he was uncertain what to do with it; it wasn't quite history and it wasn't quite horror.

Tonya found the outline among the papers on his desk and asked him about it. "What's this *Bourbon, 1769* thing?"

He explained.

"Mo, this is good. This is downright fascinating. Why aren't you drafting it as a play?"

"I'm afraid to show it to Jo. It's too . . ." He spread his hands apart in a gesture of helplessness. "I'm afraid what she'd say—what she'd think."

"Is it the sex?"

He shook his head.

"Too 'racially charged'?"

"I don't think so. She's not like that."

"Then . . . ?"

"I think it might be too close to the bone for her. It touches all the horrible things that have happened here."

"That's all the more reason to do it."

He seemed not to understand her point.

"Look, why don't you show this to Vince? I think he'll see the potential. He's been planting stories all around the region about the history of Bourbon Island and the Imperial Opera House. This is material for another one."

"I don't think I could do that. If Joanna—"

"And if he can get word out that we're doing a play about a really fascinating piece of our own history..."

"Jo won't like it."

"She listens to Vince. This will be good for business. It's that simple. And I've seen the accounts. Everything we can do to get people interested in this place will help."

"Things are that bad?"

"Let's just say I'm hoping none of the state agencies gets a look at the books anytime soon." She took the manuscript and headed toward the door. "I'm going to show this to Vince."

"Tonya, don't. I don't want Jo to think I'm—"

"When Vince gets on board, she'll come around."

And Vince did love it. "This is great. It brings so much together, all the local legends, the fact the town was deserted, all of it. And it combines ghosts and horror with history, so it covers both our areas of drama. We've got to do this."

Tonya was smug but tried to hide it. "I think it ought to be the opening night feature."

Vince liked that idea, too. He promised to approach Jo about it. But before he could get to Joanna, Mo took the manuscript back for a moment and wrote at the top, DEDICATED TO THE MEMORY OF MARK BARRY.

Joanna read it. She had her doubts. Something in the story disturbed her, and she couldn't, or wouldn't, say what. She questioned Mo about it. "How much of this is true? How much did you find in archives, and how much is your own imagination?"

He told her it was a mix; he wasn't sure he could give her exact percentages.

"If we do this as history, we'll have every historian in the region coming after us for supposedly using too much license.

Stage Fright

If we present it as a horror piece, we'll get slammed for being exploitative and sensationalistic. Opening up wounds."

Mo told her, rather petulantly, that he resented the implication he'd exploit the region's racial history. He insisted his story was accurate, at least broadly, though he admitted using some poetic license. The core of the narrative, though, he stood by.

When Vince began pressing her as well, insisting they'd never get better publicity, she finally caved. The *Bourbon, 1769* was to be their premiere presentation. But Joanna insisted that Mo was on his own crafting it into a usable script. She wouldn't have a thing to do with it. Peter Fulton agreed to work on it with him, and he took the outline back to his cabin to read. It sat on his nightstand till he was ready for bed. He had not been at Bourbon Island for most of the awful occurrences, and he'd only heard about them—some of them—second hand. Nonetheless, the scenario gave him troubled sleep.

It did not help the situation when he asked Mo, just before retiring, how much of the story was based on authenticated historical sources. Mo looked shamefaced and admitted to him, "A lot of it came to me in dreams."

> There were more and more signs and rumors [read Mo's proposal] that the Indian tribes were planning to make trouble for the people of Bourbon, and that they were after the riches that were amassing on the island; and the people were growing more and more tense. Fort Pitt was the major military post in the region, but it was sufficiently distant that the garrison there could not really provide much help. The fact that Bourbon Island sat in the center of a great river provided some protection, but not much; the Indians had their canoes, after all.
>
> But unlike most of the people who lived on or near Bourbon Island, Helen Fulton was not preoccupied with that. She was trapped in an unhappy marriage to a brutal husband. And besides, there was the plan to focus on.
>
> Helen had been attracted, more and more strongly, to some of the men her husband, Hector, trafficked in. Tall,

muscular men, with beautiful dark skin and strange music in their language. She knew that the Bible condemned them; they were the descendants of Ham, Noah's evil son. But when, now and then, she found occasion to touch one of them, it gave her such a thrill. They were good men; they had to be. As for their women . . .

Hector was too preoccupied to notice. To him, they were products, commodities, and very lucrative ones. And he was contending with two conflicting trends in the marketplace.

Some of his customers were pleased that his slave warehouse was sufficiently distant from their day-to-day lives that they did not have to see it or know what took place inside the warehouse walls. Others were pressing him to move his operation to a site closer to the business center that was growing in a town that was already coming to be known as Pitt's Borough and even, when people spoke in haste, Pittsburgh.

Helen had taken more than one of the slave men as lovers. Furtively, quietly, away from the notice of her husband and his underlings. She would find a pretext—helping her find roots or wildflowers; doing laundry when her maid was conveniently "ill." There was no concern that they would bolt; the surrounding land was wilderness, for the most part, and runaways were drawn and quartered in front of all the others. And when she had the men alone, she would find reasons to touch them, "by accident," until they became accustomed to it. And then . . .

They never seemed to know what to make of her—most of them hardly spoke a word of English, they could only speak some uncivilized African tongue—but they understood what she wanted, and they were young men raging with hormones. Despite the language barrier, their bodies spoke eloquently, when they made love to her.

And then one day the mulatto freedwoman Portia, who had learned English and spoke it eloquently, came to her and started talking to her about the male slaves and their wives or girlfriends and their children. Helen was incapable of having children of her own. Portia got her thinking about them. Helen at first refused to acknowledge the slave children were quite human. But in time, watching the little girls and boys play . . .

Finally, after months of conversation, Portia asked her to help the slaves escape and take revenge on their masters, the businessmen who traded them like cows and swine.

"But . . . but Hector Fulton is my husband. I daren't turn against him."

"You will have new husbands," Portia told her, "a great many of them, beautiful men with better, harder bodies than your present one. I am a witch. I can make it happen. I will share my power with you."

Helen resisted the suggestion, but she also resisted the temptation to reveal to her husband that there was a rebellion brewing. And she kept talking to Portia, who never failed to raise the suggestion again. And again, and again.

She promised Helen lovers. She told her she would become the mother to a great new nation. And she promised her revenge. "I know what your husband the slave trader does to you in the night. I know the whips and the knives. You can free yourself. You can make him your slave."

Portia was a witch, and all the slaves knew it. She was a freedwoman who lived in the town of Bourbon, on the Pennsylvania shore, among all the others who earned their livings at or around the island. There were the men who actually operated Hector Fulton's slave warehouse and ran the auctions. There were the ones who imported provisions for feeding and clothing the slaves. There was even a good Christian minister with a church, who had a profitable sideline selling chains and shackles. And they all had wives and children. The town was growing and prospering. Homes were being built in Ohio and Virginia [note: West Virginia was still part of Virginia at this time], and there were profitable ferry boats—owned by Hector Fulton. There were even plans to build a wooden bridge from the shore to the island, though Hector was doing everything he could to quash them.

No one was quite certain where Pennsylvania ended and Ohio and Virginia began, but Bourbon was a happy, productive American community. As for the slaves, what did they count? Did the greengrocer concern himself with the hopes and dreams of his vegetables, or the dry-goods merchant with the welfare of his bolts of cloth?

Finally, inevitably, it happened. Helen Fulton fell completely out of love with the husband who beat her and who was so preoccupied with the slaving business, and she fell *in* love with one of his slaves.

His name was Oginga, and he could speak not one word of English, but when she visited him at night, by the dark of the moon, he made her feel loved. He had been at the warehouse three months; he was reputed to have a rebellious nature, so he had not sold. Hector was torn between lowering the asking price for him or waiting till his spirit was broken and asking for even more.

Helen introduced Portia to Oginga. "Maybe you can understand his language. I've been trying to teach him English, and he's learned a few words, but . . ."

Portia tried, with some success. "The language of my grandparents," she told Helen, "is somewhat like the tongue he speaks. He says that you are the finest woman he has met since he was taken from his home. I do not know how much of a compliment that is."

Through Portia, Helen and Oginga were able to talk. And gradually, bit by bit, they learned each other's language and spoke when they were alone together. Oginga had been a shaman in his African home. His status now, as a manual laborer, was especially demeaning for him. And he was jealous of Portia's freedom—and the fact that she had access to herbs and roots that he needed for his own magical craft but could not get.

Eventually, he even began to resent Helen. To love a woman so far above him only sharpened his pain in servitude. But love her he did; and in time, she and Portia persuaded him to follow their lead and escape.

And so the plot was hatched.

Quietly, furtively, Oginga organized the other slaves. Portia promised them the protection of her magic. He would have preferred to prepare the spells himself, but there was no choice. He warned Portia sternly not to usurp his place, the man's place, as leader of the revolt.

On a hot summer night Helen stole her husband's keys. She left them at a prearranged place in the warehouse; and Oginga found them and freed the others, one by one. And, one by one, they slaughtered their jailors.

One of the slave women was in childbirth. Hector Fulton, hearing her cry out, went to investigate. And when he realized what was happening, he quickly summoned his remaining men. They surrounded the warehouse. And they set torches to it. The slaves were burned alive. Portia's magic had failed them.

With his dying breath, Oginga cursed Hector Fulton, damning him and his descendants always to inflict pain, as Hector did himself. He cursed the town, or rather, towns, of Bourbon. And he cursed Portia and Helen, the women who had led him to his death—that they would live in the wilderness and never know human kindness or warmth, except fleetingly, enough to tempt but never satisfy.

Portia, shattered by her own failure, took pity on Helen and gave her the gift of long life. She would live alone, or sometimes only with Portia herself, but she would live.

Vince asked Mo why the towns had never come to life, not even two and half centuries later.

Mo said he wasn't certain. "There was the beginning of a rebirth when Samuel Fulton built the Imperial here. A few houses sprang up, even a general store. But when the theater died, in the late thirties, so did they. I don't think anyone knew any of the history, then, but the notion that the region is cursed did survive."

"That's just folklore, Mo."

"Where is the line between folklore and history, then?"

But Vince loved the scenario. He and Mo kept working on Joanna, just to be certain she wouldn't change her mind about it.

It seemed that everything was set for the Bourbon pageant to be the premiere presentation at the Imperial. Then Joanna, after a long sleepless night, abruptly announced they would not be doing it after all. She would not explain her decision, but she spent long hours alone in her office at the top of the theater each night.

All she would say is, "The dead wouldn't like it."

Mo was disappointed quite bitterly. He spent the short summer nights sleeping in Tonya's arms and trying to make sense of it all.

EIGHT

September broke unnaturally hot. Days were blistering; the river dropped six feet below its usual level. In a way, that was helpful. It made easier work for the construction crews erecting the two bridges. By the second week of the month they were both in place.

As the opening approached, Joanna found herself more and more preoccupied with administrative duties; she relied increasingly on Peter Fulton to stage the various plays.

She changed her mind about *Bourbon, 1769*. A patriotic salute to the history of the tri-state region was to be the premiere attraction, followed closely by a set of historical plays by day and fright shows at night. Joanna had one argument after another with Mo when he pressed for *Bourbon, 1769* to be their premiere presentation.

"We need to do histories that will attract school groups, Mo. Safe, familiar stuff."

"But all those safe stories are phony. This region has a past as dark as any in the country."

"This country's past is glorious, not dark." She said it in an overemphatic tone that struck him as funny.

"Do you have any idea what an offensive statement that is? Not to mention false?"

She sighed. "Maybe we can do some of that kind of thing in time. But for now, we have to be audience friendly. This is a business. Surely you can understand that."

"So what do you want these plays to be?"

"You know all the bromides and the attitudes. This is the greatest country in the world, and always has been, and always will be. All of our presidents were good men, most were great, and all of them grew in office. That kind of thing. That's what people want to be told."

"You don't think people want the truth?"

"Mo, this is a business." She said it with surprising force.

"Even a business can be honest, Joanna."

"This is Pittsburgh. Be serious."

But she finally wore him down, and he stopped raising the subject. He dutifully gave her a series of short, "uplifting" scripts about the Revolutionary War, the Civil War, President George Washington's visits to the region, friendly relations between the Indians and the white settlers, and a half dozen more. She vetted them all, and they were all perfectly safe for schoolchildren whose parents and educators wanted to shield them from unpleasant truths.

As for the horror stories, John James Masters turned out three first-rate scripts based on local legends. There was—supposedly—a man who lived in the hills south of Pittsburgh who had been struck by lightning. It turned him green, and he moved about only by night and victimized anyone he came upon who was traveling alone. Children were a specialty of his. There was supposedly a ghost living in Panther Hollow, under a bridge on the campus of West Penn University. And there was supposedly a mad old man living along the banks of the Ohio just past Pittsburgh who had escaped from Western Penitentiary after surviving the electric chair. Like the other two figures, he preyed on the unsuspecting, mostly kids.

Joanna especially liked the one about the West Penn ghost. "Why haven't I ever heard of this?"

Mo shrugged. "I thought everyone on campus had. Frats go on drunken binges looking for him."

"Do frats need an excuse for drunken binges?"

"Evidently."

"Did one of them invent this ghost as a pretext for them?"

He looked doubtful. "Most of the fratboys I know don't have that much imagination."

"It would only take one."

"Even that pushes my credulity."

Peter Fulton liked the scripts despite the obvious similarities. He worked with his resident design team to make them seem as unalike as possible. And his cast tore into their roles with relish. He hit on the idea of having the "Green Man" played by a woman, and Megan Cantwell got the part. She said it was more fun than any role she'd ever played.

Construction at the island had proceeded smoothly. There had been a few more accidents, and a few of those were especially awful, but Harp Construction seemed able to keep the victims and their families happy.

The interior of the Imperial had been restored quite magnificently by a design firm Vince had found. All the original architectural detail was restored or re-created, down to shimmering gold leaf on the proscenium and a wonderfully restored frieze of mythical monsters above it. The new organ had been tested rigorously, and it played beautifully. When all the lights were turned on for the first time, including the lights of the great chandelier, the effect was perfectly dazzling.

The one really problematic occurrence was the fact that those subterranean rumbles continued. They didn't happen often, but when they did, they were the most alarming things. Even people who had heard them many times before would stop, freeze, then sometimes panic. What might be causing them was still unknown. Two different engineering firms were brought in, and the best guess either of them came up with was the same one everyone had heard before, that there were deep, abandoned coal mines under the island, and they were subsiding.

"They're deep enough," one engineer assured Joanna, "that they shouldn't cause any damage on the surface. And sooner or later they'll stop, once everything has settled."

"Is there anything we can do to make it sooner?"

He spread his hands to express helplessness. "Sorry."

Peter Fulton was especially unnerved when the rumblings happened. "What do we do if the place starts quaking during a performance?"

Joanna was in no mood to discuss it. "You're the director. Direct it to stay quiet."

"I'm having trouble enough with the actors you hired. And the damned stage crew—they seem to be drunk or stoned half the time. Joanna, I'm serious."

"So am I." She glared at him, then caught herself and held her annoyance in. "Look, there's not really much we can do. We'll just have to hope nothing happens."

"In an earthquake." He didn't try to hide his skepticism.

"These are not earthquakes. This is mine subsidence, pure and simple."

"What's pure about it?"

She glared. "Look, Peter, everyone says they'll pass in time. Probably soon. There's nothing we can do about it."

"Is there anything in the archives about this kind of thing happening in the old days?"

It came as a new thought to her, and an unfortunate one. "No."

"Then how are we supposed to take it in stride?"

"Are you telling me you want out? Are directing jobs that pay this well so easy to come by?"

That was her clincher, the way she won every disagreement with anyone on the staff. And, glumly, they had to admit she was right. Whatever else they may have thought about her, the company and the island, Joanna had undeniably done a brilliant job of putting everything together. Some of them who knew her mother's reputation knew where Jo got her producing skill. But they all admired her for it, frustrating as it might be for them at times.

Meantime, there was another problem brewing, one so unlikely no one had anticipated it, not even Marvin, who should have. Vince was the one who hit on it. In a stack of responses to his press releases, he found a letter from the government of East Liverpool, Ohio.

"Jo, you better take a look at this."

"What is it?"

Instead of explaining, he held the letter out to her. She read it and laughed. "This is a joke, right?"

"Does it look like one?"

"It reads like one."

"The city of East Liverpool has decided we're in their jurisdiction, and they want us to collect an eight percent amusement tax on every ticket we sell." He hesitated. "Are we in their jurisdiction?"

"They didn't think so when we needed police, water, power, sewage and all the other services they should provide."

"So . . . ?"

"Fax it to Marvin in New York. He'll deal with it from there."

"Fine."

But it wasn't fine. The next day similar notices arrived from Weirton, West Virginia, and Beaver County, Pennsylvania. The next day brought four more, two of them from places no one but Marvin had even heard of before. He dutifully informed them all that he had correspondence on their letterhead expressly denying that Bourbon Island was theirs, and that if they expected the corporation to pay taxes, they'd have to start providing municipal services forthwith. That should have ended the controversy, but several of the places promised legal action. Since the island obviously couldn't belong to all of them, Marvin suggested letting them fight it out among themselves; then he'd only have to fight the winner.

"Divide and conquer," he told Joanna gleefully. "It's one of the oldest strategies in the book. Then, if the winner persists, we countersue, demanding reimbursement for all the money we spent on facilities and amenities they should have provided to us."

"That could take years."

"At least five, if we work it right. With luck, even more."

"Marvin, will you marry me?"

"Good God, no. You're in theater."

The design firm handling all the details of the restoration had finished their work nearly two weeks ahead of schedule. Everyone agreed they'd done a wonderful job, and the old theater gleamed like a new palace. John James Masters was positively floored by it. "The Taj Mahal can't have been more beautiful. Ugly—downright hideous, in fact—but beautiful. I love working here."

The last job the crew had was to polish and point all the details on the architectural ornaments about the Imperial's façade. One afternoon one of their workmen was tending to the sphinx. Suddenly he screamed, pulled away from it and nearly lost his balance. If one of his coworkers hadn't been nearby to steady him, he would have fallen, probably to his death.

As it was, his only injury was a deep gash in his left forearm; the skin was nearly torn off. Questioned by his foreman, he insisted the sphinx had bitten him. The foreman ordered a drug test, but the man admitted he had been smoking weed. That killed any chance he'd be able to file a claim against either Harp Construction or the theater. He was given first aid, sent home for two weeks with pay, and that was that. No one took his story seriously.

But he continued to insist that the sphinx, somehow, impossible as it sounded, had sunk its teeth into him.

"That's great. But make the kiss more passionate."

Peter Fulton, who continued to claim he was not a descendant of the Fulton who's built the Imperial—and everyone asked him—was working with his cast, preparing one of the historical plays. The French army was occupying the Point at what would soon become Pittsburgh, at the fort they called Duquesne. They had established warm, friendly relations with the Indians who were native to the area. But the British wanted the land. A young French officer named Etienne Montsalvage had fallen in love with an Indian girl. They were making love under a big, full moon. But war was looming; the British were determined to have the land.

Rehearsals had been going well. This was the first time they'd done the scene on the main stage of the Imperial, complete with costumes, sets and lights. None of them had ever played on such an enormous stage before; Vince said it was larger than any of the old movie palaces in downtown Pittsburgh. The tech crew was making adjustments to the sound system, which was elaborate and intricate but could make the least whisper heard in the farthest corner of the balcony.

Jerry Early, an actor with alarmingly red hair, was playing Etienne. A pretty blonde girl named Melinda Stockard wore a black wig and played his girlfriend. They didn't like each other offstage, but they were playing the scene with conviction, and Peter was more than pleased.

Mo and Masters had written a rather tender love scene for them. But when their expressions of affection reached their sweetest, a shot was to ring out, and she was to fall dead. This was not exactly how the French and Indian War had really begun, but it worked onstage, and everyone was happy with it.

Joanna had been particularly pleased with the script. "Yeah, this is great. Just what we need."

Mo was the only one with reservations. "But . . . but this is supposed to be educational. What will the teachers and administrators say when they realize we're feeding their students sentimental hogwash instead of history?"

But Joanna took it in stride. "Are you serious? Have you ever actually *talked* to a high school history teacher? Most of them would have trouble naming all the presidents."

"But, Jo, I'm a historian. This just doesn't feel right to me. I—"

"Look, we can't tell the true story of how the war got started, can we? People would think it was sacrilegious or unpatriotic or whatever. So we cover it up with a love story. It's one of the oldest tricks in the book."

"It is?" He was deadpan.

"Just look at popular culture. Look at the movies. Every important historical event you can think of, from the Civil War to the sinking of the Titanic to the fall of Rome, turns out to be important merely as the backdrop to a love story." Realizing several of her actors were within earshot, she added pointedly, "A straight love story."

"But, Jo—"

"Even the crucifixion of Christ gets the treatment. It's all just a big, splashy pretext for Judah Ben Hur to fall in love. This script is good, and we're going with it."

That was that.

But at the next day's rehearsal, there was something strange in the air. The building seemed to groan. Odd cries came up from the basement—which had been quite cleaned out—and when people went to check, there was nothing. Early in the afternoon, just as everyone was coming back from lunch, the skies turned dark grey and it began to rain.

Despite the distractions, the rehearsal was going well, and Peter was in a good mood. Joanna was off in her office, at the top of the building. She had a little window that let her watch what was happening onstage, but today she was busy going over some revised budgets Tonya had prepared.

Jerry and Melinda did their love scene. For the first time, their kiss seemed authentically passionate. Peter let them go on, not wanting to break the mood.

Suddenly, seemingly from nowhere, another man ambled onto the stage. He crossed swiftly to the two actors, pulled them apart quite violently and began shouting something incoherent. Jerry managed to steady himself, but Melinda fell and hit her head on the edge of a prop bench. The man gesticulated wildly, as if he was trying to give them directions.

In a seat halfway to the back of the house, Mo was going over another script with Masters. When the commotion began, he looked up to see what was happening. And he froze. None of the others could have recognized the man—they had only come to the island in the last few weeks. But Mo knew him. It was Mark Barry.

Mo couldn't move. Mark, or Mark's ghost, or whatever it was he was seeing, was galloping around the stage, knocking down actors, overturning props, tearing sets apart, and attacking everyone who tried to stop him. Mark Barry, who lay sleeping in his grave, had come back to the theater and was, apparently, trying to make it his own again, in a particularly horrible way.

Suddenly Mo found his voice. Loudly he shouted, "Mark!"

Mark, if that's who it was, ignored him and continued on his destructive rampage. Finally the stagehands got their bearing and ran after him, trying to restrain him, but he was too strong. He threw them around as if they were more painted flats or balsa-wood props.

Mo ran toward the stage. "Mark! Mark!"

Then from outside there was an exceptionally bright flash of lightning, so bright it penetrated even to the Imperial's auditorium. Everyone stopped and froze. Had the theater been hit? A moment later there was a deafeningly loud clap of thunder.

The lights went out. The smokers among the cast and crew flicked their lighters on. Then a moment later the lights flickered and came on again. For a moment they were so bright they hurt everyone's eyes; then they dimmed till they were at their usual level.

Everyone looked around. The man who had rampaged was gone.

Mo was halfway up the aisle from where he had been sitting. Peter Fulton crossed to him quickly. "You knew that guy?"

"Yes. No." He was more shaken than anyone else. "I mean, I thought I did. But he can't have been who I thought."

"Who did you think he was?"

Joanna burst into the auditorium. "For Gods sake, what's gong on?" She caught sight of all the damaged scenery and props. "What on earth happened here?"

Mo took her aside and told her what he had seen.

She was plainly skeptical. "Mark? My Mark? Mo, you're seeing things."

"Everyone here saw him, Jo. Get a photo of Mark and show it around. I'll bet every last one of them will tell you it was him."

This, she clearly did not want to do.

"Joanna, there's something wrong with this place. No one knows what it is, no one can put a finger on it, but almost everyone senses it."

"Theater people are superstitious, that's all."

"I'm not theater. I'm history. You know that. And I'm telling you, something is not right here."

"Don't be absurd. Some tramp found his way to the island

and crashed the rehearsal, that's all. It can't have been anything else."

"A tramp with a rowboat. Right."

"It has to have been that."

"Then where is he? How did he manage to disappear?"

Peter had heard the last part of this and joined in, echoing what Mo had been saying.

But Jo wouldn't hear it. "You're all hysterical."

"There's such a thing as hysterical denial, Jo."

"Stop it. Drop this nonsense now. We have a theater to open."

That, it seemed, was that.

Vince was still not living at the island. When he visited, which he did regularly every two or three days, he sensed something strange in the atmosphere. But no one was willing to talk to him about what was wrong.

He had been generating more and more excitement about the impending opening. And his reports to Joanna were more and more optimistic. The afternoon after Mark came back, he met with her in her office.

"We'll be a hit. The *Sun-Telegraph* in Pittsburgh, the *Journal-Record* in Cleveland, every major newspaper in the region will be doing a spread in the week or so before we open. All we need now is a good opening night play." He smiled. "And that's not my department.

"That's all just terrific, Vince. The arts foundation doesn't know what they lost when they let you go."

"Yes, they do. They've been after me to come back."

"You're not leaving us?"

"No, of course not." He laughed. "After the way they dumped me for that kid . . . No way."

"Good."

"Besides, I think what you say all the time is right. This—what we're building here—is the future. It's not hard for me to imagine this growing into a kind of regional arts center. I'd be crazy to leave."

She kissed him, one of those "air kisses" theater people do

all the time. "With someone like you doing our PR, it could happen."

"Aw, shucks, ma'am, it ain't nothin'." They both had a chuckle, then he pulled a sheet of paper out of his pocket. "The VIP list for opening night. Two of the three governors are coming. The other one's going to be in Washington, kissing the president's ass, so he's sending his lieutenant."

"Fantastic! That alone will bring people out."

He nodded happily. "And four senators, nine congressmen, er, congresspersons, a whole slew of bigwigs from the arts mafia in the bigger cities, corporate nabobs. . . ." Vince put on the widest grin she'd ever seen on him. "We're made."

"And how! Vince, you've done such a fantastic job."

"Then how about a raise?"

It hit her why he had mentioned that the foundation wanted him back. And she wasn't happy about it; money was tight enough. Still, if he really was turning the Imperial into a regional showplace for her . . . "I can't deal with it now. Let's talk right after the opening, okay?"

He shrugged. "Strike while the iron's hot, Jo."

"It won't be that hot till after the opening."

Rehearsals continued well. Tickets for the horror plays were selling especially well; they were booked almost completely through the end of October. So Masters and Mo were working on more horror scripts. They had, after a tentative beginning, clicked together, and working on this stuff was a welcome break from history for Mo.

Masters, suddenly, seemed to be getting into the spirit of the Imperial, or at least into the spirit of its probable success. "I never knew they pay playwrights a percentage off the top of the gross. If you could see all the hitchy-switchy bookkeeping bullshit publishers use before they pay book authors . . ."

"You're kidding. I always figured people went into publishing because they love books and writers."

Masters laughed at him. "Don't be naïve, Mo. I mentioned to one of my editors that playwrights get paid off the top, and I thought she was going to have a heart attack."

So Masters, the last of the major participants in the Bourbon Island Arts & Development Corporation's theater project, finally came on board wholeheartedly and enthusiastically.

"I know a lot more local myths and legends we can use, if this stuff takes off."

Mo was fascinated. "I can't say I've ever paid much attention to that kind of . . . history."

"A couple of years ago a steel mill up in the Mon Valley collapsed. People say it was haunted. And there was a church in a little town called Mill Creek, up north of here."

"Everyplace has its local ghost stories, I guess."

"But these . . . I think they may be true."

"Be serious, John."

"I am. Everything's kept hidden. Do you think it's an accident Jo won't let us write about the island's real past? About the slaving? The whips, the lynchings, the burnings at the stake?"

Mo wasn't buying it. "I talked to her about that. It's just a matter of money, John. That stuff would never attract a wide audience."

He shrugged. "Maybe you're right. But why do they come for horror, then? What kind of horror fantasy could we invent that would be half as horrific as all that?"

Mo didn't want to think about it. He tried to change the subject.

But Masters was on a roll. "Horror writers—fantasists—and their readers are the only ones who have a serious understanding of reality. Other people think we all just have morbid imaginations. But it's not that. We're the ones who see humanity clearly, that's all."

It wasn't a thought Mo wanted to deal with. "Stop it, John."

"You know the old phrase: 'imaginary gardens with real toads in them.'"

"Yeah. Right."

"Mo . . . what do you think is going on *here*?"

It was too much for him to deal with. Mo said he needed a break and walked away. When Masters tried to raise the subject again, he ducked it.

* * *

Rehearsal. Horror. The play about the Green Man preying on children.

A child is found dead, mutilated. Parents, police, clergy gather round.

One woman in the crowd cries hysterically.

Joanna sat in the audience, watching. Peter was doing a wonderful job with it. It kept moving, the action was clear, the actors were all into their characters. This was the first time she'd watched the piece. If the late scenes, when the monstrous Green Man appeared, were as effective as these early ones, they'd really have something.

Then, in the crowd of actors, she thought she glimpsed ... no, it couldn't be. She had only had a glimpse, but ...

Yes.

It was Annie Moore. Armless. Standing there among the actors. Why did no one but Jo notice? Why didn't the rest of them ... ?

Then she saw a second man in the crowd, someone she was certain she had never hired for the company. He was a black man, tall, lean, muscular, wearing nothing but dirty cutoff shorts and battered sandals. He followed Annie as she moved through the onstage crowd.

Melinda Stockard was in the crowd, playing the bereaved mother of the child who'd been found dead. As Annie reached her, she looked back over her shoulder at the black man who was following her every step. She smiled at him, then nodded at Melinda.

From seemingly nowhere, he produced a machete. Raised it high over his head. No one else onstage seemed to notice this at all. Then he struck, hacking Melinda's right arm off. She screamed in horror as she fell to the floor and blood cascaded from the stump.

He raised his machete a second time and sliced off her left arm.

Melinda passed out. Everyone else seemed to go into a panic, running about, screaming; no one seemed to have any idea what to do. Peter rushed to the stage and tried to give orders, to bring calm, to get someone to help Melinda. In the midst of it all, Annie and the black man with the machete vanished.

Joanna managed to keep reasonably calm. She pulled out her cell phone and dialed 911. After a moment of the usual bickering about jurisdiction, she managed to persuade the Beaver County EMS unit to come as fast as possible. "Yes, the bridge is open. Yes, we're in your county. I told you."

When she was off the phone, she rushed onto the stage. One of the actors said he had had some first aid training. Peter and another of the actors took off their belts and made tourniquets for Melinda's . . . for where her arms had been. Most of the women had retreated to the wings or left the theater completely. Melinda herself was still unconscious, breathing heavily. Despite the tourniquets, she was still losing blood.

Then she stopped breathing. Her eyes were closed. Everyone became eerily still. One by one, they looked to Joanna.

"Did anyone try to stop them?" She spoke softly. "Or see where they went?"

They all looked at one another, puzzled. Peter asked, "Who?"

"The armless girl and the black guy with the chopper."

"What are you talking about, Jo?"

"Annie Moore, the actress who died here last summer. She was here."

They all looked at one another, baffled and slightly alarmed. Was the artistic director losing it, on top of everything else? A few of them said things like, "There was no one like that here," or, "You're crazy—we didn't see anyone like that." Most of them kept quiet, though.

Sensing their reaction, and not liking what it implied, Jo raised her voice. "They were here. Someone hacked her arms off. Can't you see?"

Peter said forcefully, "There was no one onstage but the cast, Jo. I'd have seen."

"They were here, dammit! We have to find them."

No one moved or responded.

Finally Jerry Early spoke up and said, "If Jo said she saw them, then she saw them. The rest of us were too wrapped up in what we were doing, that's all."

No one seemed to find this very convincing, but the guys

Stage Fright 243

and a few of the women agreed to spread out and do a quick search.

As usual, it took the police and the EMS crews forever to reach the island. They questioned everyone, and they were clearly suspicious of Jo's story.

"Look," she argued, "her arms were hacked off. Do you think that just happened by itself?"

It made no sense at all, but there was no sane explanation. There was no way anyone closer than Joanna could have missed seeing the alleged killer.

They agreed to file their report with her story included, and there would be detectives on site soon enough, but the actress's death left them completely baffled. Like everyone else. Everyone but Jo. But how could she explain? How could anyone rational believe her?

The horror of Melinda's seemingly spontaneous disintegration and death took its toll on the company quickly and, it seemed, permanently. Morale dropped, and it seemed nothing could remedy it. Jo and Tonya kept making announcements about how terrific advance sales were. "We're a hit!" Vince kept planting more and more stories about the theater and its talented company. He and Marvin had done their usual good work and kept Melinda's death out of the news; and Marvin had intimidated her family into taking a cash settlement in return for an agreement not to make trouble. But there was something wrong. Everyone knew it; no one understood what it was though, and that was the worst part of all.

Somehow, someone brought drugs to Bourbon Island. More and more of the cast smoked, snorted, or what have you, and it began to show in their work. Peter was less and less happy.

Joanna felt the need to give the company a pep talk. She told them they were the future of theater, a lively, vital group of people making art where it was accessible to everyone. "We're doing important work here. And good work. As far as I'm concerned, we're the best theater company in the world."

Everyone bought it, at least superficially. They were actors, with actors' egos, so hearing how important they were naturally played well. But they kept doing drugs, more and more of them. And at night, when they paired off—or tripled off, or quadrupled, or whatever—and went to one another's rooms, the sounds they made were not sounds of pleasure. One by one, more and more completely, they became absorbed in the concept of pain as erotic, as Joanna had with Mark. There were injuries, unintended, to be sure, but some of them serious nonetheless.

Jo realized she had more problems than just the administrative ones that had been taking so much of her time. She began to pay more attention to her actors and staff, in the most personal way she could manage.

But at night, when she was alone in her office, Samuel Fulton would come and tell her that everything was going smoothly, this kind of conflict was inevitable in a new company, actors are all fools, and on and on. Then he would produce their plaything for that night, sometimes a boy, more usually a girl, and they would whip and torture her till the long-dead impresario and the child victim vanished in the morning light.

"Jo, we're leaving." Peter, Mo and Tonya stood in a line before her desk. "We can't do these phony 'history' plays. They're wrong."

Their threat of defection hit her out of nowhere; she had actually had no idea they were so discontented. "You have contracts."

"Sue us."

"But—but—" She leaned back in her chair and sighed. "What do you want, then?"

Mo spoke up. "These plays . . . they aren't real. They don't feel right to us. To any of us, not even the cast."

"They'll sell."

"That's not the point," Peter said. "We don't believe in them."

"You don't have to believe in them to do them, do you? Aren't you professionals?"

"So many bad things have happened here, Jo." Mo took a step toward her desk. "We need to do what feels right to us."

She had a feeling she knew what was coming, but she asked anyway. "So what do you want to do?"

"*Bourbon, 1769.*" They said it almost in unison. Tonya repeated it, with emphasis. "We've been rehearsing it when you're not around."

Quietly, Jo told them, "No."

"Then we're leaving. I think you'll find half the crew and cast will come with us. We want to do something true."

That would be the end of her company. The ignominious end of her producing career. Her mother would laugh. Realizing she was in a corner, with no other option, she said, "All right. I'll have Vince change the PR for the opening night's play."

Three days to opening.

The cast was to perform *Bourbon, 1769* for a select, invited audience. It was the only chance the company had to preview their work for a group who might give them positive, useful feedback. Most of the theater faculty from West Penn were there, along with a good many undergraduates. The cast and staff who lived in the area had invited their families.

There was a delay starting. The ropes that opened and closed the curtain were stuck. A stagehand climbed up to the top of the theater, and it took him nearly twenty minutes to get them completely untangled. They had worked smoothly till then; no one could guess why they had suddenly become twisted.

Then the play started. It began with a slave auction. Jerry Early, in heavy makeup, portrayed Hector Fulton. He stood on a small podium as, one after another, shackled slaves were hustled before him and his white patrons. At one side of the stage stood his wife Helen, watching it all but not taking part. But she responded to the bodies of the male slaves, and her interest was clear to the audience.

It was a large company. Jo had hired nearly thirty actors; twelve of them were African American. It would create an imbalance in some of the later productions, maybe, but it was what this show needed. And such a large black presence was one more sign that this was "the theater of the future," at least in her mind. She had been somewhat concerned about how the male actors would feel about playing slaves, especially in a play so honest about the past. But they were professionals; this was just a "role," nothing more. Most of them seemed not to give it a second thought.

But something odd began to happen with the audience. Professor Swartz, Jo's old advisor, was the first to see something strange onstage. The man playing Hector Fulton was her grandfather, who had died more than thirty years before. She watched the actor. He was wearing heavy makeup, but it was not just a facial resemblance. There was something in the way he moved, in his posture, in his body language. When, in a later scene, he whipped one of his slaves, she even recognized the stiffness of an arthritic shoulder.

This was not possible. He was dead, he had been dead for a long time. It was a coincidence, no more. But it left her alarmed. Halfway through the performance, she slid out of her seat to the floor, limbs flailing, frothing at the mouth. The professor next to her shouted out that there was a medical emergency, and the performance was interrupted. He pushed his wallet between her teeth, and two others helped hold her down till the seizure passed. Then they carried her out to the lobby and called 911.

Joanna followed them. "I never knew she was an epileptic."

The men looked at one another blankly. "She isn't, as far as anyone knows."

The house lights went down again and the show continued.

A young graduate student in theater design saw his mother onstage, who had died in a car accident.

An African American acting student saw his great-grandfather, who he knew only from old family photos, and who had died in a lynching in South Carolina.

More and more of the audience was disturbed, deeply troubled by something they were seeing onstage. The tortures they saw were real, the cries of the victims too convincing to be acting. None of it was possible; they all told themselves it had to be coincidence and nothing more. But more and more of them were deeply unsettled by *Bourbon, 1769*.

Stage Fright   247

When the Imperial ghosts began to mingle with the actors onstage, it became even worse. Staged beatings and tortures became frighteningly convincing. Blood flowed. Limbs were twisted and burned. Eyes were gouged out of living skulls. The actors were unaware of all this, or simply oblivious to it. But the audience saw it and reacted with terror and revulsion. Two specialists in stage effects gaped at one another; what they were seeing was more real than any special effects they'd ever devised.

Joanna and Peter sat in the last row of the theater, trying to gauge the reaction. Like their cast, they did not see all the horrors happening on the Imperial stage. And they took the reaction, as it spread through the crowd, as a sign they had done their job effectively and that their play was moving people.

Afterward, at a little reception Jo had planned in the lobby with snacks and drinks, she chatted up various members of the department about what they had seen. One told her about thinking he saw a long-dead parent and finding it unsettling. It was, she told herself, an isolated incident, not a reliable indicator of the show's merit. Another talked about a history, in her Southern family, of taking part in lynchings. "I simply can't see a play like this objectively. I'm sorry." Joanna told herself it was another isolated coincidence.

It took almost an hour for the medics to arrive for Professor Swartz. By the time they arrived, she was barely breathing. But as they took her away, they told Jo they thought she'd be all right.

"We—we're not liable for what happened, are we?"

"How could you be liable for a seizure? I'm no lawyer, lady, but—"

She made a note to call Marvin. If anyone would sue, it would be Swartz.

Then later, after everyone had left, she compared notes with Peter. He had sounded out the people he knew for their reactions, and not one of them had been able to see the production objectively. "They all seem to have seen things we didn't intend. Some of them even saw things that clearly weren't there."

Jo was sanguine. "Theater people. People from my department. They probably came here hoping we'd fail."

"For them, we did. Jo, what kind of show have we made?"

"A good one, Peter. You and I both saw it, too. We know it was good."

"But—"

"Besides, it's too late for any major revisions. We open too soon for that."

"Joanna, what if the public reacts the way our audience tonight did?"

"They won't." She stared at him, as if she was daring him to press the point. "They won't. These were theater people. Theater people are all crazy. You ought to know that."

OPENING NIGHT

Vince had done a good, thorough job. Ticket sales had been brisk and, with all the VIPs attending, opening night at the Imperial was shaping up to be a genuine event. News crews wanted to cover it, and he worked with their people to provide B-roll for their broadcasts. But even with all this interest, the theater hadn't quite sold out. There were 1,200 seats in the place, only about three-fourths of them filled. He papered the media and arts organizations with comps, to create the impression the place was booked solid.

There was a dress rehearsal that morning. Vince had invited a few news operations, and their cameramen were in the audience, shooting the action from various angles. Every last one of them had showed; press coverage would be good, and thorough enough to generate a lot of interest.

Jo and Peter watched the reporters carefully, trying to judge their reactions to the dress rehearsal. But they were professionals, doing a job. They were focused on getting their footage, not on the play.

After the run-through, Peter gave his cast a quick, final round of notes for their performance that evening. Then he told them to spend the afternoon relaxing. Their call was for six P.M.

Jerry Early was the first of them to leave. He needed to

Stage Fright

blow off steam. As a matter of fact, he was horny. Really horny. None of the women in the company seemed to like him much, and they were all "spoken for" anyway. But there had been talk of some local whore or other. What was her name? Helen? Something like that. He decided he needed to find her and . . . relax.

And son of a bitch, there she was, waving to him from the West Virginia shore. She was older and a bit plumper than he'd have liked, but she had what he wanted. And word was, she worked cheap.

She waited for him at the eastern end of the West Virginia bridge. Now that he saw her close-to, she definitely wasn't what he'd have chosen. Too old, too fat, too plain. But she was there. She smiled a whore's smile at him.

"Hi. I'm Helen."

"I'm Jack." An actor's lie.

"You want a good time?"

He nodded. "You have a place around here?"

"There." She pointed. "Those bushes will hide us."

He looked. Outdoor sex had always been a turn-on for him. The bushes were visible from the island; the thought that some of his colleagues might glimpse him doing the deed was even more exciting. "How much?"

"Whatever you want to pay me."

It was getting better and better. He'd get off really cheap. But he had a thought. "There's no poison ivy, is there?"

"Don't be silly." She laughed, and it was more girlish than he'd expected. She was getting prettier by the minute, at least in his mind.

Helen actually took him by the hand and led him, as if he was one of the schoolboys who came to her now and then. She giggled. "You have nice, smooth skin."

"You, too." Hers was rough and unappealing; he was an actor.

"What do you like?"

"Just the basics, I guess."

"Blow job?"

He nodded enthusiastically.

"Rim job?"

It was getting better and better. He might actually leave her more than the ten bucks he had in mind.

They were at the clump of bushes. Not far away was a spot that looked like someone built a fire there all the time. She undid her blouse; her breasts were big, and he liked them that way.

"Guys get killed in the theater, you know." She seemed to find this funny. But Jerry wasn't sure whether she meant in the theater in general or in the Imperial Opera House in particular.

"Yeah, guys get killed. That's Shakespeare for you."

"Not in plays. For real."

"Sure." He laughed and undid his fly. She was nuts, all right.

Just as he was bending down to kick off his shoes, she picked up a large rock and pounded his head with it. He fell, dazed. She raised the rock again and again and pounded his head till it was nothing but bloody mush.

No one on the island had seen him go. They had their own sex to look after, or drugs, or booze, or whatnot. After a bit of activity, most of them slept. Jo and her staff were busy in the theater overseeing all the last minute details—props that needed touch-up painting, spotlights whose bulbs had blown. Among all of them, not one gave Jerry Early a bit of thought.

Not until six o'clock, that is, when the cast was due to report. No one had seen him; no one knew where he was. When it became apparent to Joanna that one of her principals was a no-show, she went on a rampage, shouting at everyone in sight. "Actors! He's probably drunk somewhere, or stoned. Or screwing somebody." For an instant an image of him with Helen flashed into her mind, but she dismissed it.

Peter tried to calm her down. "So his understudy can go on. We'll be fine."

"An understudy! We have to go on with an understudy on opening night! Jesus!" She rounded on him. "Have you even had time to rehearse the understudies?"

"No, Joanna. You know that's never done till after the show opens."

"Jesus fucking Christ, what are we going to do?"

He tried to get her to calm down. "Hector's a big role but

it's not a deep one. As long as the understudy knows his blocking, we'll be fine."

But she wasn't convinced. "I have to go and get dressed to greet the VIPs. Rehearse him as much as you can, will you?"

He had no intention of doing it; there was tech stuff that needed his attention. But he told her he would, and she left, not quite satisfied but at least somewhat placated. Peter made a note to himself: never work for a woman on an island again.

In their little suite at the staff building, Mo and Tonya got dressed. She put on her best gown and some ornate costume jewelry. "I hope nobody notices these are fake."

"This is the theater. Everything's fake." He smiled. "At least you're real where it counts. These actresses . . ."

"Now, don't start comparing me to actresses. I'm unhappy enough about being here."

Joanna had insisted he wear a tux, and he hated the idea. As Tonya tied his necktie for him, he grumbled, "I feel like I'm going to the junior prom."

"You are. Like you said, this is the theater. Nobody around here is grown-up, that I can see."

"You're not being helpful."

"What do you want me to tell you? Go in jeans and sneakers. Go in a jockstrap. You look better that way, anyhow."

"Don't tempt me."

In his bungalow, John James Masters was putting on his rented tux. He overheard their exchange through the thin walls, and he smiled to himself.

Joanna lit a joint and dressed in her office. She had a sleek, simple, beautiful gown in navy blue satin. It had an Art Deco line to it; she had found it in a vintage clothing store. And she had a gorgeous wig, dressed with jewels and feathers. She might have been an heiress in the 1920s, preparing to go out nightclubbing. In front of her mirror, she was able to think of nothing but herself and the way she looked. And, momentarily, of Mark. She missed him, but not too much. Their marriage would never have worked; that was clear to her now, in retrospect. But she did like him, and she did miss him. A bit.

She used the spy hole to look down from her office at the

auditorium. The lights were blazing, and the restored chandelier was perfectly brilliant. Every last detail of the place was perfect, and it all might have been new.

One of the fantastic animals on the proscenium pulled its head free of the masonry—it was quite a struggle, it seemed—and stared directly at her. She blinked. She did a double take. When she looked again, it was back where it should have been. It was nothing but plaster; there was no way it could have moved.

"Fulton?" She spoke to the empty air. "Are you here, Fulton?"

But there was no answer.

She walked to the far end of her office and looked out the window, to the Pennsylvania side of the river. The one detail that had never been attended to was parking. A large open area had been cleared there, so visitors could park and walk the short way across the bridge to the island. It might not be a usual arrangement, but it would give them a magnificent view of the restored Imperial Opera House, which would begin the evening for them in the most impressive way possible.

But the area wasn't paved. When it rained, it tended to turn into one huge mire. So far, the weather was holding; sun, fluffy white clouds, picture perfect. But the forecasters were saying there was a slight chance of rain. Joanna prayed for it to hold off—and she wasn't at all certain who she was praying to.

Vince knocked on her office door. When she opened it, he was in a tux, like the other male administrators, and he smiled an enormous smile at her. "You look magnificent. Like Peggy Guggenheim at one of her receptions."

"Thanks, I guess."

He looked at his watch. "It's nearly seven. Are the rent-a-cops here yet?"

She had arranged for off-duty police officers from several surrounding areas to work at traffic control and security. "No sign of them, but they'll be here. We're paying them more than the going rate, from what you said."

"Yeah, and enough more to make them, er . . . loyal."

"I notice they never come when we need them. And Christ knows we've had enough emergencies."

"They're cops, Jo. We're paying them. They'll be here."

"I hope so. And make sure you tell them about Helen and Portia. The last thing we need is one of those lunatics harassing our patrons."

"Will do. Is there anything else you've thought of?"

She calmed a bit. "No. You've done a terrific job. Thanks."

"Then let's get moving. We have a whole pack of VIPs to greet, and we'll have to do it just right. You know, half condescending, half obsequious."

"Just call me Uriah Heep."

Vince laughed; being theater people, they kissed each other on the cheek. He whispered, "Break a leg," and they headed downstairs. The two of them, he realized, had been the first ones involved in this project. Well, the two of them and Mark, but he didn't count anymore. And Mo, but he was . . . he couldn't think what Mo was. . . .

They checked backstage, and everything seemed to be going smoothly. They stepped out into the hall, and it looked even more magnificent than it ever had. Joanna said softly, "This is the greatest theater in the world."

Vince couldn't resist. "But it's so ugly."

"Even so."

Then the two of them stepped outside and walked arm in arm around the island. The evening was perfect. Bright, clear sky, gentle autumn breeze, birds singing in the bushes, such bushes as there were. Best of all, there was no sign of the two madwomen who seemed to haunt the region.

But just as they were about to go back inside, the ground rumbled, another of those awful shudders from the subsiding coal mines below. It passed quickly. Neither Jo nor Vince said anything, but they were both hoping silently that that would be the last occurrence for the night. Panicked theatergoers would be an absolute disaster.

There was another shudder, not as bad as the first one. The Ohio bridge seemed to vibrate slightly, and some loose debris fell from it into the river. Vince noticed; Jo was looking elsewhere. It couldn't be anything. The bridges were new, and they were solidly built. A slight tremor like that couldn't really do any damage.

At 7:05, there was no sign of the security cops. Joanna's composure, such as it was, was beginning to dissolve again; Vince hoped she wouldn't let it show to the guests.

"Where the hell are they?"

"They'll be here. Relax."

The first attendees began to arrive shortly after that. A busload of them, some damn theater group or other. Jo glared at the bus. "Where are the governors? Where are the arts people?"

"Will you relax? They'll be here."

There was no one to guide them to the parking area. Jo, absurdly in her gown, had to flag down the driver and point him to the lot on the Pennsylvania side.

More and more people came, carloads of them; it was obvious a lot of them had decided to carpool rather than make the journey on their own. Jo left Vince to direct traffic and do the greeting—no one important had shown yet—while she went to the theater and recruited a few members of the stage crew to do the traffic management.

Then she rejoined Vince and they waited at the theater entrance. He noticed that the sky was beginning to cloud up. Looking upward he whispered to himself, "No rain. Please, no rain."

Finally an actual VIP showed up, the lieutenant governor of Pennsylvania. As she saw him approaching, Jo muttered to Vince, "Where's the damn governor? He was supposed to come."

Vince shrugged. "There's nothing we can do about it. Smile and make nice."

Suddenly, around seven-thirty, a huge wave of people showed up, more than the roads and bridges could handle. There was a major traffic jam. Vince noticed several arts bigwigs caught in it and looking very unhappy. Under his breath, he told her, "We should have planned better for this."

"How could we know all 1,200 of them would show up at once?"

"You have to plan for things like that."

"Shit."

Her people did the best they could to get the traffic unsnarled, but it would take forever. Joanna had one of the guys

Stage Fright

run inside to tell everyone backstage that they'd have to hold the curtain till everyone was seated.

No governors came; they all sent flunkies, who called themselves "representatives." The press people, cameras flashing, noticed and seemed to find it funny. Vince told her he'd talk to them and do what he could to get them to play down that angle of the story. There would be more than enough good stuff, wonderful color shots of the theater's interior ablaze with light, pictures of hot, up-and-coming young actors ... more than enough, he hoped.

It was nearly eight forty-five before everyone was inside the theater, properly met and greeted, and the curtain could go up. No one seemed to be enjoying the evening so far. Jo said she could feel what they were all thinking: this play had better be damned good.

Just as she and Vince were about to go inside, Tom Douglas, the guy from the Ohio roads department, appeared out of the crowd and buttonholed them. "There's a problem."

It was the last thing Jo needed to hear. "Another one?"

"I just noticed, one of the supports for our bridge is cracked."

That rumble, earlier. It must have ... "Well, there's nothing we can do about it, Tom."

"It's dangerous. If too much traffic tries to cross it at once, it could ..." He left the thought unfinished. "You'll have to make an announcement."

"What?" She was angry and not holding it inside at all well. "What on earth can I say?"

"Explain the situation. Tell them not to use the bridge."

"Half our audience needs that bridge to get home."

"They'll have to drive north on the Pennsylvania side and cross one of the bridges at Youngstown to get back to Ohio."

"God. I can't."

"You'll have to, Jo. That bridge is damaged. You don't want your opening marred by the kind of accident that could happen, do you?"

"I ..." She was completely lost. This was nothing like the evening she'd anticipated. "I wouldn't know what to say. Can I introduce you, and have you make the announcement? You can explain it way better than I could."

A bit reluctantly, he agreed. As they were going inside, she noticed the sky again. There were more clouds, heavier ones. It was going to rain. She only hoped that it would hold off till after the performance, or at least that it wouldn't be heavy. But just as she had that thought, she saw a flash of lightning in the distance.

At least the atmosphere inside the Imperial seemed to have lightened. People were circulating in the lobby, oohing and aahing at the magnificent design. Everyone was commenting on all the brass, bronze and stone sculptures, so beautifully detailed and wonderfully restored, they seemed almost real. And the great mural, carefully spotlit, seemed almost to shimmer.

Inside the auditorium, things were even better. People were on their feet, socializing, jumping from one group of friends to the next. Nearly everyone was in elegant evening clothes, and most of them seemed in buoyant spirits. The architecture had done its job. The gods and monsters everywhere had a happy effect on the crowd; it was one huge party, with all the unmoving demons presiding like silent hosts.

There was another minor shudder from deep underground, but it was so slight, most people seemed not to notice it. Vince and Jo looked at one another, and he smiled.

"We're going to pull this off," she said, wanting to believe it.

"Get onstage to make your speech."

She glanced at her watch. It was past 8:45. The play would start nearly an hour late. She was glad it was on the short side.

Backstage, everyone was down. The cast were all in their costumes, but there was nothing for them to do. Some of them read newspapers, two of them were playing cards, a few of them were smoking. She hoped it was just tobacco. Then she remembered that they hadn't gotten approval from any of the various fire inspectors in the region—none of them were willing to admit jurisdiction, as usual. She had Vince go around and ask them—politely, no sense pissing them off at this point—to put out whatever they were smoking.

John James Masters was hitting on one of the young actors. He winked at Jo and mouthed the words, "Break a leg."

Mo and Tonya were there, playing chess. Mo kept tugging

at his collar; the fancy dress was plainly making him more and more uncomfortable. Jo gave each of them one of those theater-people hugs. "It's time to begin. Finally."

"This place is rumbling again." Tonya looked like she wanted to be anyplace else in the world.

"We'll be fine, Tonya."

While Tonya was looking at Joanna, Mo palmed one of her pawns. "What are we going to do when the rain turns that parking lot into a swamp?"

"It won't rain hard enough to mire people's cars down."

"It doesn't have to. Do you want to pay the dry cleaning bills for all the good clothes that are going to be ruined over there?"

"You two," she said in an exasperated tone, "are not in the spirit of this thing at all."

"Yes, we are. That's the point."

There was nothing to do but ignore them. She gave a cue to the stage manager. He had the house lights dimmed. Joanna stepped onto the stage, lit by a pink spotlight. From the wings Mo said to Tonya, "Her spotlight's pink. I thought that was for strippers."

"Or whores. Mo, let's get out of here."

"We can't. We have to be at the reception afterwards."

"At this rate, it won't start till two in the morning."

Onstage, Jo waited for her entrance applause to die down. "Good evening, ladies and gentlemen. And welcome to the Imperial Opera House."

She said it grandly, and she had more than enough stage presence for it to get more applause.

The notes she had made for her speech were useless. No sense acknowledging the governors and other Pooh-Bahs who hadn't shown. Instead she ad-libbed a speech about the glorious future of the arts in general and theater in particular—and it was all happening right here in the tristate area! There was more applause, polite but not overly enthusiastic. She saw several people looking at their watches. It was her cue to wrap up quickly.

But she couldn't resist plugging the company and its specific ambitions. "We plan to put the entire pageant of American history on stage here, for the entertainment and education of schoolchildren, by day, and their parents and families by night. The Imperial will welcome everyone, and everyone will find something here."

There was more polite applause. They wanted to see the play and get home. There was no way she was going to let Douglas make his announcement; it could only ruin the evening still further. She concluded with another gracious, "So welcome! And now: *Bourbon, 1769.*"

This time the applause was more enthusiastic. Finally, the audience seemed to be saying to her, we're going to get on with this.

The house lights went out completely and the curtain rose. There had been no changes since the final rehearsal. As it had then, the play opened with a slave auction. A group of slaves, meek and beaten down, stood passively, waiting for their turns on the block. Others, led by Oginga and standing slightly apart from the others, were clearly more restless. There would be trouble. Hector Fulton presided over it all, strong and imperious.

In the tenth row center a young yuppie woman sat with her husband. When she took in the onstage tableau, something felt . . . not right to her. Then she realized what was wrong. The man conducting the slave auction, this Hector Fulton, was . . . no, that couldn't be.

He was her grandfather. An alcoholic brute, he used to beat everyone in the family, and beat them terribly. He nearly killed his wife, her grandmother, once. The other members of the family all suffered that way, too, until they grew old enough or big enough to put a stop to it, or until they simply left.

It was him. Buying and selling slaves, there on the Imperial stage, giving orders to a crew of mean-looking men, and lording it over them all. Her grip on her husband's hand grew tighter, and she shifted uncomfortably in her seat. More and more often, as the action progressed, she had to look away from the stage.

The slave Oginga fought against his chains. An overseer whipped him. Stage blood flowed.

Stage Fright

And in the second row of the balcony a middle-aged, low-level arts administrator saw real blood. A gaping wound opened up in the slave's throat. The whip lashed open a huge cut in his side. The man he was seeing, unlike the actor onstage, fell to the ground, writhing in agony. In a few moments he was dead.

This was too real. The arts administrator had to avert his eyes.

The scene ended, followed immediately by a small, intimate one between Hector Fulton and his wife. They played tenderly, at one side of the stage, just beside the proscenium. She held his hands in hers and begged him to treat the slaves more kindly. He assured her that, being a lower kind of creature, the slaves did not feel things the way "we" do. She seemed unconvinced, but she kissed him lightly on the cheek.

At three different places throughout the auditorium, playgoers saw more than just simply that. The characters fondled, disrobed, made love on stage. It was salacious, it was pornographic. One of the three stood up and left the hall, as quickly as he could, taking his wife with him. She was puzzled; she had seen only what had happened onstage. The second of the three closed her eyes and waited for the scene to end. The third, a young man just out of college, watched eagerly and became aroused. When the scene ended, he was terribly disappointed; he wanted to see more. Hmm . . . this was a play about black slaves and their white owners . . . maybe there would be a rape later.

Oginga and his followers led a small rebellion. Two of them held one of Fulton's overseers while a third beat him.

Near the rear of the orchestra a woman in late middle age saw her brothers. One of them, the oldest, had accidentally killed the youngest. It brought up the most horrible memories for her. She passed out and fell to the floor. A moment later her body began to twitch. Her limbs flailed and her breathing became so labored, froth appeared on her lips.

The man next to her had the presence of mind to push his program between her teeth so she wouldn't bite her own tongue. Two ushers rushed down the aisle to her; they helped her companion carry her to the lobby, where the seizure finally passed. The man tried to call 911 on his cell phone, but all he got was static.

At the far side of the orchestra from the woman, a college student, an aspiring actor, saw his father onstage, flicking a cigarette lighter. His father used to discipline him by burning him with cigarettes. The boy cried out, "Dad, no! No, please."

The people around him shushed him.

Onstage, the actors were beginning to realize that people in the theater were not reacting to the play in anything like the expected way. A few of the cast were thrown off by it, but most of them were professional enough to carry on what they were doing.

Watching them from the wings, Joanna, Mo and the rest also began to realize that something was throwing the actors off; but they had no idea what it might be.

All through the auditorium people began to cry, to gasp, to call out. It finally became audible even to people backstage. Mo caught Joanna by the arm. "Something's wrong."

"The play's too strong for them. We've miscalculated."

"It's not the play, Jo. You made us take everything out of it that might possibly unsettle anyone, remember? This is American History Lite."

"There's nothing else it can be."

Unable to make sense of it, and helpless to do anything about it, they stood and watched and hoped things would get better.

Onstage, a black slave was tortured by his white masters. The white actors built a bonfire out of props. Then he was hogtied, hung on the end of a long, thick pole and held over a fire. The man was being roasted alive, and his agonized screams filled the theater like no sound any of them had ever heard. It wasn't in the script; there had been no such scene in the play Mo wrote and Joanna approved.

"For God's sake, Jo, stop this."

"How? I can't."

"Bring down the curtain."

Vince joined them. "What's happening? The place is going

crazy." He had meant the audience. When he realized what was happening onstage, he went pale.

Mo decided to act. He ran onstage and began to grapple with the actors playing the overseers. They quickly overcame him. It was a matter of moments before they had him tied, immobile, and began to prepare a second pole to hang him from.

Tonya shrieked. "Stop it! Stop doing that to him!"

Peter ran onstage and began undoing Mo's bindings.

Just at that moment there was the sound of thunder from outside, terribly loud. The storm had hit.

The building shuddered. The walls trembled, and the curtain fell crashing to the stage, interrupting the action once and for all. The great chandelier swayed, and one by one the bolts holding it began to work loose. The chandelier dropped a few inches, stopped, then dropped again. Before long it was hanging by only one bolt and swaying wildly.

Everyone in the theater cried out and began to riot. People fought. Others rushed for the exits, but the aisles were clogged with them, and there was gridlock. The people, unable to move—to escape—screamed and fought among themselves all the more. People were trampled underfoot. Eyes and noses were bloodied in the fighting; bones were broken and skulls crushed. Panicked people tried calling out on their cell phones, but they wouldn't work.

There was a brilliant flash of lightning, so bright it penetrated the hall. Then the power surged. Lights flared till they were painfully bright. And an instant later they flickered and went out.

There were emergency backup lights, and they came on exactly as they should. But they weren't bright enough to light the hall; they only provided dim illumination enough to show people where the exits were. The fire on the stage burned through the curtain; it gave still more light, but not nearly enough.

Onstage, Annie Moore, Jack Bilicic and Tim Myers moved among the cast, ripping and slaughtering them.

Then something else began to happen. The people were not alone. A huge figure appeared at one of the exits. It was the stone Medusa. She flailed her arms at them, knocking one person after another to the floor. She seemed determined to keep them all where they were, to prevent them from making any progress at all in their scramble to escape the Imperial. The ones who tried to push past her were bitten by the snakes that were her hair; the venom killed them almost at once.

A huge centaur appeared onstage. Flickering firelight made it seem more monstrous than it would have otherwise. It picked up the actor playing Hector Fulton and dashed his brains out against the proscenium. The other actors, finally realizing what they had been doing, coming to their senses as if they'd been in a trance, scrambled to get off the stage.

But a ferocious griffin blocked the stage left exit. It snatched the actress playing Helen and tore her limb from limb. At the opposite side of the stage, a bronze sphinx tore open the throat of the actor who had been Oginga, ate his flesh greedily and lapped up his blood.

Dragons, griffins, enormous serpents, gods and demons of all kinds moved in the near-darkness, killing, dismembering, drinking.

In all the chaos, the administrative staff lost sight of one another. When the sphinx turned on Joanna, licking its chops greedily, there was no one there to save her or to try and help in the least way. The sphinx began to tear off pieces of her while she was still alive. It thought she was especially delicious.

A unicorn impaled Vince on its horn. Then, quite violently, it shook him off and lapped up the copious blood that flowed from his chest.

Mo was still tied where his tormentors left him. Tonya ran onstage and undid the ropes, and they ran back to the wings together and hid in a supply closet.

The theater gave another enormous shudder, and half of the roof collapsed. Scores of people were crushed. The chandelier swung wildly, but that one bolt held it perilously aloft. By that time, some of the audience had gotten out. Several of them ran across the bridge to the parking lot, only to find their cars mired in thick, deep mud. Part of the Ohio bridge collapsed into the river.

The rest of them, hundreds of them, stood in the driving rainstorm and watched as the demons and monsters went back to their proper places on the façade and became still once again.

After a time, the storm began to abate. They were shattered by what they had seen and experienced. But how could they, any of them, explain it?

Mo and Tonya were the last ones out of the theater.

By sunrise the next morning, very few people had managed to escape. But a kind of amnesia set in. They remembered that something horrible had happened, and they remembered the stampede to safety, but they remembered nothing else.

Three states were slow in responding to the frenzied calls for help. Three states tried to find excuses not to investigate what had happened. But when, inevitably, the public demanded an inquiry, they set up a joint panel which, jointly, absolved them all of any responsibility. The mob had panicked. Mass hysteria had set in. Besides, there was no clear jurisdiction. What had happened was an isolated incident. No one was at fault. How could anyone be?

Epilogue

"Christ, it's really ugly."

Noichi Samaguchi stood at the tip of Bourbon Island, gaping at the shell of the Imperial Opera House. It was spring. The Ohio was running swiftly. Anyplace else, there would have been fresh, green vegetation sprouting; not here.

Beside him was Manny Lawson. "Yeah. It's perfect."

"I don't know, Manny. It would cost a fortune to repair the place. It's a worse ruin than I thought."

"Yeah, but it'll be worth it. Think of it, Noichi. Bourbon Island. What a perfect name for a rock venue. They'll love it."

"It's not the name I'm worried about. It's the building."

"The building's perfect. All those grotesque statues all around—I'm telling you, this place was made for rock."

Noichi wasn't convinced. "Have you had anyone look at it? Engineers or architects, I mean?"

"Nope, you're the first. But whatever it would cost to fix it up, it'll be worth it. Believe me, Noichi, this place was made for rock. We'll have people coming from all over the region. Maybe all over the country. Just look at the place!"

"The building partially collapsed. How can we possibly be sure it won't again?"

Stage Fright

"Listen, all that can be taken care of. Rock is the wave of the future. We can't fail."

Noichi took a step back and nearly slipped down the bank into the river. He caught himself just in time. "I think you're crazy. You know what happened here. All those people who died. People say this place is cursed."

"So much the better. Rock fans—real rock fans—are rebels. You know that. If we promote it right, they'll come here to *defy* the curse."

"Almost everyone in the theater company died when the roof collapsed. There's something wrong, some kind of old mine underneath or something."

"We can reinforce the building. It'll cost, but—Noichi, will you just look at the place? Monsters. Grotesque architecture. It's a dream."

"And people from the audience died, too, when the roof fell in. I think their families tried to sue, but there was nobody left *to* sue. None of the states would let their courts hear the cases. If we take the place over . . ."

"There's no way we could be liable. I'll have my lawyers make sure of it. We can make a fortune off this place. The Imperial Rock Palace. It even sounds cool."

"I don't know, Manny, I don't know."

They spent a long afternoon talking—arguing—and Manny finally won Noichi over. This new enterprise was as sure-fire as anything they'd ever hit on. They were riding the wave of the future; the past didn't matter here.

***The sphinxes, griffins, dragons, gorgons, all the demons of**
the past waited patiently, and so did the sad ghosts who inhabited and animated them.

They had eaten and drunk well. And now, they knew, they would eat and drink again.

Penguin Group (USA) Online

What will you be reading tomorrow?

Tom Clancy, Patricia Cornwell, W.E.B. Griffin,
Nora Roberts, William Gibson, Robin Cook,
Brian Jacques, Catherine Coulter, Stephen King,
Dean Koontz, Ken Follett, Clive Cussler,
Eric Jerome Dickey, John Sandford,
Terry McMillan, Sue Monk Kidd, Amy Tan,
John Berendt…

You'll find them all at
penguin.com

*Read excerpts and newsletters,
find tour schedules and reading group guides,
and enter contests.*

Subscribe to Penguin Group (USA) newsletters
and get an exclusive inside look
at exciting new titles and the authors you love
long before everyone else does.

PENGUIN GROUP (USA)
us.penguingroup.com